Praise for
Jenny Hale

"Jenny Hale writes touching, beautiful stories."—*New York Times* **Bestselling Author RaeAnne Thayne**

"A beautiful small-town story about family and enduring love that you won't want to miss. I can always count on Jenny Hale to sweep me away with her heartwarming romantic tales."—**Denise Hunter, Bestselling Author** on *Butterfly Sisters*

One of "19 Dreamy Summer Romances to Whisk you Away" in *Oprah Magazine* on *The Summer House*

One of "24 Dreamy Books about Romance" in *Oprah Daily* on *The Summer House*

Included in "11 Small Town Romance Books That'll Make You Feel Right At Home" in **Southern Living Magazine** on *The Memory Keeper*

"Touching, fun-filled, and redolent with salt air and the fragrance of summer, this seaside tale is a perfect volume for most romance collections."—*Library Journal* on *The Summer House*

"Hale's impeccably executed contemporary romance is the perfect gift for readers who love sweetly romantic love stories imbued with all the warmth and joy of the holiday season."—*Booklist* on *Christmas Wishes and Mistletoe Kisses*

"A great summer beach read."—*PopSugar* on *Summer at Firefly Beach*

"This sweet small-town romance will leave readers feeling warm all the way through."—*Publisher's Weekly* on *It Started with Christmas*

BOOKS BY JENNY HALE

Butterfly Sisters
The Memory Keeper
An Island Summer
The Beach House
The House on Firefly Beach
Summer at Firefly Beach
The Summer Hideaway
The Summer House
Summer at Oyster Bay
Summer by the Sea
A Barefoot Summer

The Christmas Letters
A Lighthouse Christmas
Christmas at Fireside Cabins
Christmas at Silver Falls
It Started with Christmas
We'll Always Have Christmas
All I Want for Christmas
Christmas Wishes and Mistletoe Kisses
A Christmas to Remember
Coming Home for Christmas

The Magic of Sea Glass

JENNY HALE

USA TODAY BESTSELLING AUTHOR

HARPETH ROAD
PRESS*
Nashville

HARPETH ROAD

Published by Harpeth Road Press (USA)
P.O. Box 158184
Nashville, TN 37215

Paperback: 979-8-9877115-1-4
eBook: 979-8-9877115-0-7

THE MAGIC OF SEA GLASS: A dazzlingly heartwarming
summer romance

First printing: May, 2023

For all those who have lost someone special.

Prologue

As the afternoon sun filtered through the stained glass windows of the chapel full of wedding guests, all outfitted in their pastel suits and bright floral dresses, Lauren Sutton stood at the back and swallowed the lump of sorrow in her throat. She coughed into her fist to stifle her emotions, the sound echoing in the airy sanctuary. A couple in the last pew turned their heads in her direction, clearly recognizing her, something she still hadn't gotten used to.

Lauren nodded her apologies to them, smoothing her navy satin A-line dress that complemented her chestnut hair and green eyes, the swell of sadness returning with a vengeance. This was not the time for Mason to float into her mind. She had work to do.

The preacher's voice boomed throughout the room, "Should anyone here know of any reason that this couple should not be joined in holy matrimony, speak now or forever hold your peace."

Blinking away tears, Lauren checked the time on her watch in an attempt to focus on the task at hand, but the numbers didn't register.

Inevitably, it was at weddings when Mason's memory came through the strongest. A flutter of nostalgia would distract her from her duties—usually something completely regular like the sound of him brushing his teeth in the bathroom that they'd shared in their one-bedroom apartment on the Upper West Side. Before she knew it, she'd find herself completely immersed in those everyday moments that had become little treasures.

Today, she had indulged in recalling the adoring and hopeful look in his eyes when he'd kneeled in front of her in Central Park, where they first met, an emerald-cut diamond ring glimmering between them. And now she was paying the price for allowing that memory to resurface.

The happy couple turned toward the sea of family and friends, the groom excitedly lifting the bride's hand in celebration as she gripped the custom-made bouquet of white morning frost and stone-blue dyed roses with pearl beading that Lauren had ordered for her five months prior. The crowd cheered. *Husband and wife.*

As the lovebirds took their first steps to walk back down the aisle, headed for the reception that featured Lauren's signature champagne fountains and table place cards made of edible fondant scrolls with gold lettering, the group of musicians in the balcony began a jazzy rendition of Stevie Wonder's "Signed, Sealed, Delivered" to the roar of the crowd. The groom gave the bride a twirl, her Ines Di Santo gown flowing out around her flawlessly, the dress as beautiful as the glowing bride herself.

The processional continued along the pearl white runner of the church. Lauren wiped a runaway tear, put on a smile, and waved at them as they departed, her iPad with the checklist for the rest of the evening gripped tightly in her other hand—as if holding on to it could keep her from collapsing.

"I can take over from here," Lauren's best friend and business partner, Andy Jacobs, whispered from beside her, that all-too-familiar empathy in her eyes.

"I'm fine," Lauren lied.

The concluding members of the wedding party exited through the arched doors, which led to the lush green church gardens and stone path lined with topiaries—also Lauren's idea. Then the crowd began to file out, the summer sunshine warming the area where she and Andy stood.

"You're not fine." Their earlier discussions about Lauren selling her half of the business were evident in Andy's stare. She patted Lauren's shoulder, rubbing back and forth affectionately, the gesture slowing Lauren's pounding heart in the way only a best friend's touch could. Andy had always been there for her.

A year ago, when Lauren's fiancé, Mason Bridges, had died suddenly in a head-on collision on his way to a weekend fishing trip, Andy had immediately stepped in to run Sugar and Lace Event Planning, the wildly successful business that Lauren and Andy co-owned. But in a matter of weeks, Lauren had gone back to work, pushing herself through the pain, filling her days with tasks like organizing caterers, floral design, and booking event spaces, because if she didn't, she feared she might crumble. The nights she slept without Mason, alone in their bed, were enough to torture her to the point of near insanity, and she'd needed the distraction.

One morning, after a particularly difficult night, she'd called her best friend and confided in her that she wasn't sure she could go on like she had been. She got into the wedding business because she felt there was nothing better in life than celebrating love, but after losing Mason, she didn't feel like she could be celebratory anymore. Andy had offered to buy her out, but Lauren still needed the emotional break that work provided and the promise that the world did go on, even if she didn't feel like it could.

"I'll tell the bride that we'll split the duties: you work the ceremony and I'll handle the reception," Andy said.

"I'm *fine*," Lauren repeated, her voice breaking. If she said anything more she might fall apart right there in the church. She reminded herself that she could do this. It wasn't the first time her memories of Mason had caught her off guard—she'd handled it before; she could do it again.

"Going home in the middle of one event doesn't mean you're quitting," Andy said. "I already know your position on that."

She took in a steadying breath and squared her shoulders. "I can't leave you to do the entire wedding by yourself. As your partner, I need to be here to help carry the load." But even though the words were coming out of her mouth, she knew she'd never make it through the entire event.

"Everything is finished. All I have to do is make sure each item on the list happens at the right time. Cocktail hour, cake-cutting, speeches, first dance... You know I can do it in my sleep; it's party time."

Andy was right. The actual day of the event used to always be a triumphant culmination of all their hard work—where Andy and Lauren shined. Putting out the little fires of the day and keeping to the schedule was easy, given the incredible planning that had happened in the months before. They used to toast champagne and mingle with the guests, hugging the appreciative brides, who shook their heads, baffled as to how they made it look so effortless.

But in the year after losing Mason, Lauren had found herself at these times overly fixated on whether she'd gotten all the details of the day right, or her heart would suddenly pound while she double-checked her to-do lists to be sure she hadn't forgotten something. Her mind couldn't always focus on work, so instead it became a battleground of thoughts about the things she and Mason could've done differently. And then there was the flood of memories...

For whatever reason, today was a tough one; she needed to cut her losses and admit to herself that tomorrow would be a better day. She finally surrendered, her chest aching for her life before the tragic accident. "If I go home, I won't be any better," she said, already fretting about having to navigate the silence in the apartment she'd shared with Mason. "I need something to think about, something to get my mind off… it."

Andy offered a loving pout. "Why don't you take some time today to think about what you want to do," her friend suggested kindly. "What you *really* want to do. What will make you happy, Lauren? Because I'm not sure it's this anymore."

Lauren looked around at the near-empty church, the satin bows looped along the sides of the pews, the white runner with beaded trimming leading to the altar, and none of it lifted her spirits. For the first time, she knew what Andy meant.

"You mentioned the other day about going to the Outer Banks like you and Mason had planned to do before the accident. Why don't you go before the summer ends? Maybe it could get you out of this headspace, make you feel a little lighter?"

She had considered it, wondering all summer if moving forward with their plans to visit the coast would help her to feel less like her life was just sitting stagnant in the empty space after Mason's death.

She allowed herself to recall the memory of him in the kitchen, wearing his boxer shorts with his back to her, flipping her omelet and talking, for the millionth time, about how they should move to the coast and get a dog. He always tried to convince her that they belonged in a location with a slower pace and that she'd love living by the ocean. One time, she playfully pushed him away when he ran over to her from the stove to try to convince her with kisses.

"You know I can't work from somewhere like that," she said, squealing and throwing sofa pillows at him.

"You're so stubborn!" He pawed at her while she fought him away.

"You're going to burn the eggs!"

"I don't care! Let them burn! You're much more delicious!"

She dodged him just before he got a hold of her arm.

"You'll love the beach so much that you'll want to give everything up, and we'll sail away somewhere amazing, have a boatload of kids, send everyone postcards that say, 'Wish You Were Here,' drink piña coladas, and lie in the sun until we're as red as lobsters." He reached for her, grabbing her shirt before she could get away, falling onto the sofa with her and burying his head in her neck, despite her wriggling and laughter. "Promise me we'll go one day."

"I promise," she said, wrapping her arms around him.

Andy cut in on her memory. "At least take a few weeks off before the summer ends. It's a perfect time to do it. Our biggest client right now is the Alexander wedding, and we'll be in the preliminary planning stages for the next four months. I can sit with them and choose what they want just as easily as you can."

"What about the Bakers?" Lauren asked. "They'll need work."

"It's a three-hundred-person event. I can do it with my eyes shut."

Lauren nodded, tears beginning to brim in her eyes—for what, she wasn't sure anymore. Maybe it was her memories of Mason, or perhaps it was the loss of who she'd been, the idea that all her dreams for a big family and a house full of love had evaporated in a single day. Or the fact that the company she'd built from the ground up with her best friend now felt like a burden.

"The bride's probably bustled and freshened up by now. I have to get into the reception to oversee the introductions," Andy said, putting her arm around Lauren and giving her a squeeze before pacing over to the open doors. "You going to be okay?"

"Yeah," Lauren replied. But as she gazed out the window she realized she wasn't entirely sure.

Chapter One

In her attempt to escape her old life, to go incognito and blend into the landscape of sea and sand dunes for the summer, the one thing Lauren hadn't planned on, in the middle of Nowhere, North Carolina, was to be immediately recognized.

"Hey!" an unfamiliar man's voice called, trying to get her attention from across the busy market full of sandy, barefoot patrons. Most were stopping in to pick up last-minute items before they headed back to their cottages to get cleaned up for the evening hours of cocktails and seafood.

She peeked over at him, not having a clue as to who he was. Lauren didn't want to make small talk. She'd just stopped in to grab a bite on her way through the little beach town. She'd been driving from New York since the wee hours of the morning, and all she wanted was to settle her rumbling stomach. Then she hoped to kick off her shoes in the sand and lie back on a hammock while the waves crashed onto the shore, drowning out everything she'd been through. She'd take in the sea air and allow the coastline to convince her that she'd done the right thing in finally agreeing to sell Andy her half of Sugar and Lace.

Her business that had spawned its own series on TV and was written about in *Homes & Gardens* magazine, the business that had made her name synonymous with style and glamour, bringing in A-list clients from all over the world, was no longer hers. The glossy, pre-tragedy images of her and Andy with the television show title *Tying the Knot with Sugar and Lace* splashed across them came to mind. She didn't even want to think about what Dave Hammond, the head of production at the network, was going to say… It would only be a matter of time before he would call to find out what was going on. But Andy could handle it. She was the star of the show anyway. She'd been the one to talk Lauren into doing the six-episode stint that had become an overnight hit and had the producers chomping at the bit for another season.

Lauren rolled her shoulders forward and pulled her sunhat lower, hoping the man would give up trying to speak to her. Attempting to ignore the growing curiosity from the cashier as the guy in question caused more people to take notice of her, Lauren lumped her armful of groceries onto the checkout counter: a chicken salad sandwich, a bottle of water, and two tubes of sunscreen. Out of the corner of her eye, she saw the stranger now striding down the aisle toward the checkout.

"That'll be seventeen eighty-three," the woman at the register said, gazing at her.

"Hey." A hand touched Lauren's shoulder, turning her around to face the man she'd never seen before. Towering over her, he rubbed the gold scruff on his tanned face, his blue eyes piercing against his olive skin while he squinted at her in confusion.

She stared up at him as he pulled back.

"Oh, sorry to bother you. I thought…"

Lauren braced herself, waiting for him to publicly out her.

"From over there, you looked like a friend of mine." He flashed a gorgeous smile and ran a hand through his sun-bleached, light brown hair. The depth in his eyes made it feel like he'd known her longer than the seconds they'd spent together. "You don't happen to be related to Stephanie Clark?"

"No," she said, relieved that he'd gotten it wrong while also trying to stifle the frustration that even a regular conversation caused her these days. It wasn't his fault that she had zero interest in knowing why he'd stopped her in the middle of the market. He was just going about his day happily like every other human being on the planet whose whole life hadn't been turned upside down. She used to wonder what she'd done to make the universe punish her, turning her world into an unrecognizable mess, but she'd yet to unearth an answer.

Lauren handed over her credit card. The cashier swiped it and returned it, her attention flip-flopping between her two customers.

"I apologize for bothering you," the guy said.

He rattled her, with his good looks and friendly approach. "No problem." Lauren grabbed the handles of her bag and stepped out of the line.

The man followed. "I'm Brody Harrison, by the way."

She didn't want to have to introduce herself for fear that her emotions would bubble up or that he'd finally recognize her from TV and ask her a ton of questions. But maybe she'd get lucky and he wouldn't connect the dots. With those tanned biceps and pectoral muscles showing through his T-shirt, he didn't seem like the type of guy who spent long hours in front of the TV watching wedding programs.

"Lauren Sutton," she said cautiously, carrying her bag of groceries toward the door.

Brody trailed her into the blinding sunshine, tourists moving past them, holding surfboards and beach bags as they walked along the sandy wooden sidewalk. "You new around here or just visiting?"

She tried not to draw any further attention to herself, tipping her head down as she kept walking. "Both. Kind of."

"What does that mean? You here for the rest of the summer or something?"

A pinch of anxiety took hold when he guessed correctly.

In her search for sunny destinations, she'd stumbled upon an ad for a seasonal assistant to an innkeeper and, in an act of complete spontaneity, applied. She didn't need the job, but would probably go crazy with all the free time if she just took off for the beach.

To her shock, she'd gotten an immediate response with an offer of work for the next six weeks and accepted the position. She decided that the purpose of this trip was to disappear and spend the last slip of summer away from everyone she knew, figuring out what she wanted to do with the rest of her life.

The corners of Brody's lips turned upward as those blue eyes locked with hers. "It wasn't meant to be a trick question."

"Yes, I'm here until the end of the summer," she replied before hurrying off.

"I'll have to introduce you to Stephanie if we meet again," he called.

But she barely heard him, jumping into her BMW and starting the engine.

Way out of town, down a deserted one-lane road, Lauren pulled her car past the old wooden sign that read in swirling letters "The Tide and Swallow Inn" and came to a halt in the weedy parking lot outside the towering shingled structure on stilts. The paint on the front porch was peeling, and the beds of plants were overgrown, but even with its massive size and dilapidated exterior, it still held on to a certain appeal that could only be found on the coast. She got out and stopped in her tracks when she spied the bubbling current rushing right up to the back of the inn and then retreating to the Atlantic.

"My goodness. The whole place is gonna wash away," she said under her breath.

"It's the rising tide," an older woman with a big smile and a head of gray hair tucked behind her ears said as she limped over, her unsteady steps assisted by a cane that appeared to be made of lacquered driftwood. "By about seven o'clock tonight, it'll completely cover the sand. But it won't hurt anything. At least not for a few more years." The woman made her way over to her. "I'm Mary Everett."

Surprised and slightly mortified that the woman had overheard her comment, Lauren looked out at the sparkling water. That was not really the way she'd wanted to greet her new boss.

"Lauren Sutton. I'm here for the assistant's job." She reached out in greeting.

Mary shifted her cane and shook Lauren's hand. "I'm delighted to have your help."

Lauren gave her that fabricated smile that she'd perfected over the last twelve months.

"It's getting tougher and tougher to manage every day, all by myself, with my arthritis." Mary patted her hip. "So I thought I might try having an assistant to see how it goes. I just couldn't find the right person, so the position's been empty all summer."

"I'm excited to be here." Lauren popped the trunk and began unloading her suitcases. She tugged on the heaviest one, barely lifting it over the lip of the car, letting it thump onto the pavement. "I've never visited the Outer Banks before."

"I do hope you'll have a good time here at the inn."

"I'm going to try," she said, not really sure if any location in the world could help her figure out her life.

Mary eyed the pile of suitcases. "I have a dolly we can use for your bags."

"Oh great. If you'll show me where you keep it, I can get it," Lauren said, not wanting to make the poor woman hobble all the way to wherever it was.

"It's up there." Mary waggled an unsteady finger toward the house. "Around the corner, on the porch."

"All right."

"You can wheel it down the ramp there on the side and when you come back up, head into the main house through those front doors. I'll pour us some lemonade, and I need to see Joe before he leaves."

"Joe?" she asked.

"He's a friend of mine. Comes over from time to time." She put her hands on her wide hips and gave them a playful shake. "He's five years older than I am, so he makes me feel like a spring chicken. That's the real reason I spend time with him." She winked at Lauren.

The woman's candor warmed her.

"Lemonade okay?"

"Yes. That sounds delicious. Why don't you let me help you up to the porch?" Lauren offered her arm.

Mary took it with a grateful nod.

"Is there another place where the guests park?" Lauren asked, making conversation as she peered out at the near-empty parking lot.

Mary sighed. "Nope. This is it. We never get full enough to need more parking; although, I suppose if, by some miracle, we got busy, people could park on the street if they had to."

Lauren nodded, trying to maintain her pleasant expression the way she did when something went wrong at a wedding but she didn't want the bride to know a thing. It was still summer and, if the parking lot was any indication, the place was almost entirely vacant. Given the congestion she'd seen on the ride into town, that wasn't typical.

"You couldn't have answered the ad quickly enough for me," Mary said, as they maneuvered around a bed of seagrass. "We don't have half the guests we used to have, and I'm struggling to manage."

Lauren nodded. "Why do you think you haven't gotten people in?"

Mary frowned. "This inn was always my husband's job. When he passed away, it became my job."

That familiar punch to the gut that she felt whenever someone mentioned losing someone hit her.

"Ever since I took over, it's slowly declined," Mary continued. She brightened, but Lauren could tell it was only for her benefit. "I'm hoping to get a second opinion on bringing vacationers in; maybe I'm doing something wrong."

"Perfect timing, then. Maybe I could offer my thoughts." Lauren held her steady while the woman gripped her cane. They took each step up the wide wooden staircase leading to the porch, the foamy spray of the ocean crawling across the sand under the house. "Does the water ever reach the steps?" she asked.

"Not very often," Mary replied, unbothered. "Only during storms."

While she worked with Mary to get her to the house, the sun beating down on them as they ascended the final steps, the southern humidity blanketed Lauren's skin, causing a dampness between her shoulder blades. But when they got to the top of the wraparound porch with the view of the Atlantic, the coastal breeze blew down the side of the house against them, giving her instant relief.

Mary pulled away from Lauren. "You see the dolly there?"

"Yes, thank you," Lauren replied, taking in the vast ocean, the only body of water comparable to the tears that she'd cried over the last year.

"It's beautiful, isn't it?" Mary said from beside her.

"It sure is."

"It makes everything feel okay. Anytime I need a pick-me-up, I sit out here." Mary gestured to the row of rocking chairs along the back of the house, overlooking the sparkling cobalt-blue sea. In each of the two corners, a hammock swung back and forth in the breeze while the wind chime above tinkled out a melody.

Lauren took in a deep breath of the briny air, the salt settling on her skin, and felt a little brighter than she had when she'd first arrived in town.

"I'll get our lemonade," Mary said.

"Thank you." Lauren tore herself away from the view and took the dolly over to the wooden ramp on the side of the house.

As she rolled it back to the parking lot to get her bags, a Silverado with the windows down and music playing a little too loudly pulled to a stop beside her car.

"Fancy seeing you here," Brody Harrison from the market said, cutting the engine and getting out.

A wave of something unrecognizable washed over her. Strangely, it felt good to see a familiar face, yet his personable demeanor put her on edge. She hadn't considered whether she was ready to make new friends. In planning this trip, she'd imagined that she'd be alone, working through her thoughts like she always had. Brody's presence was an unplanned surprise, and she wasn't quite sure how she felt about it.

Then she caught Brody eyeing her Louis Vuitton bags before his gaze swept over the BMW, and she could've sworn she saw judgment in his eyes. She bristled. He didn't know her; he didn't know that she'd built her fortune from the ground up. She clenched her jaw shut, trying not to let it bother her. The skill of navigating her world alone was difficult for her now. She wasn't strong enough emotionally to stand her ground in times like these.

"Did you follow me?" she asked, feeling as exposed as an open wound with no bandage to protect it.

His smile fell, and he shook his head slowly to answer. "I'm doing some work for Mary," he said.

"Oh." She scolded herself for the accusation, realizing that his truck was full of wood and tools.

The interest and concern on his face only served to make her more uneasy. It was as if suddenly he could guess what was inside her head, making her heart pound.

It wasn't like her to assume things. After losing Mason, she'd cocooned herself in her own little world with just work and the apartment that they shared, and now she was finding it hard to behave in regular life. As a wedding planner, she could fake it, smile at all the right times, rely on her schedules and clients' needs, but here there was no agenda yet, and she wasn't sure how to just be herself anymore.

"So are you a contractor?" she asked, trying to make conversation in an effort to be normal.

The corner of his mouth twitched upward, his curiosity about her clear in those eyes of his. "No, I just help her out. I'm a fisherman."

"What kinds of fish do you catch out here?" She shielded her eyes to get another view of the ocean.

"Mostly mahi and tuna, but I only fish commercially part-time. A lot of my days are spent running a fishing charter for families who want someone to take them out on the water during their vacations, and then I take the winter off."

The idea of happy families laughing and snapping photos as Brody drove them through the open sea, the wind against their faces, the spray of water on either side of the boat, lifted her mood considerably. She always imagined a full house for herself, but her career had put her plans for a family on hold. Mason had wanted to give her that family; the two of them talked for hours over coffee, teasing each other about how many kids they were going to have. He, too, had liked to fish. He'd asked her to go the day of the accident, but she'd told him she had to work…

"I'll help you with your bags. Otherwise, Mary will probably offer, and she doesn't need to put any extra weight on her joints." Before she could protest, he grabbed her largest suitcase easily, swinging it onto the cart. "So you're staying here, at the inn?" He grabbed two more bags and placed them next to her larger suitcase.

"Yes," she replied. "I'm working with Mary too. I'm her new assistant."

His forehead creased in interest. "She mentioned hiring some help. I'm glad she found someone." He went over to Lauren's car and took the last suitcases out, loading them up. While she shut the trunk, he began wheeling the cart toward the house.

Lauren shuffled up behind him as the waves crashed onto the shore just feet from the ramp. "Do you think this is okay?" She pointed toward the rushing tide near the inn. "Mary didn't seem worried by it, but it's coming awfully close."

"The coastline's constantly shifting. Eventually, she'll probably need to fill the beach in with more sand or she might even have to move the whole thing back." He waved a hand at the inn.

"Move the *building*?" she asked, walking beside him while he pushed the cart up the ramp to the upper porch.

"Yeah, it comes with the territory around here. When the shoreline changes, it's best to just move with it instead of trying to keep it where it is, or you'll work yourself to death."

She looked out at the immense expanse of the ocean, the meaning of his words running deeper for her than he'd meant them to. She was trying to move along with the changes in her life; she just wasn't sure how to do that.

"Oh hello, Brody," Mary said, holding the door open as they entered.

Brody pulled the bags off the cart, setting them inside. An elderly man with a crop of silver hair and skin that was as tough as leather was halfway through the back door leading to the porch.

"I didn't know you were coming so soon." Mary hurried over to them. "I'll make another glass of lemonade."

"Bye, Mary," the old man called, raising his hand as he left out the back door. Through the window, he rubbed his arm with a gnarled hand, the age and years of work showing in his skin.

"Is he driving somewhere?" Lauren asked, worried for a man his age to be behind the wheel of a car.

Brody shrugged. "He never goes above fifteen miles an hour anyway. He'll be fine."

Lauren tried not to think about it, taking in her surroundings instead. The first thing she noticed was the wall of old windows along the back with a view of the ocean, and then the sunshine dancing on the surface of the water in the distance, which immediately gave her a sense of calm.

"Sit, sit," Mary told them, fluttering a hand toward the old striped sofas facing each other in the open space. The room looked as if it had been decorated in a bygone era, with parlor palms and peace lilies dotting it.

Brody motioned for her to take a seat first, then went around the dark wood coffee table. A couple walked through the room, talking about one of the local restaurants, waving happily to Mary before leaving through the door next to Lauren's bags.

"So where are you from?" Brody asked.

Lauren crossed her ankles and placed her hands on her thighs, her sundress gauzy under her fingers. "New York, but I grew up in Tennessee."

That smirk returned, the sight of it making its mark on her already, and she barely knew him. "I thought I'd sensed a slight southern accent when I met you."

She allowed a smile. "It's tough to get rid of, isn't it?" The tension in Lauren's shoulders released just a little while Mary was in the other room getting their drinks; the act of conversation felt slightly easier now. The good days were the only thing that kept her above water, and she was thankful that today was one of them.

"Ah, that's why you shouldn't try," he said. "It's part of you; it's who you are deep down."

"You sound like my mom." A tiny pang swelled in her chest at the thought of her mother. With her crazy TV production and wedding schedule, Lauren hadn't been home to see her parents in quite some time. "She's always telling me not to forget who I am up in New York."

With the fame of the television show and all the big clients that she and Andy were getting, Lauren could always count on her mother, Grace, to remind her where she'd come from. Just like her name, she was always able to bring Lauren back down to what mattered, despite their differences in how they lived their lives. Her mother had never understood the absolute daily grind of her daughter's success, and it had caused tension between them in the past.

But her mom had said that she was always there to talk whenever Lauren wanted to; she just found it too difficult, so she hadn't reached out as much as she probably should have. Her mom had called her a few times recently, and it seemed like she had something on her mind, but she never said what it was, and Lauren hadn't asked. She knew that if her mother's grievance was anything other than her own absence, she couldn't be a sounding board for anyone in her state. It all just served to make her feel guilty for not being a better daughter.

"What brings you to the Outer Banks?" Brody asked.

"I needed a change from… my old job." Her answer was short and sweet—she definitely wasn't going into it.

He didn't seem to notice her unease, continuing, "What was your old job?"

She put on her brightest expression. "I was a wedding planner."

He nodded. "You didn't like it?"

She swallowed, trying to keep her thoughts on the surface level, still not allowing the deeper reasons to come through. "It's… really busy."

"Sorry for the delay." Mary wobbled in with a wrapped box and a tray of the glasses of lemonade, the liquid in them sloshing slightly with every step.

Lauren jumped up and rushed over to help her, taking the tray and placing it onto the table between them. She distributed the stack of circular coasters and set out each glass of lemonade.

"I got stopped by one of my favorite families, who wanted to know if there was an afternoon tour of the lighthouses."

"It seems like the people who *are* here really enjoy it," Lauren said, thinking back to what Mary had disclosed earlier regarding the lack of guests.

"Mary's the star of the show," Brody said. "They come for her."

The innkeeper sat down next to Brody and patted his leg adoringly, then reached over and took the box wrapped in silver paper and a blue ribbon into her hands. "I have a little something for you to celebrate your first day with us," she said before leaning over the table to offer the gift to Lauren.

"Oh my goodness," Lauren said, the gesture unexpected.

Mary wrinkled her nose kindly. "Open it."

Lauren untied the ribbon and then slipped her finger under the flap, tearing the silver paper off the small box and laying it onto the table. She opened the lid and lifted a stunning turquoise and sea-green bracelet from the box.

"This is beautiful," she said, draping it over her wrist and attempting to clasp it.

"It's supposedly made from sea glass found here in the southern states," Mary said.

Mary's mention of sea glass caused a sudden memory of Mason to slam into Lauren's mind, taking her breath away.

"Let's sell it all and travel the world," he said, pulling the flat sheet from her hand one day when she'd been trying to make the bed. "All we need is a shack and two bicycles." Mason had swept her up into an embrace, falling onto the covers.

"How will we pay for the shack?" she asked with a giggle as he hovered above her the way he always did, his sandy-brown hair falling over his forehead.

"We'll scour the beaches for shells and sea glass. You're so talented with everything you do that you can make beautiful things with it."

"Like what?" she challenged.

"Anything you want. With your talent, we'll be richer than all the millionaires out there." He pressed his lips to hers.

When Lauren surfaced, she was still fumbling with the clasp of the bracelet, blinking away tears, her frustration mounting. She wondered if she'd made the wrong choice coming here after all. She wasn't ready to throw herself into social situations like this and she abruptly felt as if she were suffocating.

Brody stood and came over to her side. "Let me get that for you." Gently, he took her wrist into his strong hands, turning it over and connecting the two ends.

The sensation of someone else touching her made her feel real for the first time in a very long time, her pulse racing.

"Thank you," she said, still recovering even after he'd gone back over and sat down across from her once more. She worked to calm her hammering heart. With a few deep breaths, she calmed herself but tried not to look over at Brody's inquisitive stare.

He watched her as if he were attempting to read her mind again, but Mary didn't seem to notice; her attention was on another couple who'd entered the room, changing the atmosphere. They waved to her and then headed toward the door.

"That bracelet is supposed to bring you good luck," Mary said after the couple left.

The innocence in her tone revealed that the woman had no idea how much luck Lauren really needed.

Chapter Two

Summer, 1957
Fairhope, Alabama

"Put me down!" The gorgeous Penelope Harper squealed with laughter, her dark hair flowing over her shoulders and along the back of her polka-dotted swimming suit.

Phillip Harrison spun her around, gripping her waist in the lapping bay water as the sun set in spectacular fashion behind them. She wriggled away from him playfully before wading back over, her emerald eyes landing on him, reminding him once more that he wasn't worthy of such a charming woman, but—somehow—the heavens had granted him her love. She draped her arms around his neck. He leaned down and kissed her, in the presence of anyone who wanted to look. He was ready to shout his love for her from the rooftops. Phillip scooped her up and carried her to their blanket on the sand while she giggled, careful to lower her down gently.

"I love you," he whispered into her ear.

"And I love *you*." Her eyes appearing as if she were drinking him in, she sat up on her elbows. "This has been the best summer of my life."

Phillip took in the glisten of water on her skin and the way her wet tendrils of hair draped along her olive-tinted shoulder, knowing he hadn't understood what happiness was until he'd met Penelope. "I couldn't agree more."

The first time he saw Penelope, she'd taken his breath away. He'd been walking down the sidewalk, outside the little bungalow where she was staying. Fairhope had been a popular retreat for artists, writers, and intellectuals for over a century, so he was used to seeing both famous and unfamiliar faces, but this girl's raw, untainted beauty blew all of those bigwigs out of the water. She was standing by her father's car, with a tattered suitcase in each hand. She flashed a vibrant smile his way that had floored him. The kindness in her eyes made him forget where he was going.

Her mother directed her away from him as if her smile had been an imposition. But he gave the striking young lady a look to let her know he'd find her again. She offered a little nod, the two of them owning that one secret moment together. They'd shared the same thoughts every single day the entire summer, never leaving each other's sides. Phillip made up reasons to go into town just to run into her, and she always seemed to find a way to be at the soda fountain exactly when he arrived.

They spent long days talking about their views on everything from the best soda flavors to Eisenhower's golf swing. Penelope was smart and witty—something he had not experienced in a woman he'd dated before. She challenged him, made him question his thoughts, and, above all, she made him laugh. With her he felt fearless, as if he could take on the whole world. And, given what he was planning, he might just have to.

Rodanthe, North Carolina

"This one is yours," Mary said, opening the door to the one-bedroom suite and handing Lauren the key.

Lauren stepped into the sitting area, running her hands along the knotty tweed sofa, punctuated on each end by pillows with faded embroidered anchors on the fronts. Despite its aging façade, the size of the suite was airy and rivaled her apartment back in New York.

"This is nice," she said, grabbing one of her bags and setting it next to a coordinated upholstered chair that only needed a slipcover to be beautiful again.

With the help of her cane, Mary paced over to a pair of draperies on the far end, pulling them open and revealing another wall of windows and a set of French doors. "These open to the porch," she said right as Brody walked past them on the outside. "You just have to wriggle the latch."

Brody did a double take, his eyes finding Lauren's immediately, unnerving her. Then he walked out of view.

"Your bedroom is through here."

Lauren rolled her large suitcase around the corner and pushed it up against the king-sized bed covered in more nautical-themed pillows from a few decades ago. The wall décor was from the same time period, featuring simple pictures of starfish and sand dollars.

"There are doors to the porch in here too," Mary said, gesturing to another set of draperies. While they did the job to darken the room, Lauren imagined how much light would fill the space if they were replaced with a gauzy set of white sheers.

A shadow walked past them on the other side, that look Brody had given her washing over her once more. She cleared her throat and turned toward Mary. "I'll be very comfortable here," she said.

With a pleased smile, Mary walked slowly to the door. "I'll let you get settled. My office is just down the hallway. Come by whenever you're ready."

"All right," Lauren said as Mary let herself out.

Once she was alone, Lauren flopped onto the bed, exhausted. For so long, she'd been on autopilot, working and then going through her rituals of eating dinner, bathing, and watching TV until she fell asleep so she could limit the thoughts about life without Mason. She didn't even have to think about what to get for lunch if she went out. It was always Giuseppe's soup and salad. But here, things were different; her routine was completely upended. Sighing, she then breathed in the new scent, a mixture of cotton, old wood, and salty air, allowed her muscles to relax, and closed her eyes...

She hadn't realized that she'd fallen asleep until something pressed hard against her face, pushing into it uncomfortably and causing her to swim out of her state of unconsciousness. On her side, she moved her arm that had been propping her head up and rubbed her skin, feeling an imprint. She'd been sleeping on the string of sea glass around her wrist. She sat up and peered down at her new gift. It was truly beautiful. The sight of it still reminded her of Mason, but after her nap it made her feel as if he were there with her—maybe it *was* good luck.

A knock at the bedroom door that opened to the porch gave her a start. Running her fingers through her long waves, she blinked, trying to focus through the bright light as she pulled back the curtains. Brody stood on the other side. Lauren unlocked the handle and opened the doors, the North Carolina humidity instantly overtaking her.

His attention went to the marks on her face from the bracelet before he met her eyes, that interest she'd seen before flickering in his gaze. "I'm replacing the boards of the porch for Mary, and I've gotten to the ones by your room. I'll be working along this side for the next few hours, so I wanted to let you know that it'll be loud while I'm cutting and hammering."

"Oh, okay," she said, still slightly disoriented from her nap, her conversational skills limited. "I was going to go down the hall to see Mary anyway."

"That's probably a good idea." He flashed that smile, his sandy-brown hair darker with perspiration. Then he turned away and got to work.

Fiddling with her bracelet for strength, she pulled the door shut and walked through the suite, headed for Mary's office.

"I enjoy spending time with the guests," Mary said, once Lauren had gotten to her office. "But bookkeeping *isn't* my strong suit, and I just cannot figure out how to get this schedule straight." Mary leaned over the desk next to Lauren in the cramped, cluttered office. The one saving grace of the small space was that it had the same view as Lauren's suite that extended past the porch to the deep blue Atlantic and its golden beach.

Brody was still outside, replacing the boards. Lauren kept catching glimpses of him through the window, obstructing the ocean that shined like a bed of diamonds in the late afternoon sunlight, and then he'd disappear. Out of nowhere, the hammering would start once more.

Wondering how Mary could get any work done with that view within reach, Lauren tore her eyes from it to take a look at the spiral-bound paper calendar full of penciled-in duties, reservations, and events. The edges of the book were bent, with some pages folded and others barely attached to the spiral casing, with sticky notes and arrows drawn across the page. Mary had all her personal appointments written in the same place as the cleaning crews' schedules, bills that were due, and meetings.

"Can you think of any way to sort this out?" Mary asked.

Lauren turned the page to find another grid full of writing. "Have you ever thought about putting all this into a computer program?"

Mary shook her head. "I don't even own a computer. My husband, Frank, used to do it all for me and when he passed away, I was left with it."

Lauren nodded. She knew firsthand what it was like to be left with a life that had once been filled by someone else. "How long has it been since…?"

Mary smiled, understanding her question. "Three years." Mary's gaze shifted to the ceiling as if Frank were there. "But we were together for forty-seven."

"That's incredible." Lauren was unable to imagine what it would be like to lose Mason after forty-seven years together. It was hard enough after four.

"It's not so incredible when you love someone as much as I loved Frank. It was easy. It's being able to live without him that's incredible."

Lauren offered a melancholy smile, knowing exactly what she meant.

"My friend Joe helps me, though. I've known him since we moved here. He and Frank became fishing buddies, and he was always around. When I lost Frank, Joe stepped in. He helps with the loneliness."

"That's good that you have someone," Lauren said, wondering if things would be easier if she had someone like Joe. She wasn't sure. To avoid thinking about it any further, she got back to the task at hand, looking down at the calendar.

"So, what do I do without a computer?" Mary asked.

"Well, I applied for this job through a digital form online, and you have a website. How did you do *that*?"

"I hired a lady to do my website for me and she took care of the form," Mary replied.

"Could she help you get all this loaded into a program?" Small slips of paper with dates scratched on them fluttered to the floor when Lauren lifted the book to try to make out what was written in there.

Mary grunted as she bent over to pick them up. "She doesn't work for me; I just paid a one-time fee. I don't have the budget for it."

"So how did you get my email about the job?" she asked, trying to ascertain what Mary had and what she lacked in the way of technology.

"I got it on my phone. I do know how to use that. I had to learn if I wanted to keep the inn running in this day and age, but it's all getting away from me—moving too fast and leaving me behind."

"I know what you mean," she said.

"And even if I could keep up, I can't physically meet all the inn's requirements by myself. It needs repairs. I'm scheduling maintenance while I'm checking guests out, managing the upkeep and who's coming in and out of the inn, keeping the crews up to date on numbers—there's just so much."

Brody popped into view again, wiping the perspiration off his forehead, and suddenly it was clear. He was helping Mary, most likely because she didn't have the money to pay for a new porch. A tickle fluttered over her wrist where his hands had been. She swallowed, realizing the tickle was just the bracelet. She'd have to get used to wearing it.

With a deep breath, she turned to Mary. "You know, for my other job, I had a program that would run all this for you and give you a daily agenda with everything you have to do that day, separated by category," she said. "It can even pay your workers for you. I still have it on my laptop."

"That sounds like heaven," Mary said. "But I'd have no idea how to set it all up or use it."

"Could I have this book for a few days? I can get all the information loaded in for you on my computer and then, once it's up and running, I can teach you how it works. And I can be the back-end person, which will allow you to enjoy what you do best—the guests." The relief Lauren felt at doing something she was used to and being out of the public eye was palpable.

"I would be forever grateful if you could do that for me."

"It would be no problem at all."

Just then Brody's face was in the window, grinning at Mary. He plugged his nose and lowered himself out of view, pretending to sink into the ocean behind him. Mary laughed, waving him off.

Amusement snaked through Lauren without warning, the shock of it as startling as the feel of jumping into an ice-cold pool. "How do you know Brody?" she asked the woman.

"I've known him since he was a baby. Frank and I sold our home in Virginia and moved here to start the inn right before Brody was born. His mother, Melinda, was one of the people I met when I first got here. We've been close friends ever since."

"Ah," she said.

"I actually got your bracelet from Brody's mother," Mary said, taking Lauren's wrist to admire it. "It's pretty, isn't it?"

"Yes." She wriggled her arm, making the pieces tinkle as they tapped against each other. "I'm still getting used to wearing it. It keeps reminding me that it's there, which is nice because it gives me another chance to appreciate it."

Mary looked out the window at the view. The sound of hammering had moved further down the decking that ran the length of the porch. "It sure is a pretty afternoon."

Lauren followed her gaze and found two seagulls floating out over the ocean, the sight distracting her from everything for a moment. They were so pure and free as they glided through the air. "It certainly is."

"Well, you should take the evening and settle in. And if you get hungry tonight, the cook is serving oysters on the half shell, crab bisque, and key lime pie for dessert."

"That sounds delicious." She closed Mary's paper calendar. "I'll get working on this," she said, holding it up before tucking it under her arm.

Mary chuckled. "I won't be expecting you to do anything tonight. Kick back and enjoy yourself."

That sounded great, but Lauren had no idea exactly *how* to do that.

Chapter Three

The rhythmic shushing of the waves and the summer heat had lulled Lauren into a dreamlike respite as she swayed back and forth in the hammock on the porch outside her suite. After unpacking her bags and adding her own little touches to her quarters, like the framed photo of her parents and two of the small house plants she'd brought with her from New York, she finally settled outside in the glorious afternoon sunshine.

She opened her eyes just enough to view the cotton-candy hues of the evening sky. The sun struggled to let go of the day, only dipping below the horizon at around eight o'clock in the evening. Had she slept that long? Her bare feet were propped on the gathering of rope at one end and her head rested on the small canvas pillow at the other. A light breeze filtered through the porch, ruffling her sundress, the stillness of it all something she wasn't sure she'd ever experienced.

Notwithstanding her tranquil state, her stomach rumbled. Relishing the silence, she'd opted to skip dinner, even though she didn't know what she was going to eat tonight. However, this being her first night in residence, she didn't feel terribly comfortable rooting around in the kitchen after-hours.

A creak at the end of the porch and the sound of footsteps caused her to come to completely. She sat up, swinging her feet onto the brand-new yellow boards of the decking that had been replaced today, the hammock creaking under her.

Brody was striding toward her with two brightly colored cocktails. He was clean-shaven, his hair combed, wearing a loose button-up with a pocket on the chest and a pair of board shorts.

"I didn't mean to disturb you," he said when he reached her. "Mary asked me to bring you a drink. I don't think she realized you were sleeping." He offered her one of the glasses full of pink liquid with a spear of fruit and a little yellow umbrella on the top.

"It's okay," she said, blinking to clear her vision, the cold glass a refreshing sensation in the heat. "What is this?"

"Rum punch. Mary's decided to put them out for the guests in the evenings, trying to keep up with the newer hotels and their bars."

Lauren inspected the summery drink.

"If you're worried about the alcohol, she goes very light on it to save on costs." He grinned at her in that friendly way of his, and she was pretty sure he was, with her, exactly the way he was with everyone.

"Thank you." She took a sip, the sweet nectar of fruit and rum going down easily, leaving a sugary taste on her tongue.

"I was on my way into town and I had to drop by some more wood, but I wanted to show you something." He set his drink on the wooden ledge of the railing and pulled his phone from his pocket. "I don't want you to think that I was trying to hit on you at the market earlier. I really do have a friend named Stephanie Clark, and from a distance, you kind of look like her. I had her text me a picture of herself to prove it."

Lauren held her hair back to combat the coastal wind, took another sip of her cocktail, and stood up. The hammock swung with her sudden movement.

Brody handed her his phone, and she immediately noticed the woman's green eyes, the brown hair, similar in color to her own, although the woman's locks were a little shorter. "I could see why you mistook me for her." She handed it back to him.

"See? I wasn't a creep."

"I don't think you're a creep," she said with a smile.

He slipped his phone into his back pocket, picked up his drink, and took a long pull of it. "Good. You had me worried."

"I did?" She stopped stirring her drink.

"You seemed a little… standoffish when we met. I worried that you thought I was trying to pick you up or something."

She shook her head, the idea the furthest thing from her mind at the time.

"So how do you know your friend?" she asked, gesturing toward the phone in his back pocket.

"I've known her since childhood. When I told her about the way you and I met, she mentioned that she's had that happen to her before too. Someone thought she was the host of a TV show once."

"Oh really?" Lauren said, laughing uncomfortably.

His gaze narrowed, immediately zeroing in on her reaction.

Lauren's pulse rose in her ears, her body burning through the slight buzz of the rum. She took another drink to chase the comforting feeling once again. "Sorry, it's just so funny. A TV show…" She was trying to explain her reaction but really only making it worse.

"Yeah," he said slowly. "A wedding show. Know anyone who fits that description?" He gave her a sideways look that made her wonder if he was onto her. Certainly he'd told this person her name and she'd confirmed it.

"I do," she admitted, her old life slithering back in, the wave of anxiety negating everything she'd just done tonight to relax. She gave him a look of warning to let him know that she'd rather not talk about it now.

He stared at her for a tick longer than she'd have liked. "Well, Mary also asked me to make sure you were fed. Wanna tell me about it over dinner?"

"Not really." She set her drink down next to his on the wide railing.

"All right. Want to *not* tell me about it over dinner? Mary said she doesn't think you've eaten anything since you got here, and she'll get on me if I don't take you somewhere."

The fact that he knew who she was would make him curious and, even if he avoided the subject of the TV show, he would certainly want to ask her things about herself over a meal. The idea of that filled her with apprehension. She did *not* want to delve into her old life because she feared that she wouldn't be able to crawl back out of it. The weight had already lifted just slightly, and if everyone would leave her alone, she might find some peace. But she was also starving. And she needed real food—not another sandwich from the market.

"Dinner's been cleaned up already here at the inn, the cook's gone for the night, and it's peak summer hours. You won't get anything in town without reservations right now," he added.

"And you magically have them?" she asked.

That smirk returned, sending her to her drink for a long swig, her nerves prickling at the sight of that elusive happiness she wanted so badly to feel herself.

"You didn't let me finish. *You* won't get anything without reservations. I, on the other hand, know everyone here. They'll seat me anywhere. I was already heading into town to eat anyway, so it's no skin off my back if you tag along."

"If I say yes, I don't want to talk about myself," she informed him.

His brows pulled together, inquisitiveness in those sparkling eyes. "Okay."

While she absolutely did not want to have to spend an evening cornered by Brody Harrison, the decision came down to emotional risk versus her primal need for nourishment. Her stomach growled again. "Can you give me ten minutes?"

"Of course. I'll be in the main room." He held up his cocktail.

Drink in hand, Lauren rushed back to her suite, tied up her hair and jumped in the shower to wash her face and rinse the car ride off her. Wrapping herself in a white, fluffy towel, she sipped her cocktail and pulled out her makeup bag, the routine of getting ready like second nature. The ease of being on autopilot was comforting, given the situation. As she applied foundation and powder, blushed her cheeks, and swiped her lips with lip gloss, she could cut herself off from the new sensations she was feeling.

At every turn, she was facing new experiences and different conversations. In a strange way, it was both draining and refreshing.

She combed through her hair and then slipped on a clean sundress, this one a pale blue with a white lace-embroidered hem, and her favorite pair of sandals. As she stood in front of the full-length mirror, it was as if she were looking at a stranger. On the outside, she was put together, poised, stylish. Yet, on the inside, she was in a complete state of disarray. With a deep breath, she grabbed her straw handbag and headed out to the main room to meet Brody.

When she walked in, he stood up, the empty drink now sitting beside him. "Hey," he said, as if he'd known her for years, something else she wasn't used to.

"Hi," she said, stepping up next to him.

"So, what do ya fancy?"

Lauren shook her head. "I don't know," she replied, taking shallow breaths as the two of them walked down to the parking lot. The idea of having a meal with a man other than Mason made her edgy, even if it was platonic. Then suddenly he stopped walking. When she turned to see what was the matter, he was observing her.

"Did you finish your cocktail?" he asked.

"No, I left it on the sink in my bathroom."

He nodded as if he could've guessed her answer. "Your shoulders are up near your ears."

She forced herself into a more relaxed position.

"If you don't have a preference, I think I've got the perfect place in mind for dinner," he said, giving her an appreciative once-over.

"Oh?"

He opened the truck door, and she climbed in. "Yeah." He shut her door and spoke to her through the open window. "It's casual."

He pulled out of the small parking lot onto the main road that snaked along the coast, the warm wind rushing in around her. She set her gaze on the cadenced push and pull of the waves, and the swell of foam as they gently splashed against the shore. She wondered why anyone who visited would ever leave.

"So, you've been here your whole life?" she asked, imagining what it would be like to spend childhood in a place like this.

"Yep," he replied.

The wind rippled his shirt, pushing it against his toned chest. She took in the strength that showed in his arms, the coarseness in his hands, and the way he managed to keep the substantial vehicle steady with only his wrist on the steering wheel.

His attention flickered away from the road—he seemed to notice her assessment of him. Caught in the act, she turned to the seagrass sliding past the window.

"I know what you must be thinking," he said. "I'm not just some small-town beach bum. I *have* been outside North Carolina."

His comment seemed to come out of nowhere, but then she remembered the way he'd eyed her designer bags when she was unpacking her car.

"I wasn't thinking anything," she said.

He didn't seem convinced, but he remained quiet, the two of them falling into silence until he pulled the truck to a stop outside a small shack of a restaurant with blue-shingled siding, bright yellow trim, and a porch overflowing with waiting guests. In the sandy yard beside it, families waiting for their tables played beanbag toss games and ladder ball, young children ran through the crowd, the boys in their cotton shirts and shorts and the girls in sundresses, their laughter infectious.

Lauren opened the truck door and hopped out onto the gravel as Brody made his way to her side. He gestured toward the porch. "After you."

They maneuvered through the throng of people toward the door. Brody held it open for her, allowing her to enter. A beachy tune of steel drums and guitars played overhead. The restaurant was packed; every stool at the tiki bar, covered in surfing stickers and bottle caps, was occupied.

"Where will we sit?" she asked, concerned that with this crowd, even Brody's connections wouldn't be enough to get them a table.

"Give me just a sec," he replied, looking over her head and raising his hand to a man with long gray hair that looked as if he'd been shipwrecked on an island for the last decade.

With a salty grin under his scraggly beard, the man leaned across the bar between two patrons, grabbed a bottle of beer, popped off the top, and made his way over to them.

"Well, look what the tide brought in," he said, giving Brody a friendly smack on the arm and handing him the bottle. "You bringin' me a fresh catch of mahi?"

"Not tonight." Brody took a long drink of beer. "I've got another 'catch' this evening. I'm tasked with getting dinner for Mary Everett's new employee." He tipped his head over to Lauren.

The whole situation was so foreign to her that she'd forgotten how to act, so she just stood there like a deer in headlights.

"Lauren, this is Lou."

"It's nice to meet you," she said, reaching out for a handshake.

Lou wiped his hand on his board shorts and then shook hers. "Pick your poison," he said.

Lauren scrambled to keep up with all the commotion around her—families laughing, patrons telling stories, couples toasting, music playing, kids coloring pictures on their paper placemats...

Brody leaned in, his woodsy scent tickling her nose, and said in a low voice right in her ear, "He wants to know what you'd like to drink."

"Um..."

"Lou, could you make her your Shipwreck?"

"Absolutely," he said, looking her up and down, clearly trying to figure her out.

"Any chance you can scare us up a table?" Brody asked. Then he addressed Lou more quietly, gesturing toward the ocean view behind all the patrons.

Lou clapped him on the back. "You know I keep a couple spots open just for friends like you. Follow me."

They moved through the crowded dining room, out the back doors, and onto a covered deck with more tables, an outdoor bar, and a panoramic view of the Atlantic. A small table sat empty at the back, with only the railing between it and the sand dunes leading to the ocean. A sunken tealight at the bottom of a glass jar flickered in the center of the table.

Brody pulled out a chair, gesturing for Lauren to take a seat. "Can you bring us a basket of your crawfish hushpuppies too?" he asked Lou. "I'll throw in an extra fillet of tuna on the next delivery."

"Done. Hushpuppies and a Shipwreck, on the house, comin' right up."

"Crawfish hushpuppies? That sounds amazing," Lauren said as Brody took a seat across from her. She placed her hands on the table, her new bracelet glimmering against the candlelight.

"They're out of this world," Brody said. "Everything here is made with fresh catch. The crawfish were caught this morning."

Her stomach rumbled. "Mm. I'm so hungry."

"I figured. And I also figured you weren't up for crowds tonight, so I asked Lou if we could sit out here."

"How did you know?"

"Well, for starters, you chose the farthest corner of the deck at the inn and didn't eat dinner. Then the look on your face when we pulled up here pretty much drove it home."

"I'm not really good in large gatherings at all…" She used to be, though.

His brows knitted together. "Don't you plan weddings for a living?"

She tensed at the mention of it. "I said I didn't want to talk about me, but yes. And that's different because I know what I need to do, what to say, and to whom."

He looked into her eyes as if there were something in them that he was trying to solve.

"Let's talk about you," she suggested. "You're from here, you said."

"Yeah." He took a drink of his beer. "Born and raised."

"And Mary said your mom's name is Melinda."

"Yep. She runs a shop in town."

Lauren held up her wrist and jingled the bracelet. "While you were out working on the porch, Mary told me she got this from your mom."

"Mom's great at finding rare treasures."

"What about your dad?"

There was a slight shift in his face when she mentioned his father. It was as if he'd gotten used to hiding it, but she caught it. He fiddled with his bottle, leaving a streak of condensation on the table. "He's recently taken a job as a professor of American history at Boston University."

"Oh," she said, seeing him in a new perspective. This gritty fisherman was the son of two people who seemed very different from him. "Boston... So your parents aren't together?"

"No, they separated last year."

"I'm sorry to hear that," she said.

"It's fine. They parted ways amicably," he said with a reassuring smile. "I think the documents my mother is finally drawing up with her lawyer say 'irreconcilable differences,' but my mother's explanation was that he was too much like his own father."

"Ouch," she said, making a face. "What was your grandfather like, then?"

"Pretentious, according to her."

Lou returned with two menus under his arm, a basket, and a hurricane glass filled to the brim with a white, frosty concoction complete with a spear of pineapple in the top. "One Shipwreck," he said, setting it in front of Lauren. "And the hushpuppies." He handed a menu to each of them. "I'll send a server your way in a second."

Lauren pinched a hushpuppy from the basket and bit through the crispy exterior. The buttery flavor of the crawfish complemented the flaky bread center perfectly.

"Hey, Brody," a flirty female voice called from behind her, cutting through the moment.

Brody looked past Lauren. "Hey," he said, raising a hand in greeting.

Lauren turned around to find a blonde with tanned skin and a perfect figure clad in cut-off shorts and tank top. The woman batted her eyelashes, and Brody smiled back. She wriggled her fingers at him as if to say toodle-oo and then headed off toward the bar. The whole exchange made Lauren question what she was even doing there having dinner with someone like Brody. She should be at the inn, where she'd planned to be. She turned back around and took an enormous drink from her straw, the coconut and rum filling her mouth and giving her brain freeze before she forced it down. When she recovered, Brody's eyes were back on her.

"I'm not allowed to ask you anything about yourself, but everything you do screams that something is eating at you and you're dying to tell someone."

She flinched at his word choice. "Well, you don't know me as well as you think, then." She took another drink, the alcohol sailing to her head on her near-empty stomach. She grabbed another hushpuppy to combat it.

"Then set me straight." He leaned back, putting his elbow on the back of the chair. She wondered what it was like to be that carefree.

"I came here to get away from my life," she admitted. "So the very last thing I want to do is to spend my free time reliving it."

He pouted, clearly thinking this over. "I can see why you'd want to escape your life."

"You can?" she asked, surprised.

"Yeah." The corners of his mouth turned upward in what seemed like empathy. "A life of busy schedules, city streets, traffic…" He shook his head. "I'd trade that every day for this." He waved a hand out at the ocean.

"Hey, Brody," a waitress said, coming up to their table to take their order.

"Hey, Molly," he returned.

She addressed Lauren. "Y'all know what you want to eat?"

Lauren scrambled to read the menu; she hadn't looked at it for even a second since they'd sat down. "I'll have the scallops," she said, choosing the first thing that caught her eye, her chest immediately tightening.

If we lived on the coast, I'd eat my weight in scallops… Mason's voice filtered through her mind as the memory of a meal they'd shared returned to her. Lauren forced herself to look up at the waitress, fiddling nervously with her new bracelet.

"And I already know what *you* want," Molly said to Brody.

Both of them said "shrimp and grits" at the same time, the two of them laughing at some sort of inside joke.

"All right, I'll get that in for ya." The waitress took their menus, leaving them alone once more.

There was a definite ease to life here, something Lauren hadn't experienced in New York or even in the small Tennessee town where she was from. People took time for one another and enjoyed each other.

And even if skirting around Brody's questions and assumptions about her was part of the experience, she was glad that she'd decided to come.

Summer, 1957
Fairhope, Alabama

"Promise me you'll meet me here first thing in the morning?" Penelope asked, her face troubled.

Phillip reached over and caressed her cheek, but it didn't seem to help. Tomorrow was her last day in Fairhope, and Phillip had yet to discuss the subject with his parents. He didn't want to spend the overnight hours away from her. He wanted to stay there with Penelope, holding her in his arms until the sun made its return the next day. He reached over and wiped a runaway drop of saltwater from her face, already envisioning his life with her.

"Of course I will." He closed his eyes and pressed his lips to hers, tasting the salt on her mouth, the electricity between them giving him the courage to broach the topic with his parents.

She pulled back and drew her arm out of the water, unfastening the bracelet made of green and turquoise glass remnants, polished smooth and strung together, holding it out to him.

Phillip opened his hand, the glass pieces cascading like a miniature waterfall into it. She closed his fingers, wrapping hers around them. "Now you *have* to meet me," she said with a giggle. "My mother will never speak to me again if she thinks I've lost this. She and I made it together."

He held the bracelet up to the sun, the light glimmering off the water droplets on each of the pieces.

Penelope leaned over and kissed his cheek, making him want to wrap himself around her and never let go. "She doesn't know I have it."

"Why did you wear it today?"

She gazed up at him with those green eyes that made his knees weak. "Because my mother said it brings her good luck."

Penelope didn't need luck. She'd already roped him right in, all on her own.

Chapter Four

Rodanthe, North Carolina

A gentle tapping sound outside drew Lauren from her sleep. She opened her eyes, an early-morning purple glow streaming in through the curtains in her bedroom. She checked her phone on the bedside table: six o'clock. With a yawn, she sat up and stretched her arms over her head. Before she even climbed out of bed, the tapping became a loud *sshh*. Lauren got up and pulled the curtains back, revealing deep gray clouds that were dumping rain into an angry sea.

Wrapping her bathrobe around her, she set the single-cup coffee-maker in her kitchenette and slipped her mug underneath it. While the coffee began to percolate, she got Mary's calendar and her laptop and sat down at the table, opening the scheduling program.

She pulled up the screen and began entering in the dates and their various codes to denote the service type. The familiar act of facilitating tasks that had nothing to do with her old life was therapeutic in a way. She could function entirely in that moment, and she knew exactly what to do. When Lauren was finished, Mary would be able to view all her day's agenda items on one page, but she could also click "Personal" to see her private calendar, "Maintenance" for improvements to the inn, and "Meetings and Agendas" for her scheduled meetings in town.

The coffeemaker gurgled and hissed as she typed, a rich scent filling the room. When the mug was full, she got up, pulled the cream from the refrigerator, and poured it in. With her steaming coffee in hand, and the rain outside, she was oddly calm. A sense of purpose took over; sitting in her little kitchen area, she sipped the rich, nutty liquid and continued her work.

After about an hour, a light knock at her door pulled her out of her focused concentration. She left her computer at the small table and peered through the peephole, finding Mary on the other side.

"Good morning," the woman said with a friendly lift of her eyebrows when Lauren answered the door.

"Good morning."

"I know yesterday was a whirlwind. I thought I'd stop by to see if you had everything you need."

"Oh, yes, thank you. I was just organizing your calendar."

Mary gripped the end of her cane, leaning on it. "Before breakfast?"

"Well, I did make a cup of coffee," Lauren countered as she opened the door wider. "Please, come in and have a seat."

Mary wobbled into the room and went over to one of the chairs in the sitting area, lowering herself down.

"Would you like a cup?" Lauren asked as she retrieved her own from the kitchenette.

"No thank you, dear. I've had mine already," Mary called back to her.

Lauren returned and sat down across from her new boss. "I was planning to get something to eat once I was ready for the day. I'm a pretty early riser so I'm used to waiting for breakfast until I'm on my way to work." She dared not admit that waking before the sun had become a ritual over the last year, because staying in bed too long would allow the thoughts about her empty future to arise, so she'd rather just get up and face the day.

"I'm an early riser, too, and with this rain, my joints had me up earlier than usual." She kneaded the knuckles on her right hand.

There was something between the two of them that settled any unease that Lauren would normally have while sitting across from someone in her bathrobe. Mary had a mothering quality to her. Even though she was Mary's employee, she was comfortable with the woman's unpretentious and friendly nature. And their mutual understanding of loss gave them an unspoken bond that Lauren hadn't shared with anyone else.

"How was dinner last night with Brody?" Mary asked, shifting in her seat until she appeared to be in a better position.

"It was nice," she replied. Since she wouldn't let him ask anything about her, he'd spent most of the night talking about the island.

"He helps me out a lot," Mary said. "I wanted to take you to dinner myself, but it's getting so hard to move around these days. I usually don't venture off the property unless I have to."

"You didn't need to arrange for someone to take me out." She curled her legs underneath her and held the mug with both hands.

"I know, but if you're going to spend a considerable amount of time here, I want you to feel comfortable."

If she only knew how difficult a task that was…

"I don't need anyone taking me on dates to feel more comfortable," Lauren said, allowing a small smile.

"Ah, I wouldn't call it a date around Brody." The woman chuckled. "Brody Harrison doesn't date."

"No?" she asked, recalling the flirty blonde and then Molly's inside joke with him at dinner. "Women seem to like him."

"He'd be the catch of the century if he let anyone in." Mary shook her head. "The ladies do love him, don't they?"

Lauren didn't want to admit how handsome he was or how kind he'd been in taking her out and asking for that table away from everyone just to give her a calmer place to eat. "Why doesn't he date?" she asked, allowing her curiosity to get the better of her.

"I asked him once, and he just shrugged, as if the mere idea were preposterous. I wonder, though, if his parents' splitting up has anything to do with it. They had a rocky marriage."

"Oh." She didn't ask any more questions, not wanting to pry too far into Brody's life. Regardless of his reasoning, the idea that Brody wasn't looking for anything did make her feel better about spending time with him. So he didn't like to date; that made two of them.

"I actually stopped by your suite in a work capacity," Mary said. "I was talking with Brody's mother, Melinda, and she tells me that she's heard you know a thing or two about planning weddings."

Great. "I suppose Brody mentioned it to her."

Mary tilted her cane a bit, leaning it against the chair to keep it upright. "I had no idea I was in the presence of a celebrity."

Lauren shook her head uncomfortably.

"Do you mind grabbing my calendar?"

Lauren got up and retrieved the spiral-bound book, bringing it over to Mary.

"Thank you." Mary opened the book and began flipping pages to the current month of August. Her attention on the calendar in front of her, she continued, "Brody has a friend named Stephanie—"

Lauren perked up at the mention of the familiar name. "Stephanie?"

"Yes, Stephanie Clark. She also knows about your wedding planning skills, and after hearing that you'll be working here for the next six weeks, she and her fiancé would like to up the date and move their wedding here to the inn. That's fantastic, since we could use the money."

Lauren could hardly get a breath in. Flashes of the woman, dressed in white, walking down the aisle toward her soulmate slashed through her thoughts, and she didn't know if she'd be able to survive that happening in reality.

"They originally decided to get married a few months from now, but since you're here, they're willing to make a change. And most of her wedding party didn't expect to travel for the wedding, so she has to plan around their schedules." Mary's eyes remained on the book that was sprawled over her lap. "She wants *you* to plan it."

If the mere request weren't enough to worry Lauren, six weeks or less would have her scrambling on a good day.

Mary scrolled a finger down the page. "I knew I had a few dates available for an event that big, but I needed my calendar to give her a concrete answer." She tapped one of the boxes. "We might be able to fit it in on the week of the seventeenth."

"The seventeenth?" Lauren leaned over Mary's shoulder, clawing through her anxiety. The weddings she'd planned with Andy at Sugar and Lace had been many, many months in the making. "That's in less than two weeks," she said, her words coming out a little more incredulous than she'd have liked. She composed herself. "I usually require nearly a year to plan a wedding."

"I can let her know that," Mary said as she seemed to notice that there was more than concern about the wedding date in Lauren's answer. "It could be great business for the inn, though. Maybe we can speak more about it later today." Mary set the calendar on the coffee table, put her cane out in front of her, and hoisted herself up to a standing position. "I'll catch up with you later."

"Okay." Lauren led her to the door, seeing her out.

Just as she'd said goodbye, her phone began to ring. She loped back across the room quickly, grabbing it and seeing her friend's name. "Hey, Andy," she said.

"Hey, Dave is freaking out and wants both of us on the show," Andy replied with no pleasantries. "I cannot change his mind."

Lauren fell onto the sofa and pulled a faded pillow into her lap, feeling like she was under water. She knew the TV producer would struggle with this. "Well, he can't ask that of me. I don't even own the company anymore. Plus, you brought all the banter anyway."

"He says you're the face of the show."

"He's just trying to make me feel guilty."

"I think he's right…" Andy said.

The uneasiness in the way she trailed off made Lauren nervous. She sat on the edge of the sofa with the phone pressed to her ear.

"I took the Maxwell wedding."

Lauren's mouth hung open. "Why did you do that?" They'd talked about this. The Maxwells were billionaires. Sugar and Lace didn't have the resources yet for an event of that size and caliber. They'd need thousands of dollars for the equipment alone that would be necessary to pull off something like that. Not to mention the helicopter patrol to keep the paparazzi away. They were doing well, but they didn't have enough money to front the massive cost while also taking on all their regular weddings.

"It's like we used to say when we were starting out: dream bigger, get bigger."

"Yeah, but you have to be able to handle it financially."

"I can if we do the next season of the show. We can negotiate for more in our contracts."

Lauren shook her head, at a loss for words.

"I need the show to fund the company, Lauren, and Dave's not doing it without you. He said he'll cancel it."

"How is any of this up to me? I'm not in the wedding business. I've taken another job, and there are people counting on me here. Not to mention—at the very least—I need a break from the show."

Andy sighed. "I know. I'm sorry I've burdened you with it. I'll figure out something to convince him that he can do it with just one of us."

"I have faith that you can," Lauren said.

"Do you miss planning weddings at all?"

"Well, funny you mention that…" Lauren squeezed her eyes shut as they began to pulse in pain and filled her friend in on the whole ordeal. "I have something like nine days, Andy. *Nine.*"

"That's crazy," Andy said with a disbelieving laugh. "Does the couple have *anything* reserved yet?"

"I have no idea."

"Can you handle this?" Andy's voice softened with the question.

Lauren took in a long, slow breath and let it out. "I don't know, honestly."

Her friend's support was evident in the stillness that hung between them on the line. "Call me later today and fill me in, okay?"

"All right."

As if she didn't have enough to deal with, she now had to think about planning a wedding *and* worry about leaving her old partner to manage the business on her own. *Sometimes, the only way forward is to take a blind step into the day*, she remembered Mason saying whenever she had a tough project. She'd take that first step. And then one more. Again and again until she didn't feel like she was going to fall apart anymore.

Summer, 1957
Fairhope, Alabama

"You can't be serious, Phillip." His mother folded her arms in the middle of the artisanal ceramic-tiled floor of their kitchen and looked helplessly at his father.

"I am." Phillip's heart thumped in his chest as he waited like a willing thief for his sentence. He knew this response would be coming, which was why he waited until the last possible minute to mention it, holding out hope that somehow he'd magically think of a reason for his parents to come through for him. "She's only here for the summer, but I want her to stay." He reached into his pocket and gripped the sea glass bracelet, the pieces as smooth as Penelope's skin. "I'd like to ask for her hand in marriage."

Phillip's mother leaned in, her eyes like lasers, her perfect red lips set in a straight line of fear. "You haven't gotten her into a… precarious position, have you?"

The bracelet fell to the bottom of his pocket and Phillip put his hands on his hips. "I can't believe you'd ask me that. She's a good girl."

"She's not…" His mother trailed off, but he already knew what she refrained from saying. Penelope wasn't a debutante. She didn't grow up the type of lady his parents had intended for him to marry.

"Say it," he urged her.

His mother took in a tight breath. "She's the daughter of a handyman and a maid. What if she's only after your money? Have you thought about that? She'll take you for everything you've got. Your entire fortune." His mother shook her head, clearly still reeling.

"No she won't. She doesn't care about any of that." He put his face in front of his mother to break her anxious stare at the wall. "I told her I'd love her forever. And I will."

"How could you be so irresponsible?" his mother barked.

His father, who'd remained silent the entire time, hung his head.

"I *love* her," Phillip proclaimed, ignoring his mother's stab at Penelope's motives. Having grown up with wealth herself and then marrying his father, heir to the most successful corporate expansion and acquisition firm in the country, she didn't understand Penelope's way of life. Phillip didn't either, if he was being honest with himself, but he wanted to.

"You don't know what love is, child," his mother said. "You're eighteen."

"Yes," he said. "A legal adult. I know how I feel about her."

His mother took a step closer to him, the lines forming between her penciled brows the way they did whenever she was upset. "In our family, you have to consider more than just your fleeting fascination. You're going to Stanford in a week. How do you propose to do that while *married*?" The word came out as if it put a bad taste in her mouth.

"I'll think of something."

His mother sucked in a long breath through her nose. "And what are we supposed to tell people when they ask?"

"I don't care! Tell them whatever you want. She'll be my *wife*. What more is there to say?"

"Son." His father stepped forward. He was a man of few words, yet he could command a room in an instant. "She will *not* be your wife. This will ruin your future."

"You don't know that to be true."

"I absolutely do." He gritted his teeth. "I forbid you to see her. And if you move forward with this, I will have no other option but to withhold your inheritance."

"You can't do that," Phillip spat.

"Oh, yes. When the fate of our family line is at stake, I certainly can."

Chapter Five

Rodanthe, North Carolina

"Right now, you've got the website set up so that people can call you for bookings," Lauren explained to Mary later that morning when she came downstairs to the office, "but I can add a feature so guests can reserve rooms and suites directly through the website, and it will automatically appear in the scheduling program."

"That's amazing." Mary leaned over to view Lauren's computer screen.

"But that's not all it will do," Lauren added, clicking a few keys. "It can automatically alert the staff of the room booking so that they can prepare for the guests, in case they need fresh flowers or little treats thanking them for their stay."

"Mm." Mary frowned.

"What is it?" Lauren asked, noticing her concern.

"Well, I'm a bit short staffed, so the rooms just get a one-time cleaning. There's nothing to prepare. Things like mints on pillows and fresh flowers don't happen here anymore."

"That's fine. You don't have to use that feature," she said. "I know you've been adding in a few things to match your competition, so this might be something small we could work toward."

"Yes," she replied, brightening, "maybe you and I can prepare the rooms."

"Not to worry. I can do things like welcome baskets with my eyes closed. But right now, let me show you the rest of the program." She hit one of the buttons on the screen. "It can also collect bills and create payments for the guests so they can check out without ever needing your assistance. Eventually, we can even move to electronic keys and they won't even have to return it."

Lauren decided not to go into all the other technological features, given the slight bewilderment on Mary's face, instead focusing on Mary's favorite topic—the guests.

"Here's something you might like: this option will give you a total number of guests that you can provide to people like the chef you mentioned. That will give you more time to focus on the needs of the guests themselves."

"And mints and flowers," Mary said, a sparkle returning to her eyes.

"Yes! I'd love to work up a plan and a budget for little amenities like that, if you're up for it."

"Definitely. We'll have to be very tight with the budget, however."

"Sure."

Mary leaned over and inspected the computer screen. "You managed to get all this ironed out in one morning? My head is spinning."

A deep pleasure filled Lauren at the idea that she could be of help. "I've had a lot of practice. It's how I managed my events company. We had, sometimes, ten weddings all being planned at the same time. If we didn't have a program to keep it all straight, we'd go crazy."

"And who's managing your company while you're away?"

The finality of Lauren's choice settled upon her, and she considered how Andy had taken that wedding that Lauren never would have. "I sold my half to my business partner."

"Why, when you're clearly so great at it?"

She turned to face Mary, wanting to explain without actually having to. "It's… a long story."

"I enjoy long stories."

Lauren produced her manufactured smile. She liked Mary, but she didn't want to have to get into the details of the last year. "Maybe one day I'll tell you all about it."

"All right. We need to focus on responding to Stephanie anyway. She's coming back into town, and Melinda would like to bring her over to introduce you two tomorrow. That might be a good time to pin down a date."

Lauren was not getting out of this. At the end of the day, she was employed by Mary, and if the woman wanted her to run the wedding, she'd have to put her fears aside and agree. "Yes, let's find a time that works to meet her."

She couldn't have the inn losing money because of her personal issues. The Tide and Swallow needed this wedding.

"How's your day been so far?" Andy asked on the other end of the phone while Lauren walked down the shore behind the inn, her arms full with a packed lunch and a blanket.

"Busy. This morning I met with the innkeeper about scheduling, and then I spent the rest of the time shadowing her, supervising the cleaning crews so I can take over those duties."

"What are you doing now? I hear wind through the phone," Andy said.

"Mary's friend Joe called to say he was coming over, so she gave me a break. I thought I'd have lunch on the beach."

"That sounds incredible."

Lauren danced through the hot sand and shielded her eyes briefly with her free hand to relieve them of the intense light. "It's not bad," she said. "But it's hot."

Andy laughed. "I'd take the coastal heat any day."

"Want to have some tomorrow?" she teased. "You could come in my place. I'm meeting the bride and groom."

"How are you feeling about that?"

"I'm not sure yet. Part of me thinks it'll never fly. We don't have enough time. You and I both know that."

"Yeah, you can probably convince the bride that there's no way and be off the hook. Show her our yearly planning itinerary where we have every task broken down by month."

"That's a good idea." She repositioned the strap of the small cooler bag on her shoulder, the sea air blowing her hair in circles.

"I didn't even get to ask on the last call, apart from the shotgun wedding, are you getting settled okay?"

"I've settled in as well as expected."

"That wasn't the answer I was hoping for. What's up?"

Lauren took in a deep breath of warm, salty air. "It's hard to assimilate into a new group of people. Most of the time, I can't escape myself."

"What do you mean?"

When she got to a flat spot, Lauren dropped her cooler into the sand and shook her blanket in the wind, the phone wedged between her ear and shoulder. "I thought I could start over and leave everything behind, but I can't. My old life is with me anywhere I go. I'm still a mess inside." She sat down on the blanket and brushed the sand off her cooler. "I think I'm damaged goods forever."

"Have you considered seeing someone?" Andy asked, her voice gentle.

"Like a counselor?"

"Yeah. Someone who could help you think through it all."

"I've already thought it through more than I'd like to. What more is there that anyone could tell me?"

"I don't know. I'm not a professional. Maybe they could get to the root of it and offer some coping strategies."

"The root of it is that I lost my entire life and I can't seem to get it back. And I really doubt any amount of deep breathing or journaling about the positives will help."

"It might be good to give it a chance before you write it off."

She fought the wind to keep the blanket flat. "You know, I think Mason would encourage me to move on. He'd want me to be happy. And I want those things as well. But even if I could give myself permission to do that, I feel like I don't even know who I am anymore. All I see is the shell of the life I was building with Mason that can no longer be."

"Think back to before the accident. Can you remember what you enjoyed doing, outside of family and work?"

Lauren looked out at the sparkling sea; there were no remnants at all of the morning storm apart from a line of sea kelp that had washed ashore. "I can hardly remember."

"Well, I can tell you what *I* saw. You were the dreamer of the two of us. You were the one with all the ideas. You saw answers where I couldn't find any."

A lump in her throat, Lauren lay back on the blanket, her knees up, her eyes closed to the blinding sun. A tear rolled down her temple and she wiped it away.

"You used to dance. In the kitchen of our apartment, before you moved out to live with Mason. You would have the music so loud that I couldn't hear myself think. You'd spin in circles, singing the lyrics of whatever was playing. I always wondered how you could be so upbeat after a long day of work."

With her eyes still closed, the bright sun warming her face, Lauren tried to connect to her former self, but she was coming up empty, her brain clouded with too much from the last year to summon anything that had transpired before. "I miss that person," she admitted.

"She's still there," Andy said.

"I'm not so sure." She sat up and cleared her throat so she didn't roll onto her side and start sobbing. "I should probably go. I need to eat lunch and get back to work."

"All right. You can call anytime; you know that."

"I'll call you back when I have a longer break. I'd love to hear how things are going on your end, and if I do have to plan this wedding, I'll need to pick your brain on some ideas."

"Okay," her friend said.

They said their goodbyes and Lauren busied herself trying to stay in the moment and not drift back to her thoughts. She opened her cooler and took out a shrimp and cucumber salad that Mary had offered the guests for lunch. She stared out at the ocean, letting it calm her. A sandpiper ran across the flat sand where the waves had retreated, leaving its footprints before it flew away with the next swell, the foam washing over them, the tracks disappearing. She pierced a cucumber slice with her fork and took a bite, the cold salad refreshing in the heat.

"Hey there," a familiar voice called in the distance.

She twisted around to find Brody walking toward her, holding a pair of flip-flops, his bare feet padding across the sand easily where she'd hopped as if it were a bed of fire.

"I came by to work on the porch and Mary said you were out here." He dropped the shoes into the sand and plopped down beside her even though she hadn't offered. She didn't mind, though. Something about him felt so comfortable, as if she hadn't just met him.

"You work in those?" She eyed his flip-flops.

"I'm just replacing railing spindles today, so my toes will be just fine."

She smiled and then turned toward a seagull that had swooped down into the ocean in a nosedive.

"She wanted me to let you know that she won't need you until two o'clock, so you can extend your lunch break."

"Did she say why?"

"She'll be at the inn, but having coffee with my mom." His broad shoulder brushed hers, the feel of it giving her arm a tingle, and she tensed in response. But she forced her muscles to relax before he noticed.

It occurred to her that Mary should be the one relaxing on the beach at her age, yet Lauren supposed she couldn't if there was no one to do her work... "Doesn't she need me to run the inn so she can spend time with your mother?"

He frowned, shaking his head. "It's slow, midday. She usually takes her break at this time anyway."

"Well, I'm here if anyone needs me."

A warm gust of wind whipped past them and she palmed the blanket to keep the edges from kicking sand onto her belongings.

"What time do you wake up in the mornings?" The silver flecks in his blue eyes rivaled the shimmering sea. He was certainly attractive, but what struck her was that over the last year, she hadn't noticed if anyone she'd met was attractive or not, so why was she noticing now?

"Around five o'clock, why?"

"Mary suggested that I help you get a feel for the area to be better informed for the guests, since she can't get around as well as she used to. I was supposed to take a family out on the boat for fishing at six, but they cancelled. So I wondered if you'd like to go before work tomorrow."

"You do a lot for Mary," she said, not answering him until she knew his motives.

He hiked his knees up and gazed out at the rushing waves. "She's done a lot for *me*."

"She has?"

"Yeah." He squinted as the sun came out from behind a white, puffy cloud. "She saved my life."

Lauren looked over at him. "Really?"

"Mm-hm." He ran his strong fingers through the sand, grabbing a handful and releasing the grains like the trickle of an hourglass. "When I was five, I fell into our family pool while she was visiting my mother. Mom had just gone inside to get a round of iced tea when I fell in. I was terrified of the water and refused to get lessons, so when I fell into the deep end, I went right under. Mary dove in and saved me."

"Wow," she said.

"She saved my life and gave me more glorious days to enjoy this earth. So I help her any way I can. And it seems that she wants you to understand this area better. It doesn't hurt my business, either, if you know firsthand about my fishing charter."

Lauren shielded her eyes from the sun once more, the turquoise glass in her bracelet glimmering against the harsh rays. "I don't like to fish," she said, her old wounds raw. The truth was that she loved to fish; she found it soothing after a long day. But she hadn't been since Mason had passed. And she couldn't say yes to Brody after saying no to Mason on that fateful day.

He leaned into her personal space, his proximity overwhelming. "Mary asked me to show you around, make you feel comfortable and teach you a little bit about the Outer Banks. But apart from that, something tells me that you *need* it."

"What?" His assessment shouldn't have taken the breath from her lungs, but it had.

"You refuse to talk about yourself, but it's clear that there is never a break in thought in that head of yours; you're always running off to be alone. I'm not completely ignorant."

She gazed into his eyes, drowning in vulnerability. "I came here to escape my problems, which is why I don't want to talk about them," she reiterated, "and if I told you, it wouldn't change anything."

"Yes, it would," he said.

"How so?"

"Because it would help me to understand, so I don't accidently offend you. I'm always around, assisting Mary, and we're going to be working together a lot. It would be nice to know a little bit about what topics are off limits."

She set her salad down beside her and faced him, fighting off tears. "You can't fix this."

"Maybe not. But we're not meant to handle life all on our own. We're meant to be with friends and people who will help us out."

"It's nothing anyone can help me *handle*," she said, turning back to the sea.

"That's fine. But it might be good to let someone understand you while *you* handle it."

The shadow of a flying seagull passed over them as Lauren dug her feet into the sand, considering Brody's words.

"I didn't talk to my dad a lot, but one time, he told me something that *his* father told him: 'The key to a happy life is to never let anything go unsaid or undone.' Things are different here. We support each other. It's who we are." He stood up and grabbed his shoes. "I'll see ya tomorrow at six."

She opened her mouth to protest, but his back was already to her and he was headed toward the inn. She wrapped her arms around her knees, the wind blowing the pieces of her bracelet, the tinkling sound echoing in her busy mind as she debated how she was going to get out of this one.

Chapter Six

There was a knock at Lauren's door, sharply, at 6:00 a.m. She'd been up since four, staring at the dark ceiling, unable to sleep, finally surrendering and climbing out of bed around five. And now, she sat on the sofa in a baseball cap and her cut-offs, the kind of thing she'd have worn with Mason on their summer walks in the park.

She eyed the sea glass bracelet on the coffee table—a reminder that she was somewhere new, trying to remake herself. Lauren got up off the sofa and answered the door.

"Good morning," Brody said on the other side, handing her a to-go cup while he held a second in his other hand. "Mary said you liked coffee."

She took it from him gratefully.

"I put cream and sugar in it. I hope that's okay."

It was perfect. "Thank you," she said.

"Ready?"

"Yep."

"Off we go." He gestured toward the hallway and she let herself out, locking the suite door behind her.

A short, quiet drive later, in the purple haze of early morning, they traveled over the bridge to the village of Manteo, and arrived at the marina. The water lapped gently against the wood as they walked down the creaking dock toward the center-console fishing boat tied to the post at one end. The moon, still out despite the sun's nudge, gave the planks a white glow. Lauren walked carefully over them. Once they made it to the boat, Brody jumped onto the vessel, and she surveyed the thin slip of orange swelling ever so slowly on the horizon.

He held out his hand to help her board. She took it, appreciating his strong grip, and made an unsteady step onto the boat, trying not to drop her cup of coffee. The boat rocked under her, and she leaned against the side with her elbow to steady herself. Brody gripped her tightly until she was stable.

"There's a ton of rockfish out here right now." He grunted slightly when he lifted the heavy rope off the post, untying the boat from the dock. "We should catch some today. And we should definitely see lots of flounder." The boat grumbled underneath them after he started the engine. "But I digress." He flashed that smile of his. "Mary says I'm supposed to teach you about the area, right?"

He pulled away from the dock, the cool early morning breeze against her skin.

"This is the largest lagoon on the East Coast," he said, the boat whirring toward the open waters. "It's home to dolphins and sea turtles, both very popular with the kiddos."

The corners of his eyes wrinkled with fondness and the image of him playfully tossing a child in the air flashed across Lauren's mind without warning. It made no sense, given what Mary had told her about him. He definitely wasn't a family man. Although, she was willing to bet that he'd be a great one.

When she surfaced from her thoughts, she realized the boat had slowed.

"You think a lot," he said, shifting gears.

"I don't like it when you do that," she informed him, in a knee-jerk reaction to his comment.

"When I do what?"

"When you make assumptions about me." She tried not to focus on the friendliness in his blue eyes because it was more than she could handle.

He slowed the boat and stepped away from the wheel. "Why?"

She gripped her coffee cup so tightly that the side bent inward. She set it down on the bench seat of the boat and crossed her arms, fixing her stare out at the pink and orange horizon.

"I don't have any agenda. I just want to be honest about what I see," Brody said.

She faced him. "My emotional state isn't your concern," she said, barely able to get the words out, a lump forming in her throat.

"I know it isn't." He cocked his head to the side. "I only said you think a lot. I never mentioned your emotional state. But now that *you* have, why don't you tell me about it? I'm curious."

"Because I'm a private person."

He shook his head. "I've never understood private people. I guess it's because I'm an open book. I take things as they come."

"Is that so?" she asked, relieved to have the focus move away from her state of mind. "Okay, if you're so open and let people in, then why did Mary tell me that you won't date anyone?"

"What?" Brody laughed and then grabbed one of the fishing rods from the holder, flipping open a large cooler and retrieving the bait. "She said that?"

"Yep."

"Why, were *you* asking if I dated people?" He bobbed his eyebrows up and down playfully while he baited the hook.

"The conversation was definitely not for myself," she said, a flutter of amusement tickling her lips against her will. The lighter banter relaxed her a little bit.

"Why did you say '*definitely*' not?" He handed her the fishing pole.

"Because I'm not in the market for a date."

"Well, that makes two of us. Need help?"

He walked over to her, ready to put his arms around her to assist her as she cast the rod, but she pulled away.

"I've got it." She flipped the reel open, took a step back and then tossed the bait into the water with one fluid motion, the line whirring out into the small wake.

He eyed her, clearly taking in the ease with which she handled herself. "You've done this before."

"Yes," she said, her attention on the line. She let out the slack a little, the way Mason had taught her, and then held it steady.

"I thought you hated fishing."

Lauren didn't reply.

"Did you grow up fishing with your dad or something?"

"My fiancé taught me," she replied, trying to keep her voice even. If she didn't offer him an explanation, he was bound to just keep asking.

"Oh," he said, baiting his own line, her answer visibly surprising him.

She could tell that he was holding back for her benefit. When his gaze flickered over to her left hand, she knew exactly what he was looking for. But the only jewelry on that arm was her new sea glass bracelet. She'd taken the ring off the day after the funeral, the sight of it too much to bear. It sat in its box in the drawer of her nightstand back home in New York.

Her line suddenly tugged, pulling her toward the edge of the boat. "I've got something," she said.

Brody set his pole against the captain's seat and moved over to her. "You got it?" This time, he didn't attempt to assist.

She reeled in the line, the pole bending against the fish's struggle. "Yes," she replied, engrossed, winding furiously, giving it everything she had. All on her own, she pulled against it, struggling, until finally the fish lifted above the water.

"It's a speckled trout," he said, grabbing the line while the fish flailed about. "It's a good size." He took hold of the fish's body and wriggled the hook free. "Look at you, getting the first catch of the day. Want to kiss him?"

"What?"

He held the fish out to her.

She darted away, making him laugh, and the sound of it took a weight off her shoulders.

"It's supposed to be good luck." He held it out once more.

"There's no such thing as good luck," she said.

He stared at her for a second, clearly wondering about her comment. "All right," he said, and she knew by the lift in his forehead that she'd surprised him again. "What do you think? Dinner or let him go?"

"Let him go," Lauren replied.

"She saved you," Brody said to the fish. Then he leaned over the edge and released it. The trout darted away out of sight, under the yellow beam of morning sun that was now crawling across the water's surface. For an instant, she wondered what it would be like to be that fish—saved and headed for anywhere it wanted to go.

"I can't believe you gave everything up, only to be wedding planning again," Andy said through the phone.

"I couldn't avoid it." Lauren rocked back in Mary's desk chair, a mere ten minutes before she was to meet Stephanie Clark, her fiancé, and Brody's mother, Melinda. Brody made a loud smack out the office window, knocking out railing slats with his hammer. She turned away from the view. "I have to go in a second so I can meet with her."

"Think she really resembles you or was that guy at the shop just trying to pick you up?"

Lauren pressed the phone to her ear. "I could see where, from across the room, he might make that mistake." A slight pinch formed in her chest. "What if, when she's dressed all in white, she looks *too* much like me? How will I manage that? Not to mention that I'm going to be working here at the inn, and you know as well as I do that planning a wedding on a *regular* time crunch will be a full-time job." She chewed on her lip, still debating her next question. But if she didn't ask, she'd never know. "Do you think you could plan it for me? I'll pay you for your time..."

"I wouldn't make you pay. But I can't do it. I've got the Baker wedding this month."

"Shoot," she said, remembering the small wedding they'd been planning before she left.

"And I've already met with the Maxwells. We're starting this month. We're in preliminaries, so I'm sure you can imagine what I'm dealing with."

"Preliminaries" was their term for documenting logistics. They had a full interview where they charted all the basics they'd need before beginning, to plan the event. Prior to preliminaries, they researched and personally visited at least twenty venue options and then documented parking for each option, travel routes, security, accommodations for guests, and the staff that would be required for the event, along with the pricing and fees for each, just to name a few of the items that went into it. And that was for non-billionaires.

"I could send a couple of team members," Andy suggested.

"That's a great idea. Tabitha and Rachel could do it."

"Rachel would love nothing more than a free trip to the beach," Andy said with a laugh.

Lauren smiled, thinking of their employee who had a different pair of sunglasses for every outfit. "I'll run the option by the couple," she said, praying for a miracle. While she'd do the wedding if she had to, she knew it would be better for everyone involved if she allowed someone else to do it.

She straightened a row of pens on the desk. "How about you? Has Dave chilled out about the show at all?"

The sound of Andy's huff on the other end gave the answer. "No. In fact, with the Maxwell wedding, he wanted to get started this week. He's really putting the pressure on to have you there. I told him, flat out, that you aren't with Sugar and Lace anymore, but he won't let up. I'll have to come up with a plan to make him see that it can be done with just me."

"Did you explain to him that I've taken another job?"

"I didn't mention it."

"*Explain* it to him. He doesn't have to know that my job here is temporary. Tell him I've got my own wedding to plan here at the inn and that I cannot, under any circumstances, leave North Carolina."

"You're okay with me telling him that?"

"Of course."

"Okay. Maybe it'll help him to understand. The Maxwells have already agreed to the TV crew being there. I just need Dave's okay to get started. I need that show so much… But it's my own fault. You warned me."

"Hopefully, Dave will get it together and move forward with the show. He's just throwing a little temper tantrum because things aren't going the way he planned and he likes things the way he likes them."

"Yes," Andy said.

Lauren looked at her watch. "I should probably go."

"All right. Call me again soon."

"Okay." Lauren ended the call and headed out to the main room to wait for everyone.

Summer, 1957
Fairhope, Alabama

"Penelope, have you seen the sea glass bracelet?" her mother called while digging through her suitcase.

Penelope stood with one foot out of the open screen door of their summer bungalow. "I haven't," she replied, her face flushing with warmth. "I'll be right back. I just want to take one more walk."

"All right, dear, but we're leaving in about an hour."

"Okay, Mama. I'll be back by then."

With excitement, Penelope stepped through the door and into the sunshine. The skirt of her baby-blue dress puffed out around her thin legs, making her feel like a real lady. After seeing it in a shop window in town, she'd saved all her money from babysitting that summer to buy it. It had a belt that showed off her waist and two buttons with a delicate lace collar at the neck. She put on her favorite perfume that smelled just like the expensive ones she'd sampled in the department stores, and purposely left both her wrist and her ring finger empty of jewelry.

Today, Phillip would return the bracelet, and she was nearly certain that he planned to propose. They'd had long talks about it while lying in the grass under the oak tree at the house and they even window-shopped at the jewelry store in town. She'd pointed out a gold band, despite his attempts to persuade her to get a diamond. She told him that a diamond wouldn't make her love for him any more. Neither of them understood how they'd fallen so quickly for one another after only a summer together, but they both knew without a doubt that they were perfect for each other.

Given their age, however, she told him that she'd give him one final chance to make up his mind. If he met her at their spot, she'd marry him, but if he didn't show up, she'd let him go. Wanting to savor only the wonderful times she had experienced in Fairhope, if their whirlwind romance were to end, she'd rather it end in silence than a dramatic breakup. But she didn't worry about that at all, because he'd assured her that he'd be there.

Meeting Phillip had been fate. The summer in Fairhope was a complete surprise. A family friend recommended her father for renovations on a client's old bay house. He was delighted to not only bring in a steady salary that summer, but that they could live there while he finished the repairs. Their mother had taken a leave of absence from the cleaning service she worked for and Penelope had enjoyed a summer holiday, something she never had before, given her family's meager income.

By the time Penelope arrived at the bay, where Phillip promised to meet her that morning, she was nearly out of breath. She sat down on the bench swing in the shade of an old oak tree. The Spanish moss, dripping from the knotty branches, swayed in the breeze. Crossing her feet at the ankles, she rested while taking in the sparkling water of Mobile Bay. Soon, this would be her home. She hadn't told her mother and father about their plans for marriage just yet, and she had no idea what they'd say, but it didn't matter. She was eighteen and if she had to press the issue, what could they say? Her life was her own.

As the seagulls squawked overhead, a couple walked by holding hands. Penelope's skin prickled with anticipation when she greeted them. Love certainly was all around. She pushed against the ground with her little blue flats and let the swing sway back and forth, the bay breeze blowing her hair. She'd pinned her curls in place all night so that she looked perfect for this moment. Unable to hide her happiness, a smile crept across her face as she peered over the walkway. Phillip was about five minutes late, but it took a while to get from his mansion of a house on the hill, so she'd need to give him time.

But as the minutes ticked by—ten and then fifteen—she rubbed her empty wrist, her smile sliding into a look of apprehension. That wasn't like him. She stood up and faced the direction that he always came, but the path was empty. She wondered if anything had happened. Should she run back to the house and phone him from the fancy rotary phone? She'd have to figure out how to use it first. She took in a deep breath of salty air and closed her eyes. *Calm down*, she told herself. *Any minute, he'll come jogging my way, apologetic for being so late*. He'd have a good reason, and she'd throw her arms around his neck and forgive him.

The longer she waited, however, the clearer it all became. She had to have been waiting for almost an hour already and she needed to get back to her family. He knew exactly what time she was leaving. So there was only one explanation: he'd changed his mind.

As she stared at the vacant path, it felt as if someone had grabbed hold of her heart and ripped it from her chest, and inside, she was gasping and straining to get it back. A tear rolled down her powdered cheek, which she quickly wiped away. Today was the first time in her young life she'd experienced real heartbreak, and she didn't know how she would ever recover.

Chapter Seven

Rodanthe, North Carolina

Lauren walked into the main room of the inn with Mary to meet Stephanie, her fiancé, and Brody's mother, Melinda.

Stephanie's hair was longer than it had been in the photo on Brody's phone, and she had on the type of sundress Lauren would've bought. With their similar styles, she could definitely understand how Brody had mistaken her for this woman. It made Lauren feel, without a doubt, that there would be no way she could make it through planning her wedding. She was certain that the woman's wedding tastes would favor hers, and she knew she wouldn't be able to cope with the task of sending Stephanie down the aisle.

Upon seeing Lauren, Stephanie clapped her hand over her mouth, her eyes wide.

Lauren reached out in greeting to the woman. "Hello, I'm—"

"Lauren Sutton, yes, I know," Stephanie said, shaking her hand overzealously. "I've seen you on TV. I've watched every single episode. Twice!"

The man next to Stephanie with curly brown hair and kind eyes offered his hand as well, and Lauren shook it. "Mitchell James,

Stephanie's fiancé." He was tall and thin like Mason, but, thank goodness, that was where the similarity ended.

Melinda took Lauren's wrist and admired the sea glass bracelet. "That suits you."

"It's lovely." Lauren gave it a little jingle.

"It has an *interesting* story," Melinda said. "I'll have to tell you all about it sometime, but today, we're here to talk about weddings, aren't we, Stephanie?"

Stephanie took Mitchell's hand, beaming.

"Yes, yes, everyone have a seat." Mary gestured to the tray on the coffee table. "I've made us all sweet tea."

"So how do you two know each other—just through Brody?" Lauren asked to make conversation, wagging a finger between Melinda and Stephanie. She was curious as to why Melinda would be helping a friend of Brody's with something so intimate as a wedding.

Melinda gave Stephanie an affectionate smile before turning her attention back to Lauren. "That's quite a story as well, actually."

Stephanie returned the woman's loving gaze and leaned forward to retrieve a glass of sweet tea. "I've lived here my whole life, and I've always known Brody's family. Then my parents passed away suddenly in an accident when I was eighteen."

"I'm so sorry," Lauren said, the tug of loss grabbing hold of her.

Stephanie nodded the way Lauren was used to nodding when people expressed their sorrow and took a slow sip of her iced tea.

"With no other living family members, she leaned on Brody for support," Melinda added.

"He was so caring and thoughtful—you know how he is." She shook her head. "And Melinda took me under her wing, too." Her features lifted. "Brody's like a brother to me. After the Harrison family got me back on my feet and helped me with managing by myself, I went on to college, and that's where I met Mitchell." She patted Mitchell's knee, positively glowing with affection for him. "He proposed two years later, and here we are."

Mary clasped her hands together. "And here we are!" she repeated excitedly.

"We couldn't be more ecstatic to have you plan the wedding," Stephanie said to Lauren.

This was the perfect time to interject—before they all got their hopes up too much. "Speaking of planning the wedding, I was thinking that two of the Sugar and Lace team members might be a good fit for this, since I'll be so busy with duties here at the inn."

Stephanie's face crumpled. "What do you mean—instead of *you*?"

"They'd be able to devote more time than I would."

"Nonsense," Mary said. "I'll pull back on your duties if I have to. This is wonderful PR for the Tide and Swallow."

"It's important to note, though," Lauren countered carefully, trying not to let her emotion show, "that if people begin to take notice, I no longer own Sugar and Lace, and won't be available to provide wedding services to future guests. This would be a one-time event. That is, unless I pull in the Sugar and Lace team and get them involved. Then they can be available if anyone else wants to get married here."

"You don't own it anymore?" Stephanie asked, her eyes wide with surprise.

"I don't," Lauren confirmed. "I sold it to my business partner, Andy."

Stephanie put her hand to her chest. "I had no idea. I teased Mitchell that he better get used to the fact that he might be on the show, just in case they wanted to shoot our wedding." She laughed. "I'd have been all for it."

"It just wasn't for me anymore," Lauren said, producing her best smile while taking a glass of sweet tea and holding it in both hands nervously. "I never really got used to being on the show."

"Well, I'd love it if you could plan the wedding instead of the team," Stephanie said. "You're the reason we moved locations." Stephanie's anxiety over it was clear, despite the fact that she was smiling to cover it up.

Mary's head bobbed in encouragement. "I was thinking we could have it on the week of the seventeenth." She addressed Lauren. "Think it can be done?"

Lauren sat holding her glass, all eyes on her, waiting for her to answer. To them, she had absolutely no reason not to do this for Stephanie. "Yes," she replied, with not a clue as to whether it could really be completed the way the couple would expect it to be. "And not to worry, I'll plan it."

Stephanie jumped up with a squeal and ran over, throwing her arms around Lauren. "This is so exciting," she said.

"What's exciting?" Brody walked in just then and kissed his mother on the cheek.

"Lauren's going to plan our wedding," Stephanie told him as he offered Mitchell a friendly handshake and a clap on the back.

She racked her brain for a silver lining. If only she could recall some genius words from Mason to give her strength, Lauren thought to herself, although she doubted that anything he'd said to her could make this feel less difficult.

Just then Brody leaned down and picked up something off the floor. "Looks like you lost your bracelet," he said, holding it out to her.

"Oh, it must have come unclasped when Stephanie hugged me."

She held her breath when Brody took her wrist and draped the string of sea glass over it, fastening it for her once more.

"Well, no harm, no foul. It's back where it belongs." He flashed her a grin before turning to Mitchell. "So we'll have a lot of time to fish while the girls are off planning."

"That sounds fantastic," Mitchell said.

"Not so fast." Stephanie stopped them. She poked Brody's chest. "*You* are the best man in the wedding, remember? We'll need you to be working on the best man duties."

"I already ordered all the tuxedos; Mitchell said he doesn't need a bachelor party, so we're just going out for beers; and I've got the wedding party's arrival organized."

Stephanie got up and gave him a kiss on the cheek. Then she turned to her fiancé. "And you'll need to focus, too, which means the two of you will be modeling your tuxedos before thinking about fishing."

"We can do both," Mitchell insisted.

"Just not at the same time," Brody teased. "Although, I am really great at multitasking."

Stephanie gave him a playful punch in the arm.

Brody laughed. "Don't worry, Stephanie. We'll be all ready to go *before* the ceremony. Promise."

"You'd better," Stephanie said with a playful warning.

"So we've got ourselves a wedding!" Mary said as she clapped her hands excitedly. The others were beaming—even Lauren, but she was quite possibly the only one panicking on the inside.

"You'd like Mary, Mom, she's really nice."

On her midday break, Lauren held the phone with one hand as she brushed the sand off the bottom step of the boardwalk leading from the inn to the beach and took a seat. Her eyelids were heavy from the long morning, the sun too much for them.

Things with her mother had been a little strained since she'd lost Mason. Unable to handle her grandparents' death when both of them had passed within a few months of each other during the last year, she'd only made a couple of fleeting trips home from New York. She'd been so consumed with her own grief over Mason that she was barely able to console her mother, and this put a huge strain on their relationship and filled her with guilt. Her father, John, told her that he'd look after her mom if Lauren promised to look after herself. She tipped her head back and closed her eyes.

"I'm glad you found someone kind to work for," her mother said, though her voice sounded off, as if she were distracted. It had seemed like that a lot these days. "And how's the actual job?" she asked with a note of uncertainty in her tone.

The last time Lauren had spoken to her mother had been when she'd told her that she'd sold Sugar and Lace. Right now, her mother didn't seem any more convinced that Lauren had done the right thing than she had then.

"I think it's helping me, for the most part," said Lauren.

"For the most part?"

Lauren told her mother about the wedding she'd been roped into planning and how she wasn't looking forward to it.

"The truth of the matter is that you're a fantastic event planner," she said. "You were able to take your little company and turn it into a massive organization. That talent is what you need to tap into now."

She'd always admired her mother's no-nonsense approach—until this past year. That was when she needed a little coddling and empathy. But she hadn't gotten it. It wasn't her mother's fault; she just wasn't built that way.

"Yeah, you're right," she said, though she knew her mother's words were easier said than done. "Are you okay, Mom? You seem distracted, like you have something you want to tell me."

The hesitation gave her pause.

"No, nothing," her mother said.

There was another beat of silence. Lauren dug her feet into the sand, her toes landing on something smooth. She leaned down and ran her fingers through the spot in question, retrieving a bottle-green piece of rounded glass.

"Well, honey, I should probably go. I've got to get the roast into the oven."

"Okay," Lauren replied, guessing she'd misjudged her mother's tone. Perhaps she was just holding her tongue about Lauren's recent life choices. She lifted the piece of glass up to the light and admired its translucency. "Yeah, me too. Mary's coming to get me as soon as she's done helping an elderly couple find transportation to one of the tours of the island."

"You couldn't help her?"

"She forced me to take a break."

"Maybe she senses that you need it," her mother said.

"Maybe," Lauren agreed, still appreciating the rare find. "I'll call you later. Tell Dad hi for me," she said before ending the call. She stared down at the clear, oblong piece of glass with little bubbles inside that made it look as if it were full of champagne, and her mind went immediately back to the evening of her engagement to Mason.

"I still can't believe we're getting married," she'd said as he handed her a fizzing glass of bubbly on the small terrace of their apartment that overlooked the bustling street below.

"Think you can put up with me forever?" he asked with that grin of his that could melt her heart in a second.

"I don't know," she teased him, "that's a long time."

If she could go back to that moment, she'd have told him, "Yes. Forever. I'll take nothing less."

"You found a piece of sea glass," Mary said from behind her on the walkway, pulling her from her memories.

"I thought that's what it was," she said, comparing it to the beads on her bracelet as she stood up to face Mary.

Mary leaned over Lauren's hand, examining the stone. "The salt in the water is what gives it that frosted look." Plucking it out of her palm, Mary flipped it over between her fingers. "By its green color, I think it might have started as a soda bottle." She handed it back.

Lauren rolled it around in her fingers. "It's so beautiful."

"Yes. And I consider the owner lucky to find such a piece."

Lauren slipped the glass into her pocket and turned her attention to Mary. "Why's that?"

"Because the whole process makes it almost impossible for that one shard of glass to end up in the palm of your hand." She grabbed Lauren's arm and guided her down the walkway toward the inn. "A bottle has to be abandoned and shattered—completely lost—and then each piece is gathered up, caressed, and meticulously smoothed by the ocean. It takes years—sometimes a *hundred* years—to etch the glass into the smooth shape you find on the beach." She let go of Lauren, her cane wobbling on the uneven planks of wood under their feet. "The nature of it alone makes it feel like hope from a broken past, to me."

"A broken past…" Lauren said, the memory of her engagement coming back into focus once more. She pushed it out of her mind.

Mary took hold of the railing to keep herself steady. "It's as if the universe is rooting for you and leaving a message of hope in your path."

"That's a nice idea," Lauren said. "But that notion of something beyond us, cheering for us and guiding our way, just doesn't seem possible to me most of the time."

"So we have a skeptic." Mary gave her a knowing wink.

"I like to think that I'm more of a realist," Lauren corrected her.

Mary stopped walking and faced her. "Can I let you in on a little secret?"

Lauren turned her head to keep the warm wind from blowing her hair into her face. "Of course."

"Life's little treasures are only visible to the ones who are open enough to see them."

Lauren rolled those words around in her mind. She hoped the idea to be true. "So then," she said as Mary resumed walking once more, "have you ever received a gift like that?"

"All the time," Mary replied, so matter-of-fact that Lauren almost believed in her crazy idea of messages for a second.

"Tell me about it."

"Well, when my husband, Frank, passed away, I had no idea how to be… my own person."

A wave of understanding crashed over Lauren. She saw herself in Mary and wondered if the emptiness that she felt now would still be with her when she was Mary's age.

"I'd spent nearly fifty years as half of *us*." Mary squinted toward the ocean. "If we went out to dinner, he always ordered for me because he remembered my favorite dishes at each restaurant longer than I did." Her gaze moved up to the bright blue sky as if the memory were playing out above her. "One day, on the advice of a concerned acquaintance, I went to one of those restaurants by myself to try to enjoy something Frank and I had shared together. But I stared helplessly at the menu, tears welling up—not because I was alone, but because I missed my best friend."

Lauren cleared her throat, grief swelling in it. *Yes*, she wanted to say, but it was stuck inside her, locked within, unable to come out.

"My hands were trembling, so I set the menu down. That was when I noticed the quarter on the floor. It was on tails. I picked it up and said it out loud: *Tails*. And then I remembered that Frank always ordered me the lobster tail there, because I loved the dipping sauce that came with it."

Lauren smiled for Mary's benefit, taking in the woman's honest expression. She was pretty sure that it had been just a lovely coincidence. But without warning, before she could suck the words back in, she heard herself say, "The way you felt at the restaurant—I feel like that all the time." She bit her lip to keep it from wobbling. "I lost my fiancé." The words had finally come unstuck and tumbled out.

"My dear child," Mary said, her eyes becoming glassy. "How?"

"It was a car wreck. We kept it private, out of the public eye."

Mary shook her head, eyes wide, both her sympathy and surprise clear. "The pain doesn't go away," she said, her hand on her heart. "But the love they had for you doesn't either. You just have to learn which one you want to breathe into your lungs every day."

"I'm not even there yet," Lauren said. "I always feel like I'm suffocating." She turned back toward the shore, closing her eyes for a moment and letting the air coming off the ocean blow against her face to keep from crying. "I came here to try to escape it, but I think it's always going to be a part of me."

"Yes, it will, but it does get easier. I mentioned before that that's how I got so close to Joe. He was a kind shoulder when Frank passed away. Joe has experienced loss as well at a young age, and he was a supportive person. He guided me through it."

Lauren couldn't help but compare how she'd met Brody at a similar time in her own life. But his purpose wasn't to teach her about loss—what did he know about that? While he was a kind person, she was on her own with this.

"What was your fiancé's name?" Mary asked.

As the sun dipped behind a cloud, Lauren turned toward the woman. "Mason."

"And what do you think Mason would say to make you feel better if he were here right now?"

A tear escaped down Lauren's cheek and she wiped it away, the answer coming to her instantly. The first time she'd heard him say it was when she'd had a bad day at work. She ordered the wrong bouquet for a client and they let her have it. He'd taken her hands and pulled her into the living room, sitting her down on the sofa. She could hear his words as if he were there with them right now. "He'd say, 'Come on, kid, the sunshine's stronger than the storm. Know how I know that? Because if it wasn't we'd all have drowned by now.'"

Mary grinned at her. "I like Mason."

Lauren wiped another tear. "Me too."

Just then the sun came back out from behind the cloud. She didn't want to admit it to herself, but in that moment, she felt like Mary could be right and he might be sending her a message.

Chapter Eight

"I don't know what to do," Mary said, her eyes on the budget displayed on Lauren's laptop. "We're barely breaking even."

"I'm so sorry, but I felt I had to tell you," Lauren said. She'd spent the rest of the afternoon inputting all the expenditures and profits into her program. The numbers after her calculations weren't promising.

"I shouldn't have bought all that wood to replace the deck," Mary said, worry etched on her features. "Brody chipped in, but it was still too much to spend."

"I don't think that was a bad idea at all," Lauren countered. "The boards were weathered and replacing them is a matter of safety for your guests."

"I know. We just can't compete with the newer accommodations in the area—they're all so beautifully decorated and spacious. Adding a new deck and evening cocktails is nowhere near enough to entice people to come." She moved a stack of papers on the desk and folded her hands. "I'm hopeful about the wedding bringing people in, but there's not enough here to keep them coming back."

Lauren clicked a few numbers on the program's spreadsheet, thinking. When she and Andy started Sugar and Lace, they had a very tight budget. The wedding venues they could afford at the beginning were dreary, and they had to work their budgets and prioritize what would be their best investments. "I'm thinking you could save a little money here and there by making just a few small changes," she said. "If you'd like me to, I could come up with a plan that might allow you to make some improvements that will help attract new guests."

"What kind of improvements?" Mary asked.

"Well, you mentioned that the newer inns are decorated differently and more spacious. We could look at how we can achieve that with the least amount of money."

"I have no idea how," Mary said, shaking her head.

"Well, for example, the colors that make a room look large are simple and basic. White paint is cheap, right? We could start by giving the interior of the inn a fresh coat of paint. Then we could slip-cover all the sofas to give them a new, more luxurious feel. It'll be much cheaper than buying new furniture. I know a girl in New York who makes them."

"You do?"

"Yep. I used to use her to redesign event spaces. She probably has enough on hand that we could buy her out and re-cover every sofa and armchair in the Tide and Swallow."

"But how would we afford even those things?"

Lauren, in her element, clicked on the "Miscellaneous" tab on the screen and scanned the inn's extra expenses. "For starters, let's look at your costs at the farmer's market." She tapped the screen. "Wedding catering deals with this all the time. What if we saved money by getting the basic food items from a wholesaler instead? You can still get the star ingredients from the local markets, but for the big items—flour, sugar, salt, spices—it might be more economical to buy in bulk."

"I wouldn't know where to start looking," Mary said.

"I do. Working in weddings, I have tons of contacts. I could even write out the inn's needs in a pitch and we could get bids. They'll lower their prices if they know they have competition."

Mary brightened a little, although Lauren could tell that her apprehension remained. "I'd love your help with that."

"I've got tons of ideas already," she said, the swell of purpose filling her as her ideas started flowing like the tide. "For instance, what about raising money for the inn for further renovations?"

"Who do you have in mind that would donate money?"

"You don't need a specific person. We could raffle off a free room for twenty dollars a ticket. With a little investment in marketing, we could raise some serious cash *and* promote the Tide and Swallow."

"I don't have any marketing money, though," Mary said, suddenly seeming overwhelmed.

Lauren looked into her eyes. She knew that Mary wasn't used to doing all this. She wasn't savvy with computers, so she couldn't research any of it, and she probably wouldn't know what to begin searching if she *could* use one. Fiddling with her sea glass bracelet, Lauren considered how kind Mary had been to her and how comfortable she was beginning to feel helping the woman. The truth of the matter was that Lauren knew absolutely what to do, and what a fantastic investment it could be. Plus, she also had the money she'd received from selling Sugar and Lace to spend.

"I have a proposition for you," she said.

Mary's eyebrows went up. "What is it?"

"What if *I* invested in the Tide and Swallow?"

Mary immediately shook her head. "Oh no, I'm not a charity. I can't take handouts."

"No," Lauren said, stopping her. "It would be an *investment*, not a donation. To get the Tide and Swallow back to its best."

"I don't know… What if you lose your money?"

Lauren smiled, already getting excited. "I don't think I would. With a little investment, I think you will have a goldmine in the Tide and Swallow."

"Really?" Mary stared at her. "I wouldn't know how to manage it all or how I could ever repay you."

"I can make all the calls, schedule the contractors, and take everything off your hands that you don't want to worry about, using my money until the inn is turning a better profit. Then maybe you can pay me back."

She took one look at that million-dollar view out the window, praying her gut was right. She then turned back to Mary. Was that look on her face trepidation or enthusiasm?

"You've been so kind to me, I'd like to repay you for that. And I'd *really* like to do this." When was the last time she'd thought that about anything? Lauren wondered.

"You're an angel," Mary said, tearing up.

At the mention of the word "angel," Lauren slipped her hand into her pocket and grabbed hold of the sea glass, gripping it in her fist and praying that Mason was actually out there somewhere and could help her actually make a miracle happen.

Late Fall, 1957
Fairhope, Alabama

"I read about Stanford's Interfraternity Council's growing opposition to discrimination in the newspaper," Phillip's father said while the family sat together at the dining table, their first meal since Phillip had returned home from the university for a weekend.

"Times are certainly changing," his mother said before taking a drink of her sherry, the taper candles in the centerpiece flickering in front of her. "For the better."

Phillip dipped his spoon into his Burgundy beef stew silently, ladling a potato and a few carrots as he contemplated his mother's comment. He was pleased that she said she was against racial and religious discrimination, but he'd had no idea she even possessed an opinion on the matter. Her little elite world was so small, she didn't often discuss much more than the latest recipes for parties or the change in attire for her neighborhood bridge club. She hadn't even accepted Penelope in his life simply because her family was poor; yet there she was, with her big opinion over dinner.

Tensions had remained ever since his parents had forced him to stay in his room, guarded by their butler, Jackson, and his father like a prisoner last summer to keep him from meeting Penelope at the bay. She'd probably gone back home to North Carolina with her parents, and without a phone in her home or Phillip knowing her address—neither of which he'd ever expected to need—he had no way of contacting her. His parents had shipped him out to Stanford the next week.

"You'll thank us later," his mother had said as she'd kissed his cheek at the train station.

He had yet to experience any gratitude over the situation.

His father buttered a roll, his face turned downward toward his hands as the butter melted in the steaming bread. "One fraternity lost its charter," he commented. "Is your fraternity involved?" he asked Phillip.

"No, sir," he answered before draping his cloth napkin next to his plate. "May I be excused?"

His mother looked up. "But you've barely eaten."

"It's been a long journey," he said to appease her, when really, he had no appetite, sitting with the two people who'd ruined his life.

"Probably better that you get some rest," his mother said. "Alicia Morton is coming over for drinks later tonight with her family."

The glimmer in his mother's eye made his skin crawl.

"She's quite the catch," his father added.

Phillip stood up. "All right," he said.

"I'll send Jackson to get you when she arrives. You'll want to greet her in the salon. Don't make her wait; it wouldn't be good manners."

"Yes, ma'am," he answered. Then he excused himself, heading upstairs.

When he reached his bedroom, he closed himself inside and stood there, staring into the darkness through the window. He knew what was expected of him tonight with Alicia. As he turned his gaze back inside the room, it was as if he were a stranger standing there, living a life he didn't want, and wondering—forever—what could have been.

He went over to his dresser, opened the small drawer and retrieved Penelope's bracelet. He held it up to view it and then shut his eyes, remembering her olive skin and the dainty wrist that the sea glass beads used to adorn. He gritted his teeth to keep the sadness from returning.

Over the weeks that he'd been at Stanford, Phillip had attempted to rationalize the situation, wondering if perhaps it had been fate stepping in, saving them both from some sort of a disaster. Or maybe Penelope was meant for someone else. And then in the wee hours of the morning, when he'd tossed and turned over it all night, he wondered if she'd even shown up to meet him that day. Could his parents' actions actually have saved him from even bigger heartbreak? For whatever reason, he and Penelope were denied the chance to be together, and he had to force himself to move on, one painful step at a time.

He moved to his desk, took a seat, and peered out the window at the vast darkness that seemed to stretch on forever, the anger that he had toward his parents, toward the world, only brewing stronger, despite his attempts to justify the situation.

Lost in his thoughts, running the bracelet through his fingers, he wasn't sure how long he'd been there when their butler, Jackson, knocked and his bedroom door opened.

"Hello, sir," Jackson said from the other side.

"Come in," Phillip called.

Jackson took a step in through the open doorway, his squared shoulders prominent in his suit. "Miss Morton and her family are here, sir."

"All right, thank you. Please tell them I'll be down in just a minute." He slipped the bracelet back into his drawer, not yet ready to part with it.

With no other options, he was prepared to resume his duties as heir to his father's acquisitions company. Maybe, in time, it would all somehow make sense to him. He left his room and paced down the hallway. When he ascended the grand staircase, he met the innocent Alicia Morton, waiting with her gloved hands clasped in front of her tailored beige dress, a string of pearls fastened at her neck.

"It's so lovely to see you," she said shyly, her blonde hair pinned into an updo that accentuated her bright blue, unassuming eyes. She was nothing short of stunning, and while she wasn't the one he loved, he knew from their childhood together that she had a kind heart and a good soul.

He smiled to ease her nerves. "Shall we?" Phillip led her into the salon.

Rodanthe, North Carolina

"You've outdone yourself," Mary said, as she, Brody, and Lauren went out to admire the finished deck. "It's just gorgeous."

"It really is," Lauren agreed, noticing the craftmanship in the details of the woodworking. Against the bright pink sky at sunset, with the bulb lights strung along the covered roofline overhead, it looked like a postcard.

Brody pridefully folded his arms, peering out at his handiwork. "Thank you."

"This boy can do anything he sets his mind to," Mary said to Lauren as she put a hand on Brody's broad shoulder and patted it. "Did you know that he built an entire cabinet in my closet for me, with shelves, little compartments, and boxes with latches?"

"Wow," Lauren said.

"She couldn't reach her shoes the way her closet was configured," he said, with a chuckle. "Something had to be done about that."

Mary squeezed his arm, fondly.

Just then an idea occurred to Lauren. "What other type of work are you good at?" she asked him.

Brody turned his attention to her, the late sunshine giving his stubbled face a warm glow. "Minor construction, painting, some electrical work… I've held almost every job on the island at some point when I was in my twenties. Why?"

She nodded, her wheels turning. "I'd like to run some ideas by you and get your thoughts. But right now, I suppose we should get inside to greet the dinner crowd." Lauren consulted her watch for the time.

"No, no, no." Mary shooed her off. "You've worked enough, and you must be starving. Grab a seat in the dining room with the guests and let me take over for the evening."

Lauren still didn't feel terribly comfortable eating dinner with everyone, and she was about to say so, when she noticed Brody regarding her.

"She doesn't like to eat in crowds," he said to Mary but his gaze was still on Lauren. "I can get you dinner."

"Again?" she asked, wondering if they could fill another evening with idle chitchat. At some point, she'd have to tell him more, and she didn't really know if she wanted to yet.

"Not out," he replied. "No crowds. And you can tell me whatever it was you wanted to run by me."

Mary clasped her hands together. "That's a perfect idea."

"And where will we eat with no people, in this area?" Lauren asked.

"My place." Brody turned to Mary. "Tell her. It's clean and quiet, isn't it?"

Mary nodded happily. "It's just lovely. And he'll be a perfect gentleman, I can promise you that."

"Definitely. I'll even ask Stephanie to come, too, if it makes you more comfortable. Mitchell's off working, so she'll probably jump at the chance to do something for dinner."

Lauren deliberated. She did have some things to ask Stephanie…

"I'll pick you up in an hour."

"All right," she relented for the sake of doing business. She made a mental note to get some groceries tomorrow so she didn't have to put herself in this position again.

"You're not going to believe this…" Andy's voice came through the speaker on Lauren's phone as she ran a comb through her hair to get ready for dinner. "Dave has agreed to six more episodes of *Tying the Knot with Sugar and Lace* with me on my own and he's using the Maxwell wedding to launch the season."

"That's fantastic," Lauren said, relieved for her friend. She'd kept the books at Sugar and Lace, and she hadn't wanted to say it, but without the show, she knew that Andy definitely wouldn't have been able to afford to pull off the Maxwell wedding. So this news was incredible all around.

"But there's one condition."

Lauren picked up her blush and dipped her applicator into the powder, applying a light dusting to her cheeks. "What's that?"

"Well, when I told him about your situation and where you were, Dave got that excited twitch in his voice."

Lauren bristled with alarm. Dave Hammond only got that little tremor, where his words broke just slightly at the end, when he was on the verge of a huge project or a big new idea.

"Dave will only *allow* me to do the show by myself if you agree to shoot a pilot episode of a new show called *Wedding Scramble*. He wants to be there to manage it. They're going to rush production, send a second crew out for the Maxwells' ceremony with his partner Stan Clements to oversee it, since I know the drill, and Dave wants to be on the premises for Stephanie's wedding planning and ceremony."

The blush brush fell out of Lauren's hand. "Come on," she said, her shoulders falling before she leaned down to pick it up. "He can't be serious."

"He definitely is. He said he'll shoot raw footage himself with a handheld camera and edit it later if he has to. He wants you for a twelve-episode show, but specifically for the pilot to pitch to the network."

"When you explained, did you tell him that I wanted to leave the wedding planning and limelight behind?"

"He didn't hear a thing I said once he heard that you had a wedding to plan in nine days."

This put Lauren in a terrible position. She was nearly certain that Andy would falter if she didn't get those six episodes. The Maxwell wedding would send the company into utter oblivion *and* cutting corners on a wedding like that spelled disaster. Bad press from the Maxwells would ruin their reputation. While none of that was Lauren's fault, it still weighed heavily on her. She didn't want to let her friend down or watch the company she'd spent so many years building crumble with one bad decision. But she also didn't want to be in front of a camera again.

"I'm seeing the bride in about an hour," she said, shaking her head in disbelief at what was coming out of her mouth. "I'll ask her if she wants to do it."

"Are you sure?" Andy asked.

What else could she say? This was Andy, one of her oldest friends and the person who had looked out for her the most over the last twelve months. She had no other choice. "Yeah. I'm sure."

Lauren scanned her notes from the last hour, twisting her new bracelet absentmindedly. She'd pulled up the spreadsheet of required tasks for the wedding and compiled a list of questions to ask Stephanie at dinner. While she still wasn't sure how she would handle the ceremony emotionally, or if she'd fall apart while plastered across people's televisions, she decided that the event was small enough that she could probably get through it.

She got up and checked her reflection in the mirror once more. On the outside, she seemed more casual, relaxed. Her hair was tucked behind her ears and she'd put on her matte lip gloss the color of the sunset. But inside, she wasn't quite as calm as her exterior. She straightened her shoulders and studied her mannerisms in the reflection, hoping to pull off the part. Then she spun around and headed down to meet Brody.

The coastline boasted its most brilliant rainbow of evening color yet. She stood on the porch and faced the water, bracing herself emotionally for the night. Two seagulls swooped down just above the waves, their wings spread gloriously. She leaned on the new railing, stretching her fingers out against the wood, and inhaled the warm air. Mason had been right: this truly was paradise.

Brody's truck growled as it made its way into the lot, the sound pulling her attention to the front of the inn. She rounded the corner and headed down the steps to greet him.

When she reached his car, he leaned over and opened her door.

"Hungry?" he asked.

"A little," she replied, climbing in.

"As expected, Stephanie can't wait to hang out. She said she'll meet us at my house."

"Oh shoot, I need to go back in and get my laptop," she said, reaching for the door handle. "We need to talk about wedding planning."

"Or, we could *not* talk about work," he said.

She sank back into the seat, the wedding deadline and the looming TV show like weighted chains around her ankles.

"Tell me something," he said as he turned out of the parking lot. "What were you hoping for with this job at the inn?"

"What do you mean?" she asked.

"From what I know so far, you left a very lucrative career in New York to come here to the Outer Banks to fold towels and complete entry-level administrative tasks. And while all of that is perfectly fine, if that's what you want to do, I was just wondering what the big picture was for you."

It was a simple question, but one without a simple answer. She wrestled with how to respond to it, his blue eyes on her with no judgment. The reality was that she didn't want to talk about Mason because she didn't really know how. All that ever came out was the pain of it, shocking everyone in its wake. She didn't want to put Brody in that uncomfortable position.

Letting him in might put a damper on the whole evening. Would he be able to handle her truth? But if she didn't tell him, he'd keep asking, and they had a lot of time still ahead of them. She'd have to eventually spill the beans. "My fiancé died last year," she finally admitted. "I came here to try to find my way through it, and it's proving more difficult than I'd ever imagined."

Brody drove silently, probably trying to figure out how to reply to what she'd just told him.

"I can't begin to understand what that's like," he finally said, his voice so soft and tender that it almost brought tears to her eyes.

The sympathy was taxing as well. It was as if she were being given permission to grieve, and everything she tried to bottle up in an attempt to act like everyone else came tumbling out. With a deep breath, she tried to push the emotion back down, focusing on the view out the window as the coastline slid past them. She inwardly scolded herself for telling him now. It didn't impact just tonight. The last thing Lauren wanted to do with this news was to cast a dark shadow over Stephanie's wedding.

"I'm glad you told me," he said.

She swallowed to force herself to speak. "Why?"

He pulled the truck to a stop at a red light and looked at her. "Because it's a step. It's the first step I've seen you take since you got here. Now you can tell me anything, since I know *that*." He gave her an encouraging grin, a clear attempt to make her smile. "And I'm kinda fun to be around if you'll ever hang out with me."

She smiled back. "It's hard to see the lighter moments sometimes."

His face fell to a more thoughtful expression. "Maybe we can look for those moments together. Just a tiny ray at first, and then eventually, one day, the sun will peek through."

"And the storm will pass," she heard herself saying, the memory of Mason's advice bubbling to the surface.

"It always passes."

If Brody was anything, it was optimistic. She couldn't imagine a day when she would wake up feeling okay. The heaviness had become a part of her, and it had been with her for so long now that she couldn't reach who she'd been before. But as she took in Brody's calm nature and the way nothing at all seemed to ruffle him, she wondered if maybe—just maybe—he might be the perfect person to help her see the brighter side.

Chapter Nine

Brody pulled the truck onto a gravel drive nestled in the woods and parked next to an old Winnebago outside a small cabin with a detached garage. They were so far from the coast that the stillness was almost shocking. As they came to a stop, Stephanie hopped off the hood of her jeep where she'd been waiting for them.

Lauren eyed the large vehicle beside them from the passenger seat.

"Like my vacation home?" Brody asked, following her line of sight to the Winnebago.

She nodded while she took it in. The body style gave away its age, but it had a coat of new paint and looked to be in good condition.

"It's been my little project over the last few years. I got it for nothin' and then fixed it up," Brody said.

Lauren let herself out of the vehicle.

Brody got out as well and greeted Stephanie. "I'll run in and get us all a beer. Y'all feel free to go around to the back deck and I'll meet you out there." He bounded up the few porch steps and headed inside, the screen door clapping shut behind him.

"It's great to see you tonight," Stephanie said, meeting her in the middle of the driveway.

"Likewise." Lauren followed her up to the stone path that led around the back of the house, past a line of fishing rods leaning against the log wall of the cabin. "I have to admit, having another female presence around is nice. You're the first woman I've met here who's similar in age."

Stephanie gave her a big smile.

The change in scenery lifted Lauren's mood. This little cabin in the woods felt calming, but she should've expected it from Brody, given his laidback personality.

Stephanie opened the gate to the fence that encircled the backyard and, when she did, a big ol' hound dog came plodding toward them with a sluggish howl.

"Who's this?" Lauren asked, pushing away the thought of Mason pleading for a puppy that popped into her mind. She couldn't hide from her memories of him. Even his love of dogs came through.

The dog howled once more.

"That's Milton."

At the mention of his name he stopped barking and turned his head to the side, his tail wagging.

Lauren bent down and reached her hand out to Milton. "Hey there, boy," she said.

The dog walked over to her, and instead of sniffing her fingers the way she'd expected, he put his head in her hand and looked up at her with longing in his eyes.

"Oh my goodness," she said, the dog's gesture surprising her. "Aren't you just the sweetest thing?"

She stood at the sound of the back door.

"He's a hell of a guard dog," Brody teased, coming down the steps with the necks of three beers in his fist. He handed one to Lauren and then another to Stephanie. Then he addressed Milton with a shake of his head. "What if those two are here to rob us? You got a backup plan?"

Undeterred, Milton returned his attention to Lauren and pressed his head against her leg.

"Your backup plan is to kill them with kindness. Okay." Brody led them up the steps to the back porch as Milton followed.

Stephanie sat down on one of the wooden Adirondack chairs that faced a stone exterior fireplace.

"You said you grew up here, right?" Lauren asked.

"Yep." Stephanie leaned over and clinked her beer with Brody's. "The two of us have lived here all our lives except for college. And now look at us—both here again."

The sun cast an orange glow through the leaves in the sweeping expanse of trees, the absolute solitude of it as relaxing as the ocean view from her suite at the inn. "I can see why. It's incredible here."

Milton finally made it over to where they were sitting and went straight to Lauren, who bent down and gave him attention.

As she ran her fingers through the dog's soft fur, Lauren took in an earthy breath of air, reveling in the quiet atmosphere, when she caught Brody looking at her, a soft smile on his lips. They shared a moment, and she felt at peace with him knowing the burden she carried. In a strange way, maybe because he was the first person she had met in the Outer Banks, he suddenly felt like her protector here. And she knew that she was safe with him.

"Brody tells me we can't talk about the wedding tonight—no work," Stephanie said, pulling Lauren back to the conversation.

"Yes," she agreed as if he weren't part of the discussion. "He told me the same thing." She tried not to think about the TV show pilot or everything she wanted to get done for the actual ceremony and reception. Instead, she knew that she should follow Brody's advice and try to relax. If anything, it was a skill she needed to practice.

"I think he just doesn't want to talk about weddings," Stephanie said, giving him a playful grin. "He hates marriage."

"Hate is a strong word," he said. "I just don't believe in it—for myself. *You* can do whatever makes you happy."

Having spent her entire adult life planning weddings, this idea made absolutely no sense to Lauren. She'd been drawn to planning weddings because the overwhelming happiness of the day was enough to carry her through an entire week. She teased Andy once, saying to her that all they needed was a wedding each week and they'd live in bliss for the rest of their lives. "Why don't you believe in it?"

"He doesn't like to discuss it," Stephanie cut in.

Lauren gave him a look that said he had no excuse not to answer after what she'd told him on the way over. Didn't he say, himself, that he was an open book?

Brody took a pull of his beer. "I'm not going to divulge my thoughts to two women who both believe in it. That wouldn't be fair or respectful to either of you."

"I'm a grown woman. I can take it," Lauren challenged him.

Stephanie leaned forward, her forearms on her thighs, the beer dangling from her fingers. "Yeah, you won't change *my* mind. But I am interested in hearing this. You've never told me why you don't ever want to get married."

He leaned back, his chest filling with air as if he were wrestling with the best way to say whatever it was. "I come from a line of divorce. My family isn't really close, apart from my mother and me. My grandparents divorced. And now my parents have split up. I've been too close to failed marriages to believe that there's anything beneficial in marriage for me. The odds are against it."

"But despite that fact, there *is* a proven fifty percent success rate—I made an entire career out of it—people still take a chance on love," Lauren said.

"The percentage of failure is the same. I don't see the point. It's easier to avoid it altogether and protect yourself from so much disappointment."

Was he onto something? She certainly wouldn't be dealing with her loss if she'd never put herself in that position. But then the smell of cotton sheets came back to her, Mason's fist balling them up in an attempt to pin her to the bed while she squealed in laughter one morning.

"You can't go to work," Mason had said, reaching for her playfully as she tried to escape.

"I have to! I have a couple coming in at nine."

"But I'm the love of your life and I need you." His fingers found her bare sides and tickled her, making her shriek. He pulled her close and pressed his lips to hers.

She forced herself to return to Brody and Stephanie. "What if you're one of the exceptions, and it *does* work out?"

"I doubt it."

"Why? You don't deserve to have the opportunity to be happy with someone?"

He chuckled. "I'm very happy now. I don't need a marriage to be happy. And I have Milton."

The dog perked up and waddled over to him, dropping at his feet with a huff.

"See?"

"I've stopped trying to convince him," Stephanie said.

"Yeah, you won't change my mind about this." Brody got up, sending Milton to his feet before the dog had even settled. "I'd much rather do my own thing. When my work slows after the summer, I've got my cross-country trip planned for the off-months. I'm free as a bird." When he said it, she could've sworn she saw uncertainty flash in his eyes.

"You're going all by yourself?" Lauren asked.

"Yep. I'm pretty self-sufficient." He crossed over to the cabin's door in one stride. "I'm going in to prep for dinner. Any objections to cheeseburgers?"

"That sounds delicious," Stephanie said.

Lauren agreed.

"There's more beer inside if you need one." Brody let Milton in first and then shut the screen door behind him. "Just come on in."

"He's so set in his ways," Stephanie said quietly, once Brody was inside.

Lauren took a sip of her beer, the light, bubbly liquid going down easily in the humid air. A gentle rustle through the trees reminded her that she was near the coast, even though she had no view of it.

"So where in the Outer Banks do *you* live?" Lauren asked, making conversation.

Her face lit up. "Mitchell and I have been living in South Carolina, where he's from, but we've actually just bought a house here. I never thought I'd move back, but I'll be honest—there's just nothing like this town. Everyone knows one another and we're like a big family."

"I've noticed that." Lauren wiped the condensation on the bottle with her hand.

"It was the weirdest thing… We had no plans to move here, but then a friend of mine texted me that my favorite house—the one I've always loved since I was a kid—was for sale. The owner had to get rid of it as soon as possible, and she knew of three other people who were interested in the property. I had to act quickly. I showed the house to Mitchell and he loved it. Before I knew it, he and I made an offer, and it was accepted. Then I found out that you were working at the Tide and Swallow—what are the odds? It's as if my whole life is coming together right in front of me, and I'm not doing a thing."

"That's unbelievable." Lauren could only hope that her own life would come seamlessly together in the same way one day.

"Yeah, it's funny how things work out. I applied for three jobs and the third time was a charm. The local real estate firm has hired me part-time. And Mitchell does investing. He works from home. It seems a little too perfect, you know?"

Lauren did know. She'd had that perfect life once. Would she ever be fortunate enough to have it twice? She couldn't help but think it was a long shot.

"I keep waiting for something to go wrong," Stephanie said.

"Nothing is ever certain. All you can do is focus on this moment and making it the best it can be." Lauren wasn't sure where that advice had come from. She certainly hadn't followed it. Maybe it was Lauren's way of protecting Stephanie from the very thing she, herself, was dealing with now, although there was no real way to shield anyone from what life threw at them.

"You're right," Stephanie said. "I guess I'm just a typical nervous bride."

"All the big changes that we make in life are sort of like jumping out of an airplane and just hoping the parachute opens." Lauren considered her own journey up to this moment. She'd sold her biggest accomplishment in life, walked away from a career she'd built, and left everyone she knew. Now, she was free-falling, praying for the sudden jolt of safety.

Stephanie grinned wistfully. "At least I have Mitchell. I know for certain about him."

"And the two of you will get through anything together," she said, her standard line for jittery brides on their big day.

Stephanie's smile widened. "Yes." With a sparkle of newfound hope in her eyes, she held up her bottle. "This is empty. Should we get another one? If not, we can go in anyway and pester Brody."

"Sure." Lauren got up and followed Stephanie inside.

The cool air and smell of sautéing onions and peppers hit her when she walked in. Milton, who was flopped on the floor at Brody's feet, lifted his head. Stirring the pan, Brody turned around, greeting them over the sizzle of the vegetables.

"It feels amazing in here," Stephanie said, throwing her bottle in the trash can near the counter. She then dropped down on one of two leather sofas flanking another stone fireplace in the living room that was open to the kitchen. "It's so much cooler." She leaned her head back.

Lauren admired the vaulted ceiling with rugged beams that arched across it. There was something about his place that felt entirely comfortable, even though she'd never lived anywhere like this before. She set the remainder of her beer down on the counter and went over to Brody. "Need any help?"

"Want to stir these while I make the hamburgers?" Brody handed her the spatula.

"Is that for tonight?" Stephanie popped back up and pointed to a large watermelon on the counter.

"Yeah," Brody replied. "I've got a knife in the third drawer to the right if you want to slice it for us."

As Stephanie hunted down the utensil, Lauren stirred the mixture, the savory, salty smell of the vegetables making her stomach rumble. While Brody began to form patties at the kitchen island, Lauren's gaze roamed the counter beside the stove. It held a couple of bananas and his truck keys, but at the far end sat a small metal bucket full of seashells.

"What are those?" she asked, curious.

"When I go fishing, sometimes I find some pretty cool things." He set a patty on the plate beside him and waved a finger toward the pan she'd been stirring. "You can probably turn those vegetables off now and go take a look."

Lauren twisted the knob on the stove to cut the burner off and went over to the bucket. "Wow," she said, digging through the beautiful shells that filled it. She picked up one with a swirl of iridescent colors on the inside, the outside rough and full of barnacles. Another one was pristine white and almost a perfect half circle with little ridges. But something sparkling among all the shells caught her eye. She pinched the pink sphere delicately and pulled it from the rest. "Sea glass?"

"Yep." Brody washed his hands and came over to her. "I found that one the day you came into town."

"You did?" She rolled it around in the palm of her hand.

"Yeah... I wondered what it must've started out as with that pink hue to it. I've never found one that color before."

"May I see it?" Stephanie asked, coming over to them.

Lauren held it out to her.

She let out a little gasp. "It almost looks like a gemstone."

Lauren inspected it, noticing the little glimmers of light that seemed to radiate from the inside of it. "You're right," she said. "It does... It's so gorgeous."

"Why don't you keep it?" Brody suggested.

"I wouldn't want to take it from you," Lauren said.

Brody frowned with a shrug. "It doesn't have any sentimental value to me, but you seem to really like it, and I found it right when you got to the island. I feel like maybe I found it to give to you, somehow."

She liked the idea that it could be meant for her. "You know, I found a piece of sea glass too. It was on the beach outside the inn."

"Maybe it's your lucky charm," Stephanie said, going back to her watermelon.

Lauren looked down at her bracelet, considering the fact that she seemed to be surrounded by sea glass lately. The idea warmed her. It had been a long time since luck had made its presence known in her life. As she took in the stunning piece of glass, she did have to admit that it was nice to have such beauty around her. Maybe it *was* lucky.

"You know that dance the kids are doing—that wiggle, wiggle, turn thing?" Stephanie asked Lauren as she sat with her knees pulled up on Brody's sofa, her fourth glass of wine in her hand.

The wine had been Brody's suggestion, since he didn't have any other dessert, apart from the watermelon.

"I don't know it," Lauren replied, taking a drink from her glass. She'd lost count of her own number of glasses, but she had the mellow buzz of normalcy that came from sipping it slowly, which she gladly welcomed. Even though she knew the feeling wouldn't last after the wine wore off, she was thankful for the moment of peace.

"Yes, you have to know it." Stephanie jumped up and set her glass on the table. "Do *you* know what I'm talking about, Brody?" She put her hands in the air and wriggled around, nearly falling over and making Brody lurch forward in response. Lauren reached out and steadied her.

"Definitely not in my repertoire," he said with a chuckle.

"This is ridiculous," she teased, pulling out her phone and scrolling through social media. "You all have to have seen it." She turned a video around toward them.

"Oh, I *do* know it," Lauren said, a plume of amusement rising up at the sight of it. "It's like this," she said, getting up and demonstrating the dance for Brody. As she waved her arms overhead, the sparkle in his eye relaxed her even further. "Stand up, I'll teach it to you—it's easy."

Chewing on a smile, Brody complied and followed her lead.

"Wait!" Stephanie stumbled across the room and clicked on the radio, tuning it to a pop station. "This'll work."

The music thumped throughout the room.

"Put your foot out like this and then back in," Lauren instructed Brody.

He did as he was told.

"And then put your hands out like this. One, two, three." She waved her hands in the air, laughing when Brody did the same, the amusement coming effortlessly tonight.

"Now turn a half turn and do it again."

Brody kicked out his heel and then put his hands up. "This is definitely not rocket science."

"But you have to show him how it fits when the two of you do it together," Stephanie said.

Lauren stepped in front of Brody, his woodsy scent wafting toward her. "When you put your right foot out, I'll put my left foot back. Then we'll throw our hands in the air, lock fingers, and turn together." As the music pounded loudly around them, they moved in unison, and before she knew it, his strong hands were holding hers, the two of them rotating as their arms slid down by their sides. His breath was at her cheek, their bodies moving together. He put his hand on her back and they began dancing right there in the middle of his living room.

Finally satisfied, Stephanie fell back onto the sofa and picked up her glass. "I want to be sure we include that in the reception. It's so much fun. It's been on my mind for weeks."

Lauren let go of Brody, breathless. "I'll make sure of it. You have my word."

A knock at the door halted the conversation.

"That's probably Mitchell," Brody said, jerking his gaze away from Lauren, clicking off the radio, and walking to the front entrance.

Stephanie looked over at him wide-eyed. "Mitchell?"

"Yes, I called him to come get you," Brody called over his shoulder.

She gave him a sleepy-eyed grin. "You're so great. Isn't he great?"

Lauren's heart hammered. Yes, he *was* great.

Brody answered the door and let Mitchell in. "Your bride," he said with a wave.

With an affectionate look at her, Mitchell came into the room and took her hand.

Stephanie pulled loose from his grip and wrapped her arms around her fiancé's neck. "I *love* you."

He huffed out a laugh and addressed Brody. "We'll see you later. And I'll bring her over to get the jeep tomorrow."

"Sounds good." He walked them to the door.

With the click of the latch, Lauren and Brody were alone. She didn't realize how much they'd all been talking and laughing until they were left in the quiet.

"Think she'll be okay?" Lauren asked.

The corner of Brody's lips turned upward. "She'll be fine." He picked up the near-empty wine bottle on the table and offered more to Lauren, but she declined. "Stephanie has never been a big drinker, so nights like these get her every time."

"How did you first meet Stephanie?"

His wine barely drunk, he set his glass beside the bottle before lowering himself next to her on the sofa. "We met when we were eight. Her desk was beside mine in school, and I kept passing her notes with little jokes on them, but she wouldn't read them. They sat there all day, and I was on the edge of my seat for her to take a look at them. Then on the bus, I saw her laughing and I knew she'd finally opened them. When I asked why she waited all day, she said she didn't want to get in trouble."

"You were a bad influence on her, then," Lauren teased, her pulse rising at the sight of his amused wink.

"I wasn't trying to be. I just would rather have been anywhere than that classroom. School was never my thing."

"But you said you went to college?"

"Yeah. My parents wouldn't have let me *not* go, even though it made no difference in what I do today." He stopped talking and suddenly, something seemed to be bothering him.

Lauren leaned forward. "What is it?"

He hesitated.

"Tell me," she urged him, her interest piqued.

"I was generally a… disappointment. At the very least, I had to go to college for my father's sake, rather than mine." The hurt he felt with those words was evident in the lines that formed between his brows.

"What makes you think that?"

He shook his head. "You don't know my family. And you don't have the length of time it would take to explain it."

"Try me."

"You're one to talk," he said with a slight glimmer returning to his eyes as he reached for his glass and took a sip of his wine. "You want me to tell you my life story when you've barely told me a thing?"

"I did tell you," she said. "I told you the *main* thing." She couldn't actually say *it* because this was the first halfway regular conversation she'd had in a year, and she needed to keep her focus on the present moment. "But fair enough. What more do you want to know about me?" Now that the biggest hurdle was out of the way, everything else would be easy.

"I heard my mother and Mary talking about your wedding company. Why did you sell it?"

"Because I couldn't handle all those happy endings anymore—one after another—given what I've been through. It made me feel like less of a person, as if it had been decided that I didn't deserve that kind of contentment." She looked down into her wineglass, knowing the alcohol had given her the ability to verbalize it. She wondered if she'd be upset with herself in the morning for being so open.

"You absolutely do deserve it," he said, the resolve in his words making it sound less of an opinion and more like fact.

She wanted to believe him. "Then why was it all taken away?"

He frowned, as if contemplating her question. "The day my dad left us, he told me that his own dad had told him, and he was telling me now, 'Some people come into our lives to help us get where we're going, but they were never meant to stay.' I believe it to be true."

"Was your dad speaking about himself?" she asked.

"I think so. But it applies to your life as well. You're allowed to love your fiancé and to miss him. But you're also allowed to find your own peace and be happy. I believe that's what he'd want for you."

"How do you know he'd want me to move on?"

He took her in for a moment, his lips turning upward just slightly. "Because I've only known you a few days and I already want you to be happy."

A flutter of exhilaration took hold of her chest. "Why?" she asked softly.

"From what I can see, behind all that silence, there's a very compassionate person."

For the first time in an incredibly long time, it felt as if someone could actually see her. "Thank you," she said, deciding that maybe opening up to the right person might actually be therapeutic. She took a moment to take a mental snapshot of him right then so that she could draw on it when things worried her. It was definitely a moment worth remembering.

When she emerged from this small shift in thinking, his gaze was on her in a way that made her wonder if she would be strong enough to resist if he made a move. It was undoubtedly the wine weakening her resolve, and if she gave in she'd surely be upset with herself in the morning.

"I should probably get you home," he said.

Was he thinking the same thing?

"Yes," she agreed as she settled into the delicious feeling that had come over her tonight, wondering how long she could hold on to it.

Chapter Ten

"How was dinner last night?" Mary asked as Lauren helped her set up the coffee station in the lobby the next morning after they'd split the supervision of the cleaning staff.

"It was actually really nice." It had felt like decades, not years, since she'd been able to be herself, and last night, a small piece of her soul had returned. She was glad, however, that she hadn't made any moves with Brody. That could've really impacted her professional life, and she'd never forgive herself for that. It was good to know that even under the spell of alcohol, she had her wits about her.

"I'm delighted to hear that." Mary handed her a stack of paper napkins, and Lauren placed them next to the silver coffee urn.

A few people were gathered in the lobby, so Mary ushered them over.

Lauren stacked the white coffee mugs on the linen tablecloth next to the window, her to-do list running through her mind. She wanted to try to plan a budget for the mints and flowers she'd talked with Mary about for the rooms, and Stephanie was stopping by soon to begin going over all the details of the wedding. Lauren would also need to tell Stephanie about the TV offer. And she had to hurry because Dave would certainly be calling since she hadn't given the green light for production of the pilot yet. Knowing him, he'd show up, contract and pen in one hand and his camera in the other. The whole idea of it made her want to crawl back into bed. "Are you going to be okay out here for a little bit while I work on a few things?"

"Yes, dear. Of course."

"All right, then. I'll be in your office. I've got to find a dress online for the big day and I'm planning to organize the space for you, by the way." She'd barely finished speaking before Mary was already happily chatting with a couple from Colorado.

Lauren headed down the hallway with purpose. There was a lot to do to get ready for this wedding, including getting started on renovations to the inn as soon as possible. Having not spoken to Brody about her plans last night—since she'd been instructed not to talk about work—she decided to make use of the personal cell phone number he'd given her when he dropped her off last night. She dialed it to run a few of her ideas by him.

"Hello?" he answered, his voice staticky and far away. A tingle of happiness ran through her at the sound of his voice.

"Hi, it's Lauren."

"Oh, hey." The wind rustled through the line, loud in her ear. "I'm on the boat, getting ready to dock. Everything okay?"

"Yes," she replied. "I wanted to talk to you about some work I have in mind."

"All right, I'll come over after."

She reminded herself not to get too attached to his kindness. He was like that with everyone. "Thank you."

"Yep. See you soon."

As she hung up, she thought about the fact that Brody had stayed up, talking to her after Stephanie left, and then driven her the twenty-minute ride home, when he clearly had to work early the next day. He'd never even mentioned it. Then her mind went back to the way she'd responded to him when they'd first met. She had no idea then that he had such a kind heart. She was indeed lucky to have met good, decent people here.

Summer, 1959
Kill Devil Hills, North Carolina

"I'll marry you," Penelope said as she stood in front of her childhood best friend, Joseph Barnes, on the old fishing dock behind the little shack her parents owned.

He'd been asking her for months, and she knew that he didn't expect her to suddenly agree, out of nowhere, so she braced herself for the response. She thought that perhaps he'd jump for joy or throw his arms around her and knock her down in manic laughter, but instead he turned to her, his brows pulled together, with that love for her radiating through every feature on his face.

"Why now?" he asked.

She put her hands into the pockets of her smock dress and looked into his patient brown eyes. "I just figured that I needed to take the next step, leave my childish ways behind, and become a woman. You deserve that."

His head fell in disappointment.

"What's wrong? I thought you'd be elated."

His jaw clenched as he looked out over the rippling water, the sea air rustling his dark brown hair. "That wasn't the answer I was hoping for."

"And what did you wish to hear?"

"That you want to marry me because you *love* me."

Guilt swarmed her, and she reached out for him. He was the kindest human being on the planet. She'd known him all her life, and ever since they were little children he'd loved her unconditionally. She stepped in front of him, forcing him to look at her. "I thought you already knew that."

A smile burst across his face then. "So you do love me?"

"Of course I do."

With that, his shoulders relaxed, and he pulled her into a cuddle and kissed her. "We won't have any money," he warned her. "I have no idea how I'll support a wife on a fisherman's salary."

"I'm not too proud to work," she said. "I can clean houses like my mother."

His honest look took her breath away. "I just want to be sure I can make you happy."

"You can," she said, putting her arms around him and pulling him close once more, her attention on the window and the light she'd left on in her bedroom where she'd read the newspaper that was still sprawled on her bed with the headline:

Aria Acquisitions Heir Phillip Harrison
to Wed Alicia Morton of the Warner Sax Dynasty

Rodanthe, North Carolina

"How are we feeling?" Lauren asked Stephanie when she walked in, amusement over last night's dancing surfacing without warning.

Stephanie ambled into the empty dining room at the inn with measured steps and sunglasses shielding her eyes. She dropped into a chair opposite Lauren's laptop. "Last night was so much fun that I didn't pay attention to how much I was drinking."

Lauren totally understood the happiness that being around Brody could bring. In fact, it was unnerving, and she wasn't sure how she felt about it. For so long, she'd wanted something or someone to take her mind off the last year, even if only for an instant, to give her some relief. But then when it actually happened, it was terrifying. She didn't know if she was ready to feel anything again. When she thought back to last night, she'd enjoyed herself. But that just seemed wrong, given the circumstances. How could she allow herself to be happy when she'd lost the best thing she'd ever known?

"I'm okay, though. I can focus," Stephanie said, sliding off her sunglasses and rubbing her eyes. She stifled a yawn.

"Well, before we start, I need to discuss something with you."

Stephanie squinted as if focusing were difficult. "Okay…"

Lauren launched into the story of her phone calls with Andy. "The show's called *Wedding Scramble* and since we've only got about a week to get it all together, I'd say we fit the bill."

Stephanie lit up, looking more alive than she had a minute ago. "I'd love to!"

"All right. I'll give them a call." She took in a steadying breath, knowing full well the circus that lay ahead. "Let's get through the preliminaries." Lauren felt much more comfortable focusing on planning the wedding than her own opinions about the TV pilot, which was saying something. She opened the checklist on her laptop.

Mary quietly came in and placed a cup of coffee next to each of them and then let herself out, shutting the double doors behind her.

Grateful, Lauren dug through the cream and sugar on the table for the perfect mix and dumped them into her coffee. Through the window outside, she caught a glimpse of Brody on his way up. He had on a baseball cap and a T-shirt with a faded picture on the front. She tore her eyes from him and went back to her list, taking a smooth, rich sip of her coffee.

"A few quick questions first. Have you insured the engagement ring?"

"Yes," Stephanie said, peeling off the top of the little plastic container of creamer and dumping it into her cup.

"Excellent. What about the guest list? Do you have a list for me?"

"I do."

Lauren smiled at Stephanie's choice of words, just when Brody came back into view through the window. Mary shuffled over to him, the two of them talking about something.

"And matchbooks, paper products—any of those things ordered yet?"

"Yep. We have all the giveaways and gifts ordered."

With every yes, Lauren felt a little better. She picked up her cup and took another sip of her coffee. "I'm assuming the color theme and the dresses have been chosen as well?"

"Yes, we're going with a pale blue. We've just had our last fitting for the bridesmaids. My dress is almost done, we've transferred it to a seamstress here in the Outer Banks, and all the tuxedos have been rented, according to Brody."

"Wonderful." Lauren clicked a few keys on her computer, checking off those items as Mary and Brody continued talking outside. It was strange to feel, already, that she knew Brody and Mary very well. In only a few days, she seemed to know more about the two of them than anyone back in New York. Letting the idea bring her to a calmer state, she returned to her questionnaire. "Have you registered for gifts?"

"Yes. That's all done, too, and we have a website."

"How many guests?"

"About a hundred. We're sticking with close friends and family."

"Given the time frame that we have, I'm so glad that you're organized," Lauren said with a smile.

"Yes, I really just wanted you to plan the venue, the reception, and the ceremony itself."

"Those are my strong points," Lauren said, relieved that they were on the same page.

Now that she knew Stephanie a little better, the idea of planning was also coming more easily to her. Stephanie was no different from one of her regular clients, so until the big day, Lauren knew she had it in the bag. Getting through the actual wedding would be another story, but she tried to ignore that for now. "Florists? I'm assuming not, since you're in a different state than you planned to be."

"That's right. We haven't secured a florist."

"Okay, we'll want to get that done as soon as possible." She clicked a key to mark it. "We may not have too much wiggle room, given the late date, but do you have any idea what kind of flowers you'd like?" She peered out the window again at Mary and Brody, but they'd moved out of sight.

"I'm not sure," Stephanie replied. "Maybe gardenias?"

"I'll call around to a few florists to see what's available and if they can send us some photo samples." She jotted down the note on her computer. "What about the officiant?"

"We don't have one yet."

"Okay." She added that to the list, trying not to panic. That one was a little more difficult. "Musicians?"

"Not yet."

Also a tough one on such short notice.

"We're going to need to hire a small production crew for lighting during the ceremony and for the first dance—things like that. Dave's film crew might be able to step in. I'll ask and if not, I'll get on it as soon as humanly possible. How about the cake?"

"We don't have a baker yet." Stephanie made a face, her concern beginning to show.

"Don't worry. Most major bakeries have stock cakes we can embellish if need be. I'm great at it—your guests will never know. I'll get some samples for that too."

Stephanie broke into an excited grin. "Yes, that's right! I saw an episode of your show where you worked magic with a stock cake."

"Oh yeah," Lauren said, recalling exactly what Stephanie was talking about. The couple had ordered a custom cake and the bride had picked it up to show her mother and dropped it. Lauren and Andy had scrambled to get her a cake on the day of the reception. Lauren really did have a knack for this sort of thing. She thrived under pressure. She'd just forgotten for a bit. "Have you sent invitations to the guests?"

Stephanie sucked in a breath. "No. But I did send an engagement notice that let them all know the wedding was coming. And most of them are aware that we've moved the wedding here. We just haven't formally sent anything out."

"I've had to rush this before. We'll need to get the invitations printed right now. I know a printer who can create them super quick and then overnight them to each guest. And I'll provide a digital code for the

RSVP so that we can get real-time responses. Do you have any initial designs for the cards themselves?"

Stephanie shook her head. "A simple design would be nice, but whatever you think."

"Okay, we'll do something simple in white with pale blue accents. I'll get working on that first." She picked up her coffee and took a long sip, needing the caffeine, right as Brody walked in. "Oh, perfect. You're just the person I want to see."

"That's what they all say," Brody teased. He winked at her.

Lauren tried to stifle the flutter of happiness at his light response and turned back to Stephanie. "Why don't we plan to get together again in a day or so to go over the samples for all the preliminaries? Then, once that's done, we can get into placement and production." She closed her laptop. "I have enough to get started and Brody's here because I'm planning some upgrades to the inn that I'd like to get done before the wedding."

"Oh, that sounds great." Stephanie rose from her seat and picked up her sunglasses. "I've got to run anyway so I can get to my dance lesson with Mitchell. I hope I can keep up since I'm still recovering from last night." She gave Brody a playful slap on the bicep.

"Glad to see you're up and about," Brody said to her, amusement in his tone.

"No thanks to you, bringing out all the wine when you know it's my favorite." Stephanie gave him a teasing squint before slipping her sunglasses back on. She turned to Lauren. "Keep your thumb on this one. Don't let him out of your sight." She waved goodbye and headed down the hallway, leaving Lauren and Brody in the dining room.

"So, what upgrades did you want to talk to me about?" he asked.

"I need your connections around town. I'm on a budget and in a race for time, and I want to get some work done here at the inn." Lauren gestured to the chair where Stephanie had been. "Have a seat and I'll tell you all about it."

He lowered himself into the chair and took off his baseball cap, turning it around backward and then putting it back on. Lauren noticed the way the sun had etched faint lines at the edges of his eyes. With the gold scruff on his face and the slight tan on his skin, he was undeniably handsome. She wondered what it would be like to put her hands on his face and drink in his stare. Suddenly aware of her shallow breathing, she cleared her throat and turned back to her computer, guilt over the moment flooding her. What would Mason think if he could hear her thoughts? A plume of emotion swelled inside her, and she felt lightheaded.

"Oh, I forgot to give you this." Brody reached into his pocket and pulled something out. Sliding his fist across the table, he dropped the object between the two of them: a piece of yellow sea glass. "I found it in the bucket on my counter after I got back home last night. I thought you might like it."

Lauren took it and held the bright piece between her fingers. "Thank you," she managed.

"I saw it right away, when I was on the beach about a year or so ago, because yellow isn't a common color."

Lauren had done enough springtime weddings to know that the color yellow represented happiness. *Find your own peace and be happy.* Brody's words from the other night floated through her mind like a gentle summer breeze, giving her a shiver. She wasn't ready. She still didn't know how to be happy while mourning Mason. Moving forward would mean she was leaving Mason behind, and he didn't deserve that.

She promised him she would spend her whole life with him and, while they hadn't said their vows, she'd already said "yes."

"It's funny how Mary thinks sea glass is good luck," she said, still fixated on the small piece in her hand. "I don't think I believe it. It's just a piece of glass."

Brody leaned on the table with his forearms and clasped his hands. "When I was a kid, I found a handful of four-leaf clovers one day. I ran straight home to show everyone. My father was the first to greet me. He put me on his lap and told me, 'There's really no such thing as good luck. You make your own luck.'"

"Do you think he was right?"

Brody nodded. "Yep." He drummed his fingers on the table. "I can't imagine that there's some big plan to our lives. It seems like things happen as a result of our choices."

"I agree." She couldn't imagine any sort of plan that would involve subjecting her to what she'd been through. No matter how hard she tried, she couldn't find purpose in the tragedy. There just wasn't any. But just in case she was wrong and there was something somewhere that could give her some luck, she set the piece of sea glass next to her computer for safekeeping.

Chapter Eleven

Winter, 1959
Kill Devil Hills, North Carolina

"What's all this?" Joseph asked Penelope after his shift at the docks, when he came into the small room in the little rented shack that he'd found for the two of them after they'd gotten married. It was a couple blocks from the beach, drafty and cold, and the ceiling leaked, but it was theirs.

Penelope sat in the center of the floor, surrounded by shells and pieces of sea glass. "I'm making jewelry," she said. "I haven't made any in a couple years and I thought I should get back to it." She remembered the last time she made bracelets with her mother—that summer seemed so long ago now, although her love for Phillip hadn't faded one bit. For the first few months, she grieved for the loss of their love and wondered why she'd been put in that position—falling head over heels for the man of her dreams, only to have it ripped away from her. She wondered where the bracelet was that she'd given Phillip. Certainly, he'd discarded it.

Joseph sat down beside her and picked up a piece of blue sea glass, turning it over in his palm. "You put a little hole in it."

"Yes, so I can thread the fishing line through it."

He set it back down with the other blue pieces she'd sorted by color. "You make them with fishing line?"

"I think it's the most appropriate way to fasten the pieces together, since fishing line is such a heavily used item here in the islands of the Outer Banks."

"True." His gaze followed her hands as she strung together a grouping of clear sea glass pieces. "How do you make one of these from scratch?"

She placed the string aside and picked up a piece of glass, dropping it in a basin of water on the floor next to her. "I have to put some turpentine on the end of the file to get it started," she said, unscrewing the cap of the bottle, the pungent smell filling the room. She dipped her file into it. "Then I turn the file in circles, pressing against the glass like this." She began twisting the file until she'd created a little hole in the stone. When she'd finally made some progress, she plucked it from the water and held it between her fingers to let Joseph view it.

He leaned back on his hands. "I've seen your collections of shells, but I didn't know you were planning to make these."

"I didn't really consider making them until now, but we're going to need the money."

"Why? Did something break?"

She shook her head as she set the tool down and twisted toward him.

"What is it?" Joseph asked with concern in his honest eyes, and she knew that he would take care of her until her final breath.

Penelope took his hand and placed it on her belly. "I'd better make a lot of them."

Joseph's eyes grew round, understanding dawning. "Really?" he whispered, in awe. He ran his hand over the small bump on her stomach that certainly wouldn't be small much longer.

"I went to the doctor this morning while you were at work."

With a gasp, Joseph threw his arms around her, the two of them tumbling backward to the floor, sea glass all around them. "We're going to be three," he said, breaking into an enormous smile.

She nodded.

He gave her a loving squeeze.

Penelope looked up at the young man hovering over her. He was so good to her that she didn't feel like she deserved him. "You know how I've been so sick with the flu?" She shook her head, giving him the answer. "It wasn't the flu. That's how I found out."

His mouth dropped open, clearly still in delighted shock. With an excited shout, he rolled around with her on the floor, the two of them knocking through the piles of sea glass.

Rodanthe, North Carolina

The next morning, before she'd even had her first cup of coffee, Lauren was in the office and on the phone to Dave Hammond, giving him the news that she was on board for the pilot. He'd agreed that he could do the lighting for the ceremony, which was a relief.

She'd already cleared the TV filming with Mary, who was thrilled to have the publicity for the inn. It was definitely a good thing for the Tide and Swallow, but Lauren wasn't at all sure she could get everything done in time. She'd never redecorated an inn and planned an entire wedding so quickly before.

"We only have six days," she reminded Dave.

"If I can't get there today, I'll book a red-eye into Norfolk, Virginia for tomorrow morning and then drive in. Will you send me the address?"

"We haven't even negotiated contract terms," she said.

"I don't care. I'll have everyone sign releases and get the footage. We'll hash the rest out while we're in postproduction."

"Is that in line with the company's legal requirements?"

He didn't answer, and she let it go. After all, it wasn't on her shoulders and if he already had the footage when they went to contract, she'd be in a good spot to negotiate a fair price for it.

"I'll need the release form right now," she said. "Can you email it to me? We can add it into the digital RSVP form for the guests. Any that we missed, we can catch when they arrive."

"Yep. Will do."

"All right. I'll text you the address. Just let me know when you're coming."

"All right, darling. See you soon." He made a kissing sound and the line went dead.

She grimaced at the thought of getting back into all this. TV production was a rat race, and she wasn't sure she could handle it with everything else that was going on. How in the world did she end up in the same position she'd been in before she left Sugar and Lace?

Trying to clear her mind, she began putting her design ideas for the inn into an action plan. She created a budget, which she knew would be more money than Mary had seen in one spot before. However, if her hunch was right, and Brody could help her build a crew to renovate the inn, *and* she could get some solid publicity behind it to make it a premier venue for events, Lauren would easily recoup her spend and Mary might just get a windfall.

Armed with a list of phone numbers for contractors that Brody had given her yesterday, she was ready to discuss her ideas for the inn with Mary. Once the guests had been taken care of, and the coffee service dismantled in preparation for the afternoon's infused water and cookies to be laid out, Lauren met Mary in her office.

"It already looks so much better in here," Mary said, tipping her head up to view the newly organized shelves as she leaned on her cane. Late last night, Lauren had cleared the clutter and organized her office by task. "You have such an eye. I know why you were so successful as a planner." Mary took a seat in the chair opposite the desk.

"Thank you."

"I can't wait to see what you have in mind for the inn."

Lauren rolled the other chair beside her and turned her laptop around so they could both view the screen. She clicked open her plan. "It's pretty elaborate given the timeframe, but if we get everyone going at the same time—and, this morning, I've already roughly worked out who should be where—we could get it done before the wedding." She scrolled down the list. "I'd like to begin renovating the main rooms, half at a time, to allow guests to still use the rooms while they're here. I thought we could run to the Quick Copy and get glossy signs made that say 'Excuse the mess. We're busy making your dreams come true.'"

Mary lit up. "Oh, I like that."

"And we could also include a subheading: 'We're creating a state-of-the-art visit to a time gone by.' That way, we can focus on maintaining the aesthetic of the original inn while bringing it into the twenty-first century with all the modern amenities as well as getting it up to speed with your competition. To start, I'd like to update the main rooms and the décor in all the suites, paint the whole inn, inside and out, upgrade the kitchen, and landscape the outdoor area in the front."

Mary put her hands to her lips. "That sounds expensive."

"It is," Lauren said, "but it'll be worth it. And I'm willing to invest the money."

"How can you be so sure this will work?" Mary asked.

Lauren smiled, hoping it would encourage Mary to have faith in her. "I've run some comps and there's nothing like it in the area. You have so much real estate here that you can give them that southern, small-town feel, while providing all the conveniences of a high-end resort. People will flock to be here."

"And what if it fails and you lose all of your investment?"

"It won't, I just know it. Mary, it's the first thing I've felt passionate about since Mason died. I want to do this."

Mary looked thoughtful as if she understood, their little bond strengthening. "Okay."

"Excellent," Lauren said, a kind of excitement filling her that she hadn't felt in ages. "I've got a designer that will knock your socks off. Let me give her a call and see if we can get her down here in the next day or so. She'll be a huge help and she'll get this done for us in record time."

Mary put her hand on Lauren's. "I have no idea what I've done to deserve such a wonderful gift as this, but I'm so very thankful. I don't know what I can do to repay you."

"You don't need to repay me. I'm enjoying the work. It'll be nice to throw myself into a project." Especially one that was completely different from anything she did while Mason was alive.

She did wonder if immersing herself into this undertaking was just glossing over her misery for a short time, the same way the wedding planning had displaced it early on, but nevertheless, she was glad for the reprieve, however short.

By that evening, after calling around to the various contacts on Brody's list, she had set up for three contractors and their teams to descend upon the inn the next morning. Lauren had also scheduled visits to three florists; alerted the TV production crew to the plan and asked them to bring the lighting setup they'd use for close-ups; pulled the websites of various musicians and officiants for Stephanie to take a look at; ordered the invitations and paid the rush fee to send them directly to guests; and found one local bakery willing to bring over samples on short notice. Sprawled across her bed, she'd just begun designing the graphic for the lobby construction sign when there was a knock on her door.

"Hello, dear," Mary said on the other side.

Lauren ushered her in.

Mary's attention moved to the doorway of her bedroom with the view of the laptop on Lauren's bed. "You look busy."

"I've been working on the initial renovations list and the wedding."

"Mr. Hammond has arrived, along with the film crew. I've put them all in suites."

She wondered how he'd managed to round up the entire crew and get them all on a plane. "Great," she said. Dave hadn't texted her, but that was typical of him. When he wanted something he had a one-track mind. There was no turning back now.

Twisting her wrist over, Mary pulled up her sleeve to reveal a thin gold watch. "Isn't it time to at least take a break? It's seven o'clock."

"I know," Lauren said, but the truth of the matter was that she'd found her rhythm and been able to tap into that productive side of herself. Her last days with Sugar and Lace had been a blur of going through the motions and trying not to break down, but with this, she was motivated and empowered. And while the hole in her personal life was still there, it didn't feel as jagged as it had before.

"I'm moving cocktail hour to the bottom deck tonight. It's low tide and Brody's building a bonfire for the guests out back."

"Anything you want me to do for it?"

Mary chuckled. "I'm not telling you as your boss. I'm telling you as your friend. His mother and I will be there, and I think Stephanie and Mitchell are coming over. Why don't you join us?"

"Oh, okay." She really needed to work, and she didn't trust herself with a night of cocktails around Brody. But she reminded herself that last time, she'd been fine. And given that they'd be with a small group of people she was getting to know, Lauren might enjoy herself.

"So is that a yes?" asked Mary.

"Yes. I'll be down in a minute. Thank you, Mary."

The woman made her way to the door. "I'm glad to hear it. See you in a minute."

She let Mary out and then paced back into her suite, her mind whirring with whether or not she should've just stayed in and continued working, given what she had to do. But as she tidied up her bed, still considering, a flicker of light through the double doors caught her eye. She peered out to see Milton running around Brody's legs, kicking up sand, while Brody threw logs on the fire and set up chairs around it.

Contentment swam through her. She hadn't felt happy in so long, and this was just the cusp of it, but there was definitely a lightness to living on the seashore. Turning away from the view to get ready, her attention fell upon the little assortment of sea glass that she'd collected. Each piece had its own story from her time there. She picked up the yellow one, the pale color of it reminding her of happiness now every time she saw it. She rubbed the glass, hoping to hold on to the calm she felt in that moment and not let it slip through her fingers.

After a quick fix in the mirror, Lauren went downstairs, left through the back door of the inn and grabbed a cocktail off the table, the summer air wrapping her in its warm embrace. The wind tickled her skin on the way down the wooden walkway leading to the shore. A small crowd had gathered on the beach in front of her; a few teenagers were roasting marshmallows on skewers over the bonfire. The flames danced in the coastal wind.

When she got to the end of the walk, Milton was the first to greet her. She stepped onto the sand, its surface still warm from the long summer day, and patted his head. "Hey, boy. It's good to see you again." He trotted along beside her, his tail wagging on their way over to the group.

"Glad to see you've come out," Brody said, striding over toward her. "And with a drink, no less. I'm proud of you." He gave her a wink.

That happiness she felt in her suite buzzed through her.

"Careful with alcohol around Brody," Stephanie teased from across the bonfire.

Lauren walked over to Stephanie, who was sitting in Mitchell's lap, her long legs draped over the arm of the Adirondack chair.

"It didn't end well with me last time," Stephanie said. "Good thing I've brought my voice of reason tonight." She snuggled up next to her fiancé.

"I can't let her out of my sight for two seconds," Mitchell said. "Which is fine by me." He leaned over and gave her a kiss.

Mitchell's display of affection for Stephanie was a completely normal response, but tonight, it unexpectedly hit Lauren right in that raw spot. Suddenly, she wanted to escape back to her room and continue her work.

She turned away, pretending to be distracted by a couple of elderly men next to the fire, and took a long sip from her cocktail, the strawberry sweetness of it doing nothing to extinguish the feeling of emptiness that assaulted her without warning. She waved to Mary and tried to put on a smile.

Brody looked Lauren's way, then walked over to her. "Take a walk with me?" he asked into her ear, as if he could sense her mood.

She nodded.

"We'll be right back," Brody said to everyone as he led Lauren down to the water.

Milton followed behind them, waddling happily across the sand.

"You okay?" he asked once they were out of earshot from the group.

"Yes," she said. She wasn't lying. She told herself that, in general, she wasn't falling into a million pieces or crying herself to sleep. So, yes, she was totally normal.

The surf splashed over her toes in bubbling foam.

Brody kept his gaze on her, clearly not convinced. "What are you thinking about, then?"

She stopped and faced him. "Nothing," she said.

Brody pursed his lips.

"Look, I thought I could do it, but sometimes, I still struggle to have light conversation and joke and tease like everyone else because, in the back of my mind, life is so much heavier and bigger and more terrifying than that."

"What's terrifying?"

"The fact that I'm only in my thirties and I don't have a path in life anymore. No real career of my own. Nowhere to call home. That's a little frightening."

"It's all in how you look at it," he countered.

She stared at him, not understanding his suggestion. She couldn't just switch her thoughts and view the issue a different way.

"You think I plan to be a fisherman forever?" He shrugged, the wind pushing his T-shirt against his toned chest.

She forced herself to look at his face.

"It's just what I do right now. I can do it forever if I want to, but I can also do something else if I feel like it."

"What do you plan to do when you get tired of fishing?" she asked.

"One day, I'll show you." He shrugged. "But there's no rush. I like where I am now. I get to go wherever I want and do whatever I want. There's freedom in that."

"But I *do* want a solid career and a family… and to spend more than a few hours feeling completely fine instead of on the verge of tears most of the time because I've lost *everything*." She gripped her melted cocktail. "I'm sorry. I bring everyone down."

"No, you don't." With a smirk, he gestured to Milton, who was frolicking in the surf.

She allowed a little smile but then sobered. "I do. You should be over there laughing and carrying on with everyone, but instead, you're here with me, listening to all this."

"But everyone needs someone to listen, right?"

"Most people can get along just fine on their own without dragging someone else into it."

He cocked his head to the side. "What would happen if you let yourself off the hook, even a little?"

"Off the hook?"

"You don't have to make all those things happen. You just have to be you and they'll begin to show up around you. Before you know it, you'll have the family you've wanted and the job you've been looking for." He took a step toward her. "Right now, *all* you have to do is stand across from me, right here. That's it."

She dragged her toes through the sand, drawing streaks in it. "You make life seem so simple."

"It is. *We* make it hard."

"My fiancé, Mason, thought the same thing. He wanted us to sell everything and move to the coast where we could live a less complicated life."

With a proud grin, Brody held his arms out as if to say, "Here it is."

Just then something cold washed up on her foot and she jumped.

Brody leaned over to see what it was. He reached down and plucked a shiny object from the tide. "You're a magnet for sea glass," he said, holding the clear piece of glass between his fingers. "This one looks relatively new. It's still sort of pointy on one end." He handed it to Lauren.

"That's two pieces I've found on this beach so far," Lauren said, inspecting it.

"You're actually in a great spot to find it, here." Brody turned his attention to the deep blue sea as it rushed toward them, pushing and pulling, back and forth. "The rip current can get strong in this area and it churns up all kinds of stuff. I'm always throwing away old visors and sunglasses that wash up, probably from vacationers who lose them on their boat rides."

"Well, I guess I should add this piece to my little collection." She slipped it into her pocket, feeling slightly better after talking to Brody. "Thank you," she told him.

"For what?"

"For letting me get my feelings off my chest."

He gave her a warm smile. "It's no problem."

There was something in his eyes. *Interest?* But before she could scrutinize it for too long, he turned toward the bonfire.

"We should probably get back." He whistled for Milton, who ran through the sand toward him. "And you need some s'mores."

"Me?" She stepped up beside him.

"Of course you," he said with a laugh. "Milton can't have chocolate."

"I've never had one," she said.

He stopped and faced her with wide eyes. "*What?* You've never had s'mores?"

She shook her head.

Brody linked his arm in hers, the motion startling her. "We're fixing that right now."

His fingers brushed her forearm as they walked together until they got back to the group. He let go and her skin still felt his touch where his hand had been. Mary gave them both a happy greeting when they arrived.

"Mary, Lauren has never had a s'more." Brody grabbed a skewer, and handed it to Lauren.

Mary gasped.

Stephanie got out of her chair and picked up another skewer. "You haven't?" She reached over for the bowl of marshmallows, offering it to Lauren. "Take one and put it on the stick like this." She threaded the marshmallow onto the pointy end of the skewer.

Lauren followed her lead, loading the marshmallow and jutting it into the flames, the marshmallow turning black on one side.

"Oh, save her, Brody," Mary said, waving a finger at Lauren's skewer.

Lauren compared her own to Stephanie's, and realized that her marshmallow was now on fire.

Brody came toward her. "There's an art to it," he said, putting his hand around hers and lifting the skewer from the bottom of the fire. He blew out the little flame. "You want it right about… here." He guided the marshmallow onto the top of the flame.

As he kept it steady, she couldn't help but assess the way his hand felt around her own. It was a new feeling, yet at the same time it felt oddly comfortable, like something she'd done before, even though she hadn't. But what struck her the most was that she didn't feel the instinct to yank her hand away. Perhaps it was because he'd been so kind to her tonight, or the fact that she knew he wasn't looking for a relationship of any kind, so there was nothing behind it.

"Placement in the fire is the most important part of the entire activity. You want your marshmallow super gooey, and you *don't* want it charred to oblivion." He looked down at her, and she noticed that something changed in his eyes as they locked with hers—it was as if he were only just then seeing her for the first time. He let go of her hand. "You should be good now."

Stephanie handed Lauren a couple of graham crackers and a square of chocolate, but Lauren was still focused on the zinging sensation rushing through her body after her and Brody's little moment. As she looked over at him, she wondered what those hands would feel like on her face, what those arms would feel like around her. Realizing how distracted he could make her, she focused on stacking the chocolate and marshmallow onto her graham cracker.

"Who's that?" Stephanie asked, distracted from the marshmallows by a crew of people as they trudged through the sand. *Cue the record scratch.*

"Oh. That's Dave Hammond, the producer of the show." Lauren handed Stephanie her s'more and left the group to head him off. After all, *she* had agreed to this, but she hadn't even warned everyone else yet about the filming. "Hey." She waved, trying to be friendly. "Why don't we start filming tomorrow?"

Dave shook his head. "We have less than a week, right? We need all the footage we can get." He tapped on his iPad, bringing up a form. "We'll just need a few electronic releases. Here, you go first." He handed her the iPad.

A director that she didn't know was holding a fuzzy microphone on the end of a boom pole over their heads and a camera guy had his camera rolling while the set designer and location manager went ahead of them to speak to Brody and Mary.

"Let Diane touch up your makeup for the lighting," Dave suggested, looking around. He fished around in his shoulder bag and lifted the slate out before sinking his hand back inside, presumably for the wipe-off marker he always used to label the scene. "I'm gonna need some set lighting for this. Carl!"

The man speaking to Brody turned his head.

"Think we can get a few of the lights up?"

"Yep!"

While the woman with a crop of dark hair and a crew badge— presumably Diane—jogged over to Lauren with a powder brush and a palette of makeup, Carl ran off to greet more of the crew who were filtering in with large boxes of equipment. They began setting up portable lighting units and running their extension cords up to the inn. The lights came on with a loud puff when they hit the switch.

"Just act normal," Dave called to everyone happily as the crew descended upon them like a SWAT team. He threw the black-and-white slate in front of the camera and clapped the arm on the top. "Action."

Mary looked around her from the edge of her Adirondack chair with an anxious smile while the others chatted in hushed tones.

When Diane moved on to Stephanie, Carl took over the iPad, getting everyone's electronic signatures. Then, as the cameras were rolling under the large lights plonked in the sand, Dave came over to Lauren.

"I'm just getting some initial clip options to feed into the intro reel for the opening and closing credits. Then we'll need to get with the bride and groom as soon as possible for a few candid shots."

"They're here." She pointed to Stephanie and Mitchell.

Dave followed her direction. "Funny. You're the same size as the bride. If she takes off the day of the wedding, we can do back-shots and have you fill in."

Lauren rolled her eyes at his joke, but she knew that if any of them would be running, it would probably be her and not Stephanie.

Dave gathered his equipment. "Let's set up a conversation over by the fire and you can talk about the wedding with the happy couple."

Lauren plastered on one of her polite smiles. While she'd expressed to Brody that she didn't know how to just hang out with people, suddenly she wanted nothing more than to be left alone with her new friends, not performing for the TV crew. The next week should be interesting...

Chapter Twelve

Fall, 1960
Fairhope, Alabama

Unable to get a breath, Phillip bent over, his hands on the knees of his tuxedo trousers, in the middle of the storeroom floor.

The tailor who'd been measuring his inseam leaned into his view. "Are you all right, sir?"

"I just need a minute," Phillip replied with a gasp, lightheaded as he looked at himself in the three-way mirror. Instead of his reflection, he saw Penelope's gorgeous smile flash across his mind and squeezed his eyes shut. Beads of sweat formed along his hairline and at the back of his neck. When the tailor left the room for more straight pins, Phillip tugged at the stiff collar of his pressed shirt, feeling strangled.

"What is it, darling?" Phillip's mother asked, her heels clicking closer to him. "Are you ill?"

Phillip righted himself and stared into his mother's concerned eyes. "I can't do this."

"Can't do what, dear?"

"I can't get married."

His mother pressed her red lips into that straight line she'd gotten so good at whenever she was disappointed in him, which seemed to be a lot in the past year. It used to make him feel guilty, but now he was indifferent to it.

Then she produced the strained smile, which always came next. "You just have cold feet." She rubbed his back. "It's normal for a young person. You're moving from being a bachelor to a family man, with responsibilities and a wife to take care of. It's a big step. It's only natural to feel nervous."

He looked his mother square in the face, fear mounting. "I don't love Alicia."

Her smile fell to an angry frown. "She is *perfect* for you."

"She's a very nice woman," he said, his mouth dry from anxiety over the situation. "But I don't *love* her."

Then her face softened. "You will," she said gently. "It takes time."

He shook his head defiantly.

"Phillip," his mother snapped, "you can't still be hung up on that insignificant little girl from Kill Devil... whatsit. The town's name itself should be a sign to you."

Phillip looked up. "Kill Devil what?"

His mother sucked in a breath of annoyance. "It doesn't matter."

"How do you know where she lives?"

His mother's lips were suddenly sewn shut and she glared at him, clearly not wanting to say.

He took a step toward her, trying to keep his cool. "Tell me."

"We did a little research on the young lady before we kept you away from her for good." Her shoulders fell, empathy showing on her face. "She doesn't have anything to offer financially, Phillip. She would drag you down and drain you of your inheritance."

"Or, given our resources, she would flourish," he said through his teeth.

"Our family isn't a charity, son. We found you someone who will make a wonderful wife and community member. She has a string of courters waiting in line for her, but she accepted *your* proposal. She adores you."

"And what *I* want means nothing?"

"You don't know what's best for you."

Phillip stripped off his shirt, startling her, and she turned away as he stomped toward her bare-chested. He kicked off his shoes, took off the tuxedo trousers, and lumped them on the chair next to the mirror. Then he threw on his street clothes and stormed through the room toward the door.

The house was empty when he pulled into the drive. In a flash, he got out, raced up to his bedroom, and threw open the top dresser drawer. He rooted around in it until his fingers landed on the cool, smooth surface of the stones. He retrieved the sea glass bracelet, put it into his pocket, and got back into his car.

Rodanthe, North Carolina

Lauren lay in a cold sweat in her bed, the scent from the bonfire still lingering from when she'd opened the double doors after returning to her room. She'd needed some fresh air to clear her head, but it hadn't helped, the fragrance only reminding her of the evening.

These difficult nights would spring up out of nowhere, blindsiding her every time. But this episode was different; she had new issues that were most likely the culprit. Drowning in guilt for feeling something tonight for Brody, and for allowing herself to get into this situation with the TV pilot, a lone tear meandered down the side of her face and onto her pillow. She stared at the dark ceiling, her eyes aching and her head pounding.

She clicked on the lamp and sat up. Her gaze fell on the top of the dresser and the little pile of sea glass. Shame and frustration swarming her, she crawled out of bed and put on her robe. Then she marched over to the pieces, scooped them up into her fist, left her suite, and headed down the staff hallway toward the kitchen to dump them somewhere so she didn't have to look at them, and to see if Mary had any ibuprofen.

"Oh, hello," Melinda said, standing by the kitchen table as Lauren entered, startling her.

"Hi," Lauren returned, surprised she was up so late.

"That was quite exciting tonight."

Lauren offered a smile, hoping her eyes weren't red enough for Melinda to notice her distress. "Yes."

"It's the biggest thing to happen to this little beach town in decades. Wait until the locals find out about it; they'll be lining up outside the inn to get a peek at the filming."

The idea of it only served to add to Lauren's trepidation.

"Mary and I decided to have a nightcap to talk about it, and she's just gone to bed. I told her I'd clean up after us." She walked over to the counter with two used mugs dangling from her fingers and rinsed them in the sink. "Can't sleep?"

When Melinda turned away, Lauren rubbed her eyes, hoping to eliminate any last evidence of her tears. "I had a headache, so I came down to see if Mary had anything I could take for it."

The sink still running, Melinda waved a dripping finger toward one of the cabinets next to the old, commercial-style oven. "She keeps a little stash of medicine in there. You'll probably find something."

Lauren padded over to the cabinet and fiddled with the bottles inside, until she found what she was looking for. After that she leaned across the counter toward the small trash can that the chef used for scraps and dropped her fistful of sea glass into it. She didn't believe in good luck. The idea of it hadn't gotten her anywhere but muddled and confused. Lauren opened the bottle and dumped one of the small pills into her hand.

Melinda pulled a glass from the cabinet, filled it with water, and handed it to her.

"Thank you." She swallowed the pill.

"Got a minute for a chat?" Melinda asked.

Not wanting to retreat to her silent room where she'd be consumed by her thoughts, Lauren lowered herself into one of the chairs at the table and gestured to the seat across from her.

"I never got to tell you the story about the bracelet that Mary gave you."

"Oh, yes," Lauren said.

She didn't have the heart to throw that away, since Mary had given it to her as a gift. She'd left it in her room, but decided that she'd slowly taper off the times that she wore it until everyone had forgotten altogether that she had it. Then she'd put it into her jewelry box as a memento of her time at the beach, but nothing more. The idea that it held any special power at all was just a false hope that she'd held on to for a brief moment in time.

"My father-in-law, Phillip, had it in his dresser drawer," Melinda said as she sat down across from Lauren. "He and my husband never had the best relationship. Phillip had been a distant father, somewhat bitter about life, always preoccupied when my husband was growing up. When Phillip was around eighty, he got cancer, and we were the only family there to take care of him."

Lauren hung on Melinda's every word. She couldn't imagine what the dynamics must have been like, nursing a man who'd barely been present for his own son.

"Before he died, while I was taking care of him in his final days, he got up and pulled out the bracelet from his drawer. He told me that he'd intended to give it to his wife, but never got the chance to."

Lauren gripped her water glass. "How come?"

"He didn't say. His wife, Alicia, had left him by then, so we'd originally guessed that he must have bought it just before." She leaned forward. "However, later, when I asked him where it had come from, he said that he'd gotten it in the Outer Banks of North Carolina when he was passing through as a young man. There was something in his eyes that made me wonder if he was giving me the whole story of it. He said the artist told him that it was good luck, although he was adamant that, for him, it was anything but."

Lauren sucked in a little gasp. Her inklings about it had been right. "So it isn't good luck at all?"

"Well, that was his assessment. I can only assume that he'd decided it didn't bring him luck because things hadn't worked out with Alicia." She shook her head. "He fell into my embrace, in tears. He said he'd wasted his life, angry for too long at the cards he'd been dealt."

Lauren could certainly sympathize.

"He also mentioned survivor's guilt, which I didn't understand. Then he offered the bracelet to me and said he owed it to the artist to strip away any negative feelings associated with it. It was meant for something better, he said. He asked me to give the bracelet away to someone who was full of life and possibility because then the luck that had missed him was sure to find the right person." She smiled, a little chuckle rising up. "He said that if he could, from heaven, he'd tell me who the right person was."

"Why not Stephanie? She's full of life."

"Stephanie had already gone off to college when he died, and it hadn't occurred to me. But when Mary said that you were coming, and she couldn't find the right gift to get you, something in my gut told me you were the one who should have it."

Lauren wasn't sure she was the right person at all. Was she full of life? Definitely not.

"It's silly, but I felt like Phillip was urging me to give it to *you*." Her face fell into a more serious expression. "When you went up to your room early tonight, I was worried about you. Brody told me about your fiancé."

The hairs on Lauren's arms stood up with the mention of Mason. His memory had found its way to her even while she'd tried to avoid the thought of him by coming down to the kitchen tonight.

"It's all a bit unreal after hearing about him."

"What's unreal?" Lauren asked.

"Phillip explained to me that night that life *is* that sea glass: broken, jagged pieces, left to the elements. And yet, in the turbulence of the storms they are made beautiful. He said he could see the beauty now, but it was too late for him. He'd wasted his life being angry."

Lauren's breath was shallow while she absorbed Phillip's explanation of the sea glass. Her own storms were overpowering her now, but were they also smoothing her, polishing her up for a better life? She certainly didn't feel like it, although it was a nice thought. "Why was he angry? Did he tell you?"

She shook her head. "But he took both my hands and looked directly at me, and that was the moment that I realized that all the bitterness I'd seen in him over the years was actually fear. Of what, I'm not sure. Tears welled up in his eyes and he told me to go get my husband, Chuck. He sat with him that night and pleaded with Chuck to forgive him for being a terrible father."

"Wow," Lauren said, floored by the sadness of Phillip's story.

"I do wonder if he had some hand in you getting it, or at the very least if there's something bigger than us at work—call it luck, intuition, karma."

"If I'm being honest, I don't believe people can give us signs. Or that a bracelet can bring luck. I don't believe in any of it at all."

"What *do* you believe in?"

Lauren hadn't considered that question since the day Mason died. She hoped that there was somewhere he'd gone to. There were times she swore she could feel him near her. "I believe in God, but it seems sometimes as though I've been overlooked."

"Why?"

Lauren found herself opening up due to Melinda's sincerity and the late hour. She explained exactly what happened to Mason and how she was managing. "I'm stuck and I don't know what to do."

"You've sold your business, changed where you live, started to work a new job, met new people. You're only stuck in here." She tapped her temple. "But I understand. I've been there. When Brody's father and I didn't work out, I was lost. I felt like I'd done something wrong to be abandoned. I still love him..." Her voice faded away as she drew inward.

"He left you?"

She nodded. "Last year. From the moment we married, he was barely there. I should've seen the warning signs then. But I thought that when Brody was born he'd change. Growing up, Brody barely knew his father—Chuck worked all the time. And they were so different. The only time Chuck would talk to him was to tell him that he needed to apply himself if he was ever going to succeed in life. He wasn't around enough to see that Brody approached life differently than he did.

"I pleaded with him to stop spending so many hours at work. I tried to explain to him that he needed to have quality time with his son if he ever wanted a relationship with him. But Chuck hadn't really had one with his own father."

"That's so terribly sad," Lauren said. She'd seen firsthand that Brody was a good man.

"Yes. I do know, however, that like his father he has a good heart deep down, and he loves Brody. He's just not great at showing it. I've left messages for him, telling him that. I just hope he doesn't wait until the bitter end to see it, the way Phillip did. And my biggest fear is that the same trait was passed down to Brody."

"Brody mentioned that he didn't want to get married."

"I know." Melinda shook her head. "He doesn't realize that all relationships aren't like the one that Chuck and I had."

"I can't imagine never knowing the kind of love I had with Mason."

"I wish Chuck had known it." Melinda frowned. "I wish *I'd* known it."

"Maybe you will," Lauren offered.

Melinda perked up. "Is that hope I hear from you?" She smiled at Lauren. "Maybe I'll get lucky?" She gave her a wink. "Unlike you, I *do* believe in luck. And I believe that it finds us when we least expect it."

Chapter Thirteen

The sun sent glorious beams through Lauren's curtains the next morning, so she pulled them back and opened the French doors in her bedroom as she made the bed. After her talk with Melinda last night, she'd been able to get some sleep and woke up feeling refreshed. She moved to the dresser and picked up the sea glass bracelet, turning it over in her hand, recalling Phillip's story.

On her way downstairs to get the address for the printing company, she had a new pep in her step. When she got there, the film crew was already camped out in front of Mary's office. They scrambled to attention, while Diane came over and got Lauren camera ready.

"We've been wondering if you'd ever emerge from your suite," Dave said. "I was about to knock on the door."

She remembered how her privacy wasn't hers anymore when Dave and his show were involved, but she also recalled how they couldn't do anything when she was in her private home. It was off-limits.

When she got inside, the office was empty. Mary was probably still with the guests at breakfast—lucky woman.

"Sorry to jump right in," Dave said, "but I'm squeezed for footage time." The cameraman adjusted the heavy handheld on his shoulder while another one set up a tripod in the cramped space. A portable light popped on right in her face, causing spots in her vision. They'd only just started and the heat from all the people and lighting caused a prickle of perspiration at the back of her neck. "Just carry on with what you're doing and don't mind us. We're not even here."

Trying to look as natural as she could, given what was going on, she sat down at the desk. When she did, in front of her was the pile of sea glass that she'd left in the trash last night, with a note:

Lauren,

The chef found these in the kitchen scraps bin and thought they were too beautiful to discard. When he gave them to me, I knew they were yours. I hope the cleaning crew didn't think they were garbage and strip them from your suite. Anyway, we saved them, and they're back with you, where they belong.

Love,
Mary

Lauren read the final words again: *back with you, where they belong.* The sea glass seemed to find her no matter what. She couldn't get rid of them. The sight of it was oddly comforting, though, given the circumstances. Feeling better about them this morning than she had last night, she scooped up the pieces and slipped them into her pocket.

She scribbled down the address for the printing company, grabbed her handbag, and headed out to get the printed sign so that the interior painting could begin, with the TV crew following behind her the whole way.

That afternoon, after picking up the sign from the printer and placing it in the main room, Lauren took care of a few phone calls. She chatted with the beach preservation society to see about the dwindling shoreline at the back of the inn and scheduled the exterior work. Then she packed up the room to clear it for the interior painters while Mary handled the guests.

Dave and his crew had settled at the corners of the room with their cameras rolling, and, while she didn't love it, Lauren was getting used to having them around again.

As she stood atop a chair, unscrewing the old curtain rods, Brody's voice floated over to her.

"Mary said you needed my help?" He eyed Carl and the cameraman.

She glanced down at him before she went back to the task. The feel of his touch on her arm raced through her mind, and she hoped the cameras didn't pick up on it. Dave's team was notorious for tapping into inner emotions, capturing the movement of a hand or the blink of an eye to divulge a feeling, and they were bizarrely accurate. "I didn't tell Mary that I needed help."

Lauren twisted the screwdriver with her sore hands, all the screws stripped and difficult to get out of the wall after so many years. When she turned to address Brody once more, she realized he had a ladder under his arm, a toolbox, and a toolbelt around his waist.

"She asked me to bring the basics along with some storage containers," he said, setting the ladder up next to her and then reaching into his collection of tools. He climbed up and placed a small drill over the screw she'd been wrestling with. One quick buzz and it came out of the wall.

"I could've used that four screws ago," she said, rubbing her red fingers.

He grinned at her and quickly removed another, the rod coming down. Lauren climbed off her chair and he handed the dusty hardware to her.

One of the crew members rolled his camera closer, moving between them. Dave raised a finger in the air and one camera was on her while the other tipped up to get a shot of Brody atop the ladder, and her heart fluttered. This show was not about *them*. It was about the wedding that they were renovating the inn for. The very last thing she needed was for the public at large to think there was anything going on between her and Brody. First, it would put incredible pressure on the both of them if things went anywhere, and then even more stress if they didn't work out. *And* the public still thought she was engaged. There was no way she'd ever rehash the last year on film for the benefit of the viewers. She'd have to be very careful. She turned away from Brody and dragged one of the upholstered side chairs to the middle of the room to get it into position for the painters.

"The back of my truck is full of boxes for all the stuff," he called down to her.

She peeked over to one of the cameras out of the corner of her eye and realized it was still positioned right on her face. A swell of warmth spread through her cheeks and she looked away. "Thank you."

"No problem." Brody stretched across the wall and removed another screw, the rod falling loose into his hand. "You want all these drapes taken down, right?"

"Yes, please." Trying to avoid the prying lens, she focused on scooting the coffee table out of the way, praying the flush in her face wasn't noticeable.

"I'll help for a few minutes or so and then I've got a family booked for the fishing charter."

"Any help will do. You're the best." She flashed him a wide smile. "The painter's coming this afternoon, and he's starting on this room, so I'm frantically trying to clear it out."

"Stephanie said she's coming over today too. You're a busy lady."

"Yes. I think I'm starting to find my rhythm." She stepped aside, avoiding the crew's prying lens in an attempt to keep the conversation flowing normally when everything inside her wanted to close up. But Dave gritted his teeth and widened his eyes from behind the crew, pointing down to the camera and reminding her that this was a show she'd signed up for.

"It didn't take you long." Brody moved his ladder to detach the last curtain rod and then climbed down, placing the last bit of hardware onto the table next her. "Hey, it's my birthday tomorrow—"

The camera moved closer.

"Oh my gosh," she said, surprised. "Happy almost birthday. Why didn't you say anything last night?"

Despite the camera that was nearly in their faces, the corner of his mouth turned up, revealing his amusement. "What did you want me to say—'Hi, thanks for coming out to the bonfire. It's my birthday the day after tomorrow. Want to wish me an early happy birthday?'"

His flirty expression and the assembled film crew filling the room had suddenly made her hot. She brushed a runaway tendril from her face and wiped her forehead with her wrist as one of the team rolled their light to the right of her face. "Well, you said it just now. Why didn't you say it then?"

He laughed, the sight of it lifting her mood without warning, despite their audience. "I don't know! But you didn't let me finish." He placed his drill into his toolbox and faced her. "Mom wants to come here to the inn and have a drink tomorrow to celebrate, if you'd like to come."

She inwardly debated letting him down if she said no, with the relief of retreating to her room, away from the cameras. But she enjoyed being with him. And it was his *birthday*. How could she decline?

"Mom and Mary will be there, and Stephanie and Mitchell are coming, too, so you won't have to be the center of conversation," he added, as if he were reading her mind.

"I'd actually love to go." Given the kindness he'd shown her since she'd gotten there, she couldn't *not* celebrate his birthday.

"Excellent." He folded his ladder. "I'm so sorry—I've gotta go." He surveyed the rest of the furniture she had yet to move before looking at his watch.

"I'll be fine. You've done the hard part. I'll see you tomorrow."

"I'll set the boxes on the porch."

"Thank you again for bringing them over."

"Of course. See ya later." He picked up his toolbox, tucked his ladder under his arm, and headed out, leaving her in silence with the film crew once again.

"Cut! The chemistry between you two is fantastic!" Dave said with a devious sparkle in his eye. "I didn't see that coming!"

"Dave." She put her hands on her hips. "This is a show about planning a wedding on a time crunch, correct?"

"Yes, but people will eat this up."

"Eat what up? There's nothing to eat up."

"Don't try to hide it. The two of you are amazing together. You just light up the screen with sexual tension."

"Dave!" Lauren rubbed her eyes in a mixture of frustration and mortification. "He's just a friend."

"Yeah, okay," Dave said with a chuckle.

The familiar guilt swam through her. Diane rushed over and tapped some foundation under her eyes where she'd just rubbed them; this whole ordeal was proving to be exhausting.

"Just focus on the wedding," Lauren warned.

While the film crew got a few filler shots for editing, she worked to finish the main room and then went on to the office to clear it out and finalize timings for the rest of the renovations.

"What kinds of things does Brody like?" Lauren asked Stephanie as the two of them shopped after visiting the florist to choose the wedding bouquets. With Mitchell working, Stephanie had made the final decision on a bundle of white roses with wrapped stems that she was sure he'd approve of. The film crew had gotten it all on camera, and they were now meandering through the shop while curious bystanders hovered around at the edges of the store, gawking at their little entourage.

"Anything to do with building or fishing."

"I could've guessed that." A swell of fondness for him floated through her and she glanced at the film crew. "Hang on a second." She walked over to the cameraman. "You can quit filming for a few hours. We aren't wedding planning."

The man leaned around his shoulder cam for guidance, and Dave spun a finger in the air to tell him to keep rolling. "Since it's the two of you, it's nice to see you bonding," Dave said.

"But our bonding doesn't have anything to do with the show," she countered.

"Yes it does. It adds an emotional element, and it'll resonate with the viewers."

With an exhale, she went back to Stephanie and ignored the cameras, trying to switch gears, picking up a coffee mug with a beach scene on the front, not really considering it, and then putting it back on the shelf. "What about something for Milton?" she asked, already regretting the decision to agree to this TV pilot. The money she got from it would be useful for renovations to the inn, but otherwise, it wasn't at all helpful to anyone but Andy.

"Maybe we could find Brody and Milton matching T-shirts," Stephanie teased, making Lauren laugh despite her predicament.

"If we find matching shirts, I'm buying them immediately."

Stephanie giggled before diverting her attention to something on one of the tables of the beach shop. "Look at this." She picked up a box of coasters with fishing lures on them. "These might be good. I think I'll get them."

Lauren peered over her shoulder to view them. "I bet he'll like those." She perused the table for other options, still trying to get the feelings about Brody out of her mind so they wouldn't show. Thoughts of him came to her like a movie reel: his kind smile when he looked at her, the way his eyes crinkled at the sides when he was happy, and, again, how his touch had felt. It was all so strange to experience, something she hadn't experienced in a long time. She didn't trust herself with these new thoughts and feelings. Remorse for even thinking about him at all bubbled up, and she pushed it down, moving to another table of wares as the cameras followed.

"Hey, Lauren," Stephanie called.

Happy for the interruption, she hurried over to her new friend.

"Don't you collect sea glass?"

"Sort of," she said. "Why?"

"It's an entire display of it." Stephanie gestured toward the presentation.

"Oh my goodness," she said, taking in the massive grouping of bracelets, earrings, belt buckles, and wine bottle tops. "Look at all of this. It so artfully done." She picked up a ring and slid it onto her finger, admiring it.

"It's as if someone made a table just for you."

Lauren smiled. "It does seem to find me." She put the ring back onto the table. "It's almost unreal how much of it I've seen since I've been here."

"You should treat yourself."

It was as if Lauren could see the kind of optimistic person she was meant to be in Stephanie, as if she could strip away all the pain she'd gone through and view herself untainted. "Maybe I should," she said.

"That ring looked nice on you. And it goes with your bracelet." Stephanie lifted Lauren's arm adorned with the gift from Mary to compare the two.

Lauren picked the ring back up and held it against her wrist. "It does, doesn't it?"

"It really does."

"All right, you talked me into it," Lauren said. "Now, you have to help me find something for Brody."

Stephanie laughed. "I think he'd be glad you were spending the time shopping."

"You think so?" she asked, her mind wandering again to Brody's kindness.

"Definitely."

Chapter Fourteen

"Hey, Mom," Lauren said, with the phone pressed against her ear while she wrapped the antique fishing lure art she'd found with Stephanie yesterday. After redecorating Mary's office, she'd spent her entire morning break in her suite to avoid the cameras. "Sorry I couldn't call you back until now. It's been my first real break of the day."

"Whatcha up to?" her mother asked, an indecipherable hesitancy lingering in her tone.

"I'm just wrapping a birthday present for someone."

"Already making friends?"

"Actually, yes… surprisingly." She definitely hadn't planned on it, but it had all just happened.

"That's lovely to hear."

"Except now I have cameras following me around." She explained to her mother what she'd agreed to.

"You should be excited," her mother said, of course, thinking differently than Lauren would.

"Why would that be exciting in the least?"

"Because, without even trying, look at what happened. You ran away from your old life, only to still be planning weddings and doing TV shows. That's the person you were before the accident. Maybe that's who you're still meant to be."

Lauren shrugged off the suggestion. "I'm not so sure about that." She didn't want to start a debate. "But I do feel like I belong *here*, somehow." She held the two ends of the wrapping paper together and applied a piece of tape.

"I have to admit that I worried about you living somewhere without Andy, or anyone else you know. I was scared that you'd close right up and things would get worse." Her mom became silent. There was still something unsaid hanging in the air between them that Lauren couldn't put her finger on.

"You okay?" Lauren asked.

Her mother was quiet just long enough to make Lauren pause. She stopped wrapping and sat down on the floor to give her mother her full attention.

"There's this thing I've recently learned about, and I've been wanting to tell you for a little while, but I was waiting for a good time, given your state since Mason…"

"I'm fine. Tell me."

Her mother cleared her throat. Whatever she had to say must be pretty big or she wouldn't be so hesitant—that wasn't like her mother at all. Lauren went over to the sofa and sat down, curling her legs underneath her.

"Okay… Well, you know how I've finally been going through Gran and Gramps's things?"

"Yes?" It had taken her mother months after inheriting her parents' home to begin the task of going through a lifetime of belongings. She was planning to have Lauren help, but it proved too difficult for her, so she and Lauren's father handled it.

"I found some paperwork in their house."

Lauren drew her knees up, patiently wondering what all this could be about.

"It turns out that I was… adopted."

"What?"

"They never told me."

Lauren covered her mouth. Gran and Gramps weren't actually her blood relatives? The very last thing she could handle was another unknown, another what-might-have-been. Just when she had a tiny glimpse of who she was supposed to be, her own family history was now being ripped out from under her. "Are you serious?"

"Most definitely. I can only imagine how you're feeling right now." Her mother's breath came down the line quietly, not matching Lauren's short, surprised inhalations. There was blood running through her veins that she didn't know. Why was she only finding out now instead of all the years before Mason's death, when she could've handled it better and been strong and supportive for her mother?

"While I was floored at first and confused," her mother continued, "in a strange way, I'm at peace with it. I had a wonderful life with my parents. I was loved by them and I felt fulfilled in everything I did."

Lauren's mind was going a hundred miles an hour, and she was barely able to take in what her mother was saying. It was all such a shock to her system. "Did Gran and Gramps leave any indication at all as to who your birth parents were?"

"No. I've found nothing. Except that I was adopted here in Tennessee."

"That's still so hard to believe."

"I was calling to check on how you were doing first, not to dump all our family secrets on you right away."

"I'm glad you felt like you could tell me," Lauren said, even though she was struggling to handle the news.

"You sound happier."

She looked down at Brody's gift on the coffee table, the silver ribbon trailing over the edge of the package. "I might just be getting there," she said. It was hard to say, given everything she still dealt with, but Brody made her feel happy, and that was something no one else had been able to do.

Lauren had been checking and approving the new design for the landscapers out front while the TV crew filmed her from various angles.

"I'd like to show you something before we go out to Brody's get-together," she said to Mary, as she caught the woman in the hallway. "I went to the electronics store and the home décor shop in town before my break, and I've been organizing."

Mary wobbled along beside her on her cane until they reached the office door. The crew followed them.

Lauren pushed it open, revealing the white walls with floating shelves, flowing curtains on either side of the wide window, framing the cobalt blue of the sea. She'd tucked away everything in the office into coordinated light gray boxes with labels on them; cleaned and shined the old wood floors; and slipped the landscapers a couple twenty-dollar bills to cart away the old desk. They'd helped her replace it with a slimmer one with a gray wash over the wood and a padded chair on wheels. In the center of the desk sat a sleek, brand-new computer with all the bells and whistles, and Brody's gift for later placed next to the keyboard.

Mary clapped a hand over her mouth. "This is astonishing," she said through her fingers.

Lauren smiled, pride filling her. "Like it?"

"I love it." Mary dragged a finger along the surface of the new desk as the cameraman swooped around them, Dave hovering in the doorway.

"I've got lots more planned," Lauren told her. She liked helping Mary; it made her feel whole in some way.

"I don't know what I did to deserve all this," she said, shaking her head. "I'm so blessed to have you this summer." She put her arm around Lauren.

For the first time in a very long time, Lauren felt like she had a purpose, something to get her up in the morning. She grabbed Brody's gift. "Want to head outside?"

The woman slipped her arm in Lauren's. "Yes."

The sun had dipped just low enough to cast an orange glow on the faces of the people gathered out back, on the porch of the inn. The wind chime was tinkling as it always did, and she was pretty sure that Dave would be alight with it all. He stayed quiet for the shot as the crew filed out behind them. Mary let go of her arm and walked over to say hello to Melinda.

"Cut," Lauren called, turning to the crew. "We're off the clock. No more wedding planning today. Go get yourselves a cocktail."

Dave frowned. "You can't halt production."

"All right, then you do it," she said as Brody walked up.

"You signed an agreement to allow this, Lauren. Unless you're sleeping or indisposed, nothing is off-limits."

"It's Brody's *birthday* party," she pleaded, hoping he'd have some decency.

"He signed the same release."

"It's fine," Brody said. "We'll probably bore them all to sleep anyway."

Dave beamed. "See? All fine." He turned to the crew. "Keep rolling."

Lauren didn't want any chance of Dave turning tonight into a circus, trailing after her and Brody to create some sort of love affair for the viewers. She opened her mouth to protest, but Brody redirected her, tapping on the present in her hand.

"You didn't have to get me anything," he said.

"Nonsense. It's your birthday." Lauren tried to ignore the small crowd of television folks gathered around them and held out the silver package.

He took the gift and shook it by his ear humorously, but then he gave her a genuine smile. "Thank you."

She couldn't help but notice how the setting sun sparkled in his blue eyes, making them look like the ocean. With the cameras around, she forced herself not to look. "Stephanie helped me pick it out."

"Oh no," Stephane said, walking over in a peach two-piece sundress ensemble that Lauren would've chosen for herself, while holding a cocktail. "She found that." Stephanie waggled a finger at the gift in Brody's hands. "I just went shopping with her."

Brody shot Lauren a fond look and set it on a small table next to the hammock.

"Well, it's so nice to see you three already chatting away." Mary's voice sailed toward them, her cane clicking against the new boards of the decking. "Did you want a drink, Lauren? We have piña coladas, a couple of different daiquiris, and lemonade."

"A lemonade would be wonderful, but I'll get it. Anyone else want one?"

The others declined. Mary, however, gave her a bright nod. Lauren went over to the table full of drinks, taking one of the glasses in each hand, the film crew following. Dave motioned for them to pan out on the beach just as a seagull flew over the sand. The crew began to descend the steps and Lauren used it as her opportunity to escape them, hurrying back over to the group.

When she returned, the woman was leaning forward on her cane and peering down the walk. "I wonder where Joe is."

Lauren offered her the other lemonade.

Mary took it, thoughts clear on her face. "He's usually early when I ask him to come over."

"You could call him," Stephanie suggested.

"Maybe I should." Mary set the untouched lemonade on the wide railing of the deck and paced over to the door, letting herself inside.

"Hey, tell him I'll come get him if he needs me to," Brody called after her.

Mary gave him a thumbs up and then disappeared into the inn.

"He's been having a hard time getting around lately," Brody said. "I worry about him."

Lauren couldn't help but be affected by Brody's caring nature. "That's sweet of you."

"Joe was best friends with my grandfather. He's been great to our family. When my dad left last year, he stepped in to help my mom with anything she needed, even though I could handle it. He's been like a father to me."

"He always treated me like a daughter too," Stephanie said happily over her shoulder, as Mitchell beckoned her to the edge of the deck to show her a pair of dolphins out on the horizon. "That's why I'm having him give me away at the wedding."

The crew rushed over to get the shot, staying on the beach, to Lauren's relief.

"Hey there." Melinda came over to them from a group of people in the corner. "How's the birthday boy treatin' ya?"

"Good," Lauren replied. "We were just chatting about how Joe is like a father to Brody."

Melinda gave an affirmative nod. "He's a wonderful man."

Lauren took a sip of her lemonade, the crisp sweetness of it like summer in a glass. "He was best friends with Brody's grandfather?"

"Yes. My father-in-law told me that Joe was the first person he met when he moved to the Outer Banks. It was an interesting relationship, but they seemed to understand each other."

"Interesting?"

She and Brody shared a knowing look. "My father-in-law was raised... differently from Joe."

"My grandfather was from a very wealthy family," Brody added, something lingering behind his eyes—disapproval?

She thought back to Melinda's story about how his father had worked all the time and she wondered now if Brody associated wealth with that overpowering drive to work.

He pulled two chairs over and offered them to Lauren and his mother before taking a seat across from them. "Joe was a local dock-worker, cleaning fish for the big fishing companies."

"They were definitely an unlikely pair," Melinda said, sitting down. "Brody's grandfather didn't seem to connect with anyone in his life, but he had a very strong bond with Joe. No one can understand it."

Lauren sipped her lemonade and lowered herself into the chair. "So how did they meet?"

Melinda looked questioningly at Brody. "I think they met the very day Phillip arrived here from Alabama, didn't they?"

"That's what Dad told me." Brody looked out over the water.

Cutting through the conversation, Mary returned to the porch. "Joe didn't answer, so I'm guessing he's on his way." She reached for the glass of lemonade she'd left and took a long drink.

"He'll be here soon, then," Melinda said with a smile. "Let me get you a chair."

An hour or so later, the film crew broke for a late dinner, leaving them all a bit more relaxed. Stephanie and Mitchell had settled on the rockers next to Brody, Mary, and Melinda, while Lauren leaned against the railing, the summer wind blowing warmly over her shoulders. Brody looked at his watch. "Anyone heard from Joe yet? What's he up to?"

"Maybe he's off running errands," Mary replied. "It takes him longer to get around these days. Should I try to call him again?"

Brody stood up. "The motor in his car's been idling funny too. I'll just run down the route to his house and make sure he hasn't had car trouble or anything. You know how he never carries a phone."

"I'll go," Melinda offered. "You stay here and enjoy your birthday."

Brody shook his head. "Let me go. If his car needs work, I'll be the one who can help him with it."

Melinda leaned back in her chair. "You've got a point."

Brody went over and gave his mom a kiss on the cheek. "Be right back."

After he left, Melinda addressed Lauren and Mary brightly, resuming the conversation. "How are the renovations coming along?"

"I can't believe how quickly we're getting it done," Lauren replied. "The painting's almost finished in the main room; then we're starting on the empty suites. And I've got a designer coming in soon to help with the décor."

"Can we see what you're planning?" Stephanie asked, her eyes glistening with interest.

"Oh yes," Mary agreed, rubbing her hands together in excitement.

"Sure. Let me get my laptop and I'll show you some of my mockups."

Lauren went down the porch, entering her suite by the bedroom doors, passing the little grouping of sea glass on the dresser. She stopped for a tick, glad she'd gotten those little pieces back. They seemed more vibrant today. Then she peered down at the ring she'd bought with Stephanie, the glass glistening in the evening sunlight as if it were moving with the jovial atmosphere outside. She grabbed her laptop and headed back to Mary and the others once more.

Just as she returned, Melinda's phone went off. "Oh, it's Brody." She held it to her ear and answered. Her eyes moved back and forth across the boards of the porch as she listened. Then her face turned white.

Lauren gripped her laptop, her gaze fixed on Melinda's worried expression.

"All right. I'll let them know."

"What is it?" Mary asked.

"He's at the hospital. With Joe."

Chapter Fifteen

"They think it's his heart," Brody said after everyone had arrived at the hospital to check on how Joe was doing.

Lauren was so glad they'd been able to slip out before the film crew had returned. This was no place for the show, and she was certain that Dave would eat it up, since Joe was walking Stephanie down the aisle. Sometimes, he had no boundaries. Her phone pinged with messages from him, but she ignored them.

"His truck was in the drive, but no one answered when I knocked, so I used the spare key that he hides under the old cowbell on the porch," Brody continued. "He was unresponsive when I found him in his living room, so I called an ambulance."

"I hope he's all right." Mary wrung her hands.

Lauren focused on the white in the woman's knuckles, suddenly feeling sick and shaky, her vision blurry. Melinda put her arm around Mary to comfort her, worry etched on both their faces while Lauren took it all in as if she were under water.

"They've just admitted him. The nurse said the doctor would be out to update us once they have him stabilized." Brody pulled a few of the blocky hospital chairs into a circle, and they all sat together. Lauren lowered herself into one of them, trying to keep her balance.

"I'm so worried about him," Stephanie said.

Brody nodded, his face grave. "I know."

"He's done a lot of good." Melinda took a chair next to Lauren. "He even called Chuck and tried to convince him to come home. He's always helping me, fixing things at the house while I'm at work and Brody's out on the boat, cooking the two of us special dinners on the weekends just because…"

"And he did the same for me when I lost my parents," Stephanie added. "He was right there the minute I needed someone to help. He changed the oil in my car, took care of my school fees, even though he didn't really have the money to do it, and he stopped by every few days to check on me."

The weight of being in the hospital was hitting Lauren hard. Everything had happened so quickly out on the porch, but now that she was there, with the shiny floors, the sterile smell, the beeping of machines somewhere down the hall, and the low chatter of the staff… She hadn't stepped foot in a hospital since Mason had been admitted after the crash. The different stages of her emotions that day flashed through her mind: panic, hope, exhaustion, and, finally, utter grief. Her hands trembled uncontrollably as she sat in the circle with everyone, and she felt as if she couldn't catch her breath.

Just then the doors to the waiting area swung open and she forced herself to look up. A doctor walked through with purpose, his white coat swishing at his sides. "Brody Harrison?"

Brody stood. "Yes, sir."

The doctor met him in the middle of the waiting room.

"He's stable. And he's awake, but a bit groggy. We've got him on an IV and sipping from a cup of ice chips. It was a heart attack, but he's surprisingly resilient for his age. He'll still need a few days with us, though, to be sure he's okay."

"Is he able to see people?"

"I think it would be fine, as long as you keep him calm." The doctor consulted their little group. "Are you all with Mr. Harrison?"

They nodded to confirm the doctor's question, while Lauren worked to get herself together. How lucky they all were that their news had been so different from hers a year ago.

"Shall we go see him?" Mary asked, getting up.

The rest of them followed, and before Lauren knew it she was walking behind the doctor down the long hallway to Joe Barnes's hospital room. To keep her memories at bay and maintain composure, she focused on Stephanie, who was a step in front of her talking quietly with Mitchell. Lauren matched her stride and tried to remain calm and strong. Today was about supporting her new friends. She did *not* want to turn this into some kind of pity party by breaking down. Forcing herself to stay in the present, she eyed the artwork on the wall as they neared it.

"Here we are," the doctor said, just as they stopped in front of the piece—a small row of flowers…

Lauren reached out and ran her fingers over the smooth surface of each bloom, processing what she was feeling.

"Oh, look at that. It's a mural of polished glass, right outside Joe's room," Mary said from beside her, drawing her attention away from the brightly colored pieces.

"Like sea glass," Stephanie said, her eyebrows raising.

Mary looked up at the ceiling as if she were sending a prayer of thanks to God above. "It *must* be good luck, then."

Lauren fiddled with her bracelet on their way inside the room. She'd barely seen the man before now, their paths not crossing entirely. Yet she was there to support him, so she wanted to take her strongest stance. She squared her shoulders and tried to clear her mind so that she could be strong for him and everyone else in the room.

Joe was sitting up slightly, oxygen tubes in his nose, a small paper cup in his hand. Stephanie and Lauren were the first to reach him. His attention went straight to Lauren's bracelet and then up to Lauren's face, his eyes widening.

"Grace? Where'd you get that bracelet?" he asked as he peered over at her with an astonished look.

"He might not be totally himself at the moment, but he should make a full recovery," the doctor said.

Lauren stared at the man, surprised by his blunder.

The others had now crowded around Joe, quietly chatting with him, directing his attention elsewhere. Mary was helping him get the ice from his cup with a plastic spoon while Brody asked how he was feeling.

"He called me Grace," she said under her breath to Stephanie. "Does he know someone named Grace?"

Stephanie frowned, shaking her head. "Not that I know of."

"It's just odd that he's mistaken my name for that one in particular."

"Why?" Stephanie asked.

"My mother's name is Grace."

"You didn't have much of a birthday," Lauren said to Brody when they got back to the inn.

"It's okay." He stood beside her as the two of them surveyed the back porch in the dark, the shushing of the waves and a lone stripe of moonlight on the unstill waters letting them know the ocean was still there in the void. Brody reached inside the door and clicked on the light, bright yellow beams illuminating the remains of the party.

With the late hour, everyone else had gone home. The camera crew must have given up waiting and gone to bed, which was a welcome break. Brody had insisted on following Lauren and Mary back to help clean up what was left of his celebration. After the events of the evening, Brody told Mary she could turn in for the night and he'd get everything picked up. Clearly exhausted, Mary hadn't objected.

"You didn't have to help me clear all this," Lauren told him as she threw a couple of bottles into the trash bag.

"It's fine. And I wanted to be sure that you and Mary got back safely."

"I think we could've managed," she said with a smile.

He grabbed a couple of plates off the railing and tossed them into the trash. "You looked white as a sheet in the waiting room at the hospital." He turned to her, his hands stilling as if he were giving her permission to explain. That was when she realized that he really came back to the inn with them to make sure *she* got back safely.

"It was hard to be in a medical setting after losing Mason last year."

He nodded. "That's understandable. Are you all right now?"

"Yeah," she said, glad that he'd come. His warmth and attention soothed her. To avoid blushing in front of him, she went over to another small table in the shadows and gathered a couple of paper cups.

"I overheard what you said to Stephanie about Joe calling you by your mother's name. That's peculiar, isn't it?"

"Yes," she said, stopping to face him. She'd wanted to talk about it ever since it had happened but just wasn't sure how to bring it up or whether it was even appropriate, given the situation. "How did he know that?"

"I have no idea. It was probably just a happy coincidence."

"We recently found out that my mother was adopted. All evening, I've been wondering, did he know her or her family somehow? But there's no way that I can think of that happening." She plopped down into one of the chairs and Brody followed. "Then again, he *was* fixated on this bracelet, which he has no ties to," she said with a shrug, "so maybe he just guessed correctly, and it was a big coincidence, like you say."

"It's definitely unusual, though, right?"

"Yeah." She twisted the smooth pieces of sea glass on her wrist. "Your grandfather had this bracelet, your mom said. Perhaps Joe had seen him with it?"

He stretched his fingers over his knees, leaning forward. "Possibly."

She was grateful to have Brody to talk to. He brought her to a state of calm that no one else had been able to achieve in the last year. He always responded to her with utter kindness and no judgment, even after knowing her story. As natural as can be, the urge washed over her and she reached out, putting her hand on his. He peered down at her fingers and then back up at her. A mixture of shock and delight swirled in his eyes like a hurricane. He abruptly sprang to his feet and faced the water.

"I'm sorry," she said, moving beside him, her face flaming from her boldness. "I don't know what came over me. I just like you. It was… an honest reaction."

He turned to her with intensity. "I know."

His response stunned her. "You do?"

"I've been waiting for you to let your guard down and let me in. But I guess I didn't expect you to make the first move. It took me by surprise. A nice surprise," he quickly added.

"Really?" she asked, the word barely coming out on her breath.

He looked out toward the Atlantic, his eyes unstill as if choosing his words. "You know, I was only supposed to replace half the boards on the deck, but I chipped in my own money to finish the whole thing so that I could see you more." He smiled down at her, vulnerability in his face.

In the past year she'd never thought beyond her grief, and she wasn't sure that she was even ready. Would Mason approve of this? "I don't know what to do," she said honestly.

"I don't either. I hadn't really planned on this…" He smirked. "I was fine, just fishing, spending time with Mom, and helping Mary."

She allowed a small smile in return, but their conversation the other night about how he didn't believe in marriage came back to her. While there were definitely no plans for marriage, she knew that she was too fragile to become serious with someone who didn't share her same beliefs. There was so much to learn about him. "Tell me about you and your family," she said, sitting back down.

He obliged, taking a seat as well. "What do you want to know?"

"You weren't close with your dad?"

"My dad officially left a year ago, but he wasn't ever really *there*. I blame my grandfather." He leaned back in his chair and propped his feet up on the new railing.

"Why do you blame your grandfather?" She could guess the answer, but she wanted to hear his perspective.

"He was a terrible example. He worked all the time, and while I do have a few good memories with him, he never seemed emotionally present, and I don't think he ever actually loved my grandmother. I think a lot of their years were spent together out of some sort of duty he felt."

"What kind of duty?"

"I have no idea. It makes no sense that he'd marry her if he didn't love her. Except maybe that's what was expected of him. His parents were very wealthy and tough on him."

"When did they separate?" she asked.

"They were married for years before she finally left him. Once, when I was a teenager, they were staying at our house while they got some plumbing work done. I was supposed to be asleep, but I could hear them talking downstairs. My grandmother finally asked him point-blank why he never loved her when she'd done everything right. He told her that it wasn't her. And that he was sorry. But he left that night. He didn't come around much after that."

"I'm so sorry that you had to hear their struggles."

He shrugged and looked out at the black of night, the fizzing of the waves as they hit the shore the only sound between them. "My dad was just the same. My mother told me once that she wished he'd open up to her, but he never would."

"I wonder, did *she* ever open up to him about how she felt?" she asked, realizing how much it had helped her to tell Brody about her loss.

His face crumpled in confusion. "Why would she need to open up about anything?"

"If your father didn't have the best role model, maybe he might benefit from a little coaching?"

"I don't know if coaching of any kind would help my father."

"But there could be hope for them. Your mom still loves him, right?"

"Yeah. I have no idea how."

"He could change."

"I doubt it."

"Look at your grandfather. He did finally admit his mistakes at the end of his life—your mother told me. And your grandfather was friends with Joe, right? That shows that deep down he was a good person. He couldn't have been so bad if Joe liked him. Joe seems so wonderful."

"I've always wondered how they really met, but I never asked Joe. I don't know how the two of them even struck up a conversation. My grandfather was quiet and introspective, and Joe was always talkative and ready to help someone."

"Maybe that's exactly why," Lauren said. "Your grandfather needed him, and Joe was able to help him," she said. In a way, she understood his behavior because it had been Brody's kindness that had started to make her see things differently.

She thought back to her old life, and it already felt like a lifetime since she'd lived it. Brody had definitely helped her. Now, she enjoyed the slower pace and the kindness of the people around her. And, just as Mason had predicted, Lauren wondered if she would ever want to leave…

Fall, 1960
Kill Devil Hills, North Carolina

The map of North Carolina that Phillip had bought at the state line was spread across the passenger seat of his car. He'd been driving all night and was exhausted, but his optimism for finding Penelope had kept him going. He had no idea where she was, but he knew the name of the town, and that he had to find her. He just hoped that she'd hear him out.

His dark green Packard Hawk paralleled the coast. The angry gray sea crashed onto the empty shore beside him, mirroring his emotions. But he pushed his anger at his parents out of the way and focused instead on Penelope's kindness and charm. He missed her so much.

On the drive, he decided that he was ready to give it all up for her—his inheritance, his university placement, everything. She was worth it. And then he would spend the rest of his life making up for his absence that day in Fairhope.

When he got to the town of Kill Devil Hills, Phillip pulled into the only structure within miles, a small country store, and went inside to see if anyone knew her.

"Excuse me?" he asked the shopkeeper, a grizzly old man whose weathered face looked as if he'd spent all his days out on the ocean. "Do you happen to know where I could find the home of a Miss Penelope Harper?"

The man stared at him for longer than he felt comfortable. "Yes, but do you mean *Mrs.* Penelope Barnes?"

Phillip's breath hung between his open lips as he processed what the man was implying. Then he snapped his mouth shut, swallowing against his dry mouth and taking a minute to pull himself together. "Yes," he said, clearing his throat, praying there was some kind of misunderstanding. His hand in his pocket, he gripped the sea glass bracelet.

The man gave him the address, and as Phillip left, the man called out, "Please tell Mr. Barnes we'll be thinking of them."

The comment made no sense to Phillip, but he was too busy trying to keep his cool. She'd gotten married. And he'd proposed to Alicia. And now, his impromptu plans were crumbling in front of his eyes. Two minutes ago, he'd been ready to call off his wedding, to change his entire life, and spill all of his innermost thoughts to Penelope, but now, he knew he couldn't do that.

He also couldn't simply go home. He wanted to see her, at least. He needed to be sure that happiness was evident in her eyes, and if she looked content, he'd have to take that with him. That was all he'd have of her.

Angrily brushing a tear off his cheek, he got back into his car and snatched up his map, locating Penelope's address. Not too far from where he'd asked for directions, he pulled onto her street and was met with an unusually long line of cars and other vehicles. Both sides of the road were full, people gathering outside a small fishing cottage. Was there a party of some sort going on? He squinted at the number—it was the one the shopkeeper had given him. Certainly with all these people he could get out unnoticed and have a walk around. Not wanting to cause her any pain, he'd be careful not to let Penelope see him.

He found a place to pull over and parked. Looking around to be sure she wasn't nearby, he got out of the car. A cold morning haze hung in the air as his feet ground against the gravel, his face tipped down to be inconspicuous. When he found out she was married, he should've turned around and returned to Fairhope, but something pulled him toward her. He knew what that something was—love. He loved her more than anything—more than his family, more than his money, more than his entire life.

"Hello," a voice said, drawing him from his thoughts.

He looked up to find a middle-aged woman. Her nose and the rims of her eyes were red, a balled handkerchief in her hand. "Are you here for Penelope?"

Shocked by the mention of her name, he wrestled with an answer, his hands beginning to tremble with unease. He jammed them into his pockets, the bracelet jutting against his fingers. He held on to it, trying to figure out what to tell her.

"I know, dear," the woman said, her eyes glistening. "You don't have to say anything." She took his arm. "It's unbelievable, isn't it? I can't believe she's… gone."

An electric current flowed through him with the heat of a raging fire. "Gone?"

"And now, her poor husband has to deal with this all on his own."

The blood drained from his face, leaving it clammy in the damp air. His mouth went dry once more and his head began to pound. Suddenly, his whole body was shaking. "What happened?" he finally asked. At the woman's look of confusion, he added, "I don't know a lot. I've just come into town from Alabama." He could barely get the words out, his heart feeling like it might explode in his chest.

"She died due to complications with her pregnancy."

All the oxygen left his body and he struggled to focus, his vision distorting with the onslaught of tears that suddenly pushed through to the surface. Would he wake up and realize this was some horrible nightmare? He prayed for relief. "Oh, my God." The words finally came out.

The woman wiped her eyes. "Yes, yes," she said, pulling him through the small yard up to the house. "Come inside. Let's get out of this dreary weather."

The rest of the day was a blur. Phillip stood among strangers, staring into the void of his anguish as people shared things they knew about Penelope, none of which were really who she'd been—not with him. People offered him food, but he declined. And then, as the day stretched on, he finally saw *him*, Penelope's husband. He knew right away because the man's pain matched his own. He walked over to him and introduced himself as an old friend from her summer away. The man nodded and shook his hand, telling Phillip his name was Joseph.

"I thought I'd be with her forever," Joseph said, his voice breaking. "But I suppose that some people come into our lives to help us get where we're going, and they were never meant to stay."

Phillip locked his joints to keep from collapsing into his own sorrow.

"She was too good for this world to stay very long," Joseph whispered.

"Yes," Phillip agreed, Joseph's words hitting him like a load of bricks. "She was put here to show us what goodness was like." His eyes brimming with tears once more, his heart aching for the lost time with Penelope, he reached into his pocket and pulled out the bracelet. Swallowing hard to give room for his words, he said, "She left this in Alabama. I want to return it."

"Ah," Joseph said, tears falling down his cheeks. "Please. Keep it."

As a cold rain began to fall outside, the two men who loved Penelope Harper more than life itself sat with each other, united by their sorrow.

Chapter Sixteen

Rodanthe, North Carolina

With the dawn of a new day, Lauren had a fresh perspective regarding her talk last night with Brody. She shouldn't have been so forward when she absolutely wasn't ready for anything with anyone. Especially when he was about to take off for six months or so on his road trip. And then there was the lingering shame that she was moving on... At least her gesture hadn't gone any further.

She finished up the last of the wedding details on the computer, double-checking the final RSVPs and waivers online, getting them loaded into her list for Dave. Given the time crunch, the wedding planning was going more smoothly than she'd ever expected. It helped that Stephanie and Mitchell had done some of it prior to working with her, but given all that she had to accomplish, things were moving along surprisingly well. The officiant hadn't been her first choice after seeing clips online, and she'd had to mix white roses with the gardenias for the bouquets, but other than that, things were moving right along. She went through the last few items to be sure she hadn't overlooked anything and then went out to let Mary know that the designer had called and said she'd be there in an hour.

"Where were you last night?" Dave asked, coming down the hallway at a clip. "I texted."

"There was an emergency."

"Well, you could've at least responded. What happened?"

"A friend of Mary's had a heart attack." She dared not say it was Stephanie's escort down the aisle. They'd cross that bridge when they came to it.

"Everything okay?" he asked, clearly trying to seem empathetic.

"Yes. Everything seems to be fine."

"Good to hear." Then he immediately switched gears. "We need to schedule a time to do your solo narration clips. We'll want some close-ups with you, telling us how the preparation is going."

Still not entirely sure she could make it through the wedding, which would mean that this pilot might go up in flames, Lauren stalled. "Could we shoot them all at the end?"

"Good idea. Maybe we can make a second visit for that." Dave nodded to the crew, who immediately assumed their positions, the camera now rolling. "Carry on," he said.

"Wait. Can't you just take a break or something? I'm not even doing wedding planning at the moment."

"What are you doing, then?" Dave challenged.

"I'm looking for Mary to give her a message."

Dave cocked his head to the side, the camera still rolling. "About?"

"I'm just going to tell her when the designer is coming for the interior work."

"Perfect," Dave said, snapping his fingers to pull the cameras closer. "That's preparing the venue. Something about the wedding is bound to come out." He turned to the crew. "Keep rolling."

With a deep breath, Lauren headed toward the front porch. When she found Mary, she was pointing toward the end of the street, directing a couple to town. They thanked her and walked down the steps to the parking lot. The seagulls screeched overhead while they flew back and forth in front of the sun, as if they were alerting them all to the summer heat that had already taken hold.

"Good morning," Mary said, pacing slowly toward Lauren. "I was just out here admiring the beds. They're so gorgeous."

The camera panned around them while Lauren took in the desert blooms in pinks and yellows, with pampas grass and palm trees giving height to the space, all freshly arranged this morning. Everything was perfect next to the newly planted turf grass, which was edged in driftwood-colored beams.

"I wanted to let you know the designer's coming. She'll be here in about an hour."

Mary's smile widened with glee. "That's exciting."

"Yes." Lauren stepped to the side to get out of the way of a crew member. "And I know we're pushing it, but I'm having the parking lot repaved today as well," Lauren said. "And the exterior painters will be redoing the inn in white with gray trim and painting the sign to match."

"*Exterior* painters?" Mary gave her a surprised but excited look before eyeing the camera crew, clearly not wanting to speak of the cost, which was surely on her mind.

"Yep." A fizzle of joy took hold at the idea of making Mary happy. "And I've got a conservation crew that will be bringing in sand to build up the beach. They say it'll give you at least five to eight more years, but that change won't happen until after the wedding. They want to wait until the end of the summer so they don't disturb the vacationers."

"Oh my goodness."

"I also wondered if we could extend the back and include a closed, heated glass porch with a big stone fireplace to entice people to come in the winter months."

"That would be amazing, but it's awfully ambitious." Mary wobbled her cane back. "Yours was a temporary position; I've only set aside pay for the next few weeks. Who will manage it all when you're gone?"

"Well, I was thinking…" Lauren smiled at her new friend. "I wondered if I could stay on and help you."

The initial excitement in Mary's eyes was quickly clouded with uncertainty, and after seeing the books, Lauren knew why. The future of the Tide and Swallow wasn't secure. *Yet.*

"I have plenty of money to live on," she said quietly into Mary's ear. "I wouldn't take a salary unless we could afford it. But if you give me time, I think I can make you more money with this place than you've ever seen."

Mary stared at her, hope evident in her eyes. Then she put an arm around Lauren and gave her a squeeze. "How could I say no?" Like she'd gotten accustomed to doing, Mary threaded her arm through Lauren's. "It's such a beautiful morning. I know we both have a lot to do, but walk me out to the back porch for a quiet moment." She gave the crew a motherly once-over.

Dave rolled his eyes and cut the camera. "No wedding talk whatsoever," he said.

"I told you," Lauren called to him as she and Mary made their way to the porch. "I'll let you know when you should come back. Take a break. Put your feet in the sand."

Dave blew a frustrated puff of air through his lips and rounded up the crew.

Lauren guided Mary up the ramp to the house and around the corner by the hammock. The late morning air blew off the ocean in a salty mist.

"I know you've got a lot to do, and you don't love the TV show people being here—I can tell. But you look so much happier than when you arrived," Mary noted as they came to a stop in front of the cobalt-blue sea.

"I suppose I am," she said. She'd expected to relax a little during her time there, but she never guessed she'd feel so at home. She was really settling in. And while she still had her struggles, in only a short time, life had begun to feel… normal.

Mary lifted her wrist with the bracelet. "Still don't believe in good luck?"

Lauren smiled. "Ah, I'm not sure it's the bracelet making me feel at home here. I think it might be the people." She winked at Mary.

Mary gave her a fond squint, wrinkling her nose in that now-familiar way before leaning on the new railing and closing her eyes, the sun casting an orange glow onto her weathered cheeks. "We've got work to do, but I could stand here all day and breathe this in."

"That sounds like a great idea. But you're right. I have to meet with Stephanie and Mitchell briefly before the designer shows up."

"What's on the agenda today?" Mary asked.

"Cake tasting. The baker is coming over with samples of their stock cake options. I'm floored that they were willing to put a cake together on such short notice."

"How did you do that?" Mary asked.

"I told them who I was and they rushed the order for me." It had been the first time since she'd arrived that she'd willingly put it out there that she was Lauren Sutton from Sugar and Lace. What she wanted to avoid at all costs upon her arrival had been her saving grace. "But we better not say too much without the crew here." She pulled out her phone and texted Dave to meet them in the dining room before addressing Mary once more. "The baker's coming in about twenty minutes. Want to lend your opinion?"

"It's a difficult job, trying cakes, but I suppose I can if I have to," she replied, teasing.

Mary took Lauren's arm once more, and the two of them went inside. With the breakfast crowd now gone, the dining room was closed, so Lauren put out plates from the kitchen and prepared a tray of iced tea while the crew set up. Diane powdered Mary, and Dave tampered with the lighting.

The baker arrived before Stephanie and Mitchell, a woman with salt-and-pepper hair pulled back into a bun and a faded apron that looked as though it had been around for decades of cake-baking. Dave intercepted her with his iPad for a release and then she unloaded a table full of small sheet cakes with the flavors written on the box in marker. She introduced herself.

"Nice to meet you," Lauren said.

Mary rubbed her hands together. "It looks like you've got a ton of different flavors."

"I brought the lemon meringue and key lime pie since it's a late summer wedding, but in case the bride is more traditional, I have vanilla, classic white, and buttercream. I also have the occasional bride ask for chocolate so I brought my chocolate mousse cake and threw in the red velvet."

"That's quite an array," Mary said, her eyes sparkling.

The baker began to pull small tubs from one of the bags she brought in. "And I made each sheet cake big enough to try multiple icing flavors.

Some people like vanilla cake and buttercream frosting while others prefer the cream cheese. This way, you can try them all."

"What are all the frosting options?" Lauren asked as she set places for each of them at one of the dining tables. Her phone went off with a text that Cass Albright, the designer, was two minutes away.

"I have whipped vanilla, regular vanilla, buttercream, cream cheese, iced caramel, lavender cream..." She consulted a few more of the tubs. "One I call snowberry because it has a cream and raspberry flavor, and my signature hazelnut truffle."

"Well, there's no way I will make a decision unless I try them all," Mary said.

Just then Stephanie and Mitchell arrived, coming through the double doors. "You two have got quite a decision to make," Lauren said, patting them both on the shoulder. "Mary will take care of you. I've got to catch up with the designer who's coming in to talk about décor and get ideas for the wedding layout of the main room. I'll be back in when you've decided, and I'll wrap up all the details."

Lauren hurried out to meet Cass, a lone cameraman running behind her, Dave on his heels with release forms.

They all met in the main entrance of the Tide and Swallow, and after a quick conversation to explain the show, the designer signed the form.

"Good to see you." Lauren reached her hand out to Cass for a hello.

"Oh, that's gorgeous," Cass said, momentarily distracted as she set her bag onto the floor. She reached for Lauren's arm and inspected the sea glass bracelet, running her fingers over the light green and teal pieces. "This could be our color palette, right here." Then she clasped her hands around Lauren's. "Sorry, work hazard. Lovely to see you." Her attention went back to the bracelet. "It is a perfect color combination, though."

Lauren looked around at the newly painted white walls, the furniture gone, the light wood floors clean. "It would be pretty, wouldn't it?"

"Absolutely." Cass walked the room, tipping her head up to the ceiling, taking in the size of the wall of windows as the cameras followed. "For the regular décor, I'm imagining two separate seating areas in here with a wide, wooden, padded bench that stretches under all these windows. We could fill it with seafoam-green and navy-blue pillows to frame the same colors of the ocean."

"That sounds perfect," Lauren said. "And for the wedding, I'd like to get as many seating options as possible without it being too crowded."

"It's not hard to do." Cass paced over to the hearth, assessing it. "We could whitewash the wood on this fireplace and then have just a few glass bottles in green on the mantle. And then over here, two wingback chairs in a light beige with large-knit throws and more navy pillows." She waved a hand toward the other side of the room. "We could mirror the initial design I mentioned over here. And then in the center, have two facing sofas and a coffee table."

Lauren stepped to the side of Cass to allow the cameraman to get a wide shot. "And for the wedding?"

"I'll put the furniture in storage and have my team completely reorganize the room for the wedding. We'll set up the rows of white chairs facing this way."

"That's perfect. I'd like to do all of it. I want the space to compete with larger, more prominent hotels and venues."

"What's your budget?"

Lauren considered the money in her bank account, none of it doing anything to help anyone, sitting there. "Whatever it takes. Let's make it perfect," she said. The sparkle in Dave's eye was undeniable, and she knew that this was his climax footage. "How soon can you have it done?"

"I've got a big team. It'll only take us a couple of days."

"Wonderful."

Stephanie peeked her head out of the dining room. "Hey, Lauren, can I grab you before we leave?"

"Of course."

While Cass alternated between scratching down notes and sketches and stretching her tape measure across various surfaces, Lauren met Stephanie in the middle of the room. "What's up?"

"I wanted to get your opinion on something." Stephanie turned so that her back was to the camera, but the man only moved around her to zero in on her face. She eyed him, unsure of something.

"Everything okay?"

Stephanie leaned in closely and whispered, "I'd like to ask Chuck Harrison to attend the wedding."

"Brody's dad?"

She nodded, turning her back to the crew. "Think we could talk about it... later?"

"Absolutely. I'll call you tonight."

"Okay."

Mitchell walked into the room with a cardboard box of cake. "She let us take some samples home with us," he said with a devious grin.

Lauren laughed. "See you all tomorrow."

As they walked out of the main room, she wondered what could be behind Stephanie's request.

"I've put one of the staff on lunch duty and I'm taking some chicken salad to Joe," Mary said, with a plastic sack hanging from her elbow as she stopped in the front entryway where Lauren had been refilling the water service for the guests. "Want to go with me?"

Joe's behavior toward Lauren yesterday had her curious. "I'd love to."

"Wonderful. In case you did, I had the chef make enough chicken salad for us all."

"Always one step ahead." Lauren offered her arm. "I'll drive."

The two of them walked out to the parking lot and climbed into Lauren's car. Then they headed to the hospital in the nearby village of Nags Head.

Lauren was excited to talk to Joe, wondering if he'd remember seeing her yesterday. When they walked in, and she spied the same wide-eyed look spread across his face when he saw her, she thought she had her answer, and she couldn't deny the bubble of curiosity that he might somehow know her mom. But she pushed it away. How could he?

"Hello," Mary said, setting the sack down on the small table next to his bed. "How are you feeling?"

"Better than yesterday."

"Well, you're making jokes, so that's a start." Mary patted his leg. "I brought you some lunch."

"Thank God for that," Joe said, his attention still on Lauren. "I could do with some home cooking. Who'd you bring with you?"

"I'm Lauren," she said, taking a step toward him.

He gazed at the bracelet again. "Lauren... nice to meet you."

"She came by yesterday with everybody. Do you remember us all coming in?" Mary dug in the bag and pulled out a couple of boxes, setting them on the table.

"No, I was a little out of it yesterday. But the doctor says my ticker's doing all right now."

Lauren sat down in the small plastic chair in the corner. "That's wonderful to hear, Joe." She gripped that little bit of hope that, by some miracle, he might know something about her mother. "You know, you called me Grace yesterday."

The flush in his cheeks and the shock in his eyes surprised her, her own pulse rising in response. The heart monitor attached to him began chirping with elevated beats, the little green line shooting up the screen. "You look like someone I know, that's all."

She wasn't sure if she should push him any further.

"Who's Grace?" Mary asked, squinting at the machine to see what it was chirping about.

His eyes glistened suddenly and he broke eye contact. "Someone from a long time ago." The machine resumed its regular rhythm. He looked over at Lauren and smiled.

"Do I look like her?" Lauren asked gently.

"I don't know. I haven't seen her in many, many years." He nodded toward Lauren's wrist. "Where did you get that bracelet?"

"Mary gave it to me."

Mary handed him a paper plate with a chicken salad sandwich and a pile of fresh vegetables. "Melinda had it."

Joe's interest was visibly piqued. "Melinda?"

"Melinda told me that it belonged to Brody's grandfather, Phillip," Lauren said, scooting her chair a bit closer to his side of the bed.

"Yes. It belonged to someone he and I knew very well."

Lauren remembered Melinda's story. It only stood to reason that Joe would know Phillip's wife, Alicia, since they all lived in the Outer

Banks, but then again, it hadn't actually *belonged* to her… "Phillip bought it for his wife, right?"

Confusion swam across Joe's face. "Ah, yes. It could be," he said, nodding to himself. "A friend of his that I… knew… made them for a living." He seemed to struggle for the right words.

"Who's that, then, Joe?" Mary asked.

Joe paused just long enough for Lauren to wonder what was bothering him. "My wife, Penelope."

Mary sucked in a breath and then quietly made her own plate as if she were honoring the moment in some way. "I'll bet Melinda doesn't know that Penelope made that bracelet. She never mentioned it and I'd think she would have." Mary dished out more food, filling a plate for herself and Lauren.

"Melinda told me that when Phillip had given her the bracelet in his final days, he'd asked her to give it to someone 'full of possibilities,'" Lauren said.

Joe smiled, his wise gaze moving to the hospital ceiling, as if he knew the reason. "And that's you?" he asked.

"I suppose so."

"She's definitely full of possibilities," Mary said. "You should see what she's done in a few days' time and what she has planned for the inn."

"I can't wait to get out of here and go see it." Joe took a bite of his sandwich. When he swallowed, he added, "I'm glad you were the one who got the bracelet. I hope it brings you luck."

Lauren smiled, still not entirely persuaded but somehow more willing to believe in luck now than she was before.

Lauren had just finished checking the digital RSVPs for the wedding one more time, adding in a few stragglers. She typed in the names on a master list of people who still needed to sign filming release forms for Dave, and was planning to give Stephanie an update when her phone rang. "I was about to call you," she said upon answering.

"Perfect timing, then," Stephanie said. "I wanted to talk to you about Chuck when the cameras weren't present."

"Yes." Lauren set her laptop aside and sprawled out on her bed.

"I know Brody isn't very close with his dad, and Melinda might not want him there…"

"That's true."

"But *I* want him there."

"Why?" Lauren asked, baffled, given what she'd heard about the man.

"He was absent most of the time, but whenever he *was* there, he was always kind to me. I know it isn't my place to make judgments, but I feel like he was given a poor hand in life. I'd like to invite him."

"You don't want to have any tension on your big day, though," Lauren warned. "Should we check with Brody and Melinda first to get a read on their feelings about having him there?"

Stephanie sighed. "Probably, but I do want to invite him. The gesture is important to me."

"I think you need to explain it to Brody and his mom."

"Okay. I'll call Brody now and see what he says."

Chapter Seventeen

The main doors to the Tide and Swallow were propped open, letting in the humid, salty morning air. Cass had called Lauren early this morning in a frenzy, thrilled beyond belief to have secured a full delivery of in-stock items from the local furniture store. She couldn't believe her good fortune. So now, the delivery guys were hauling the new furniture across the room while Cass directed them where to put each piece.

Lauren had opted to wait until the fall for the kitchen remodel, when she was also planning to design the glassed porch out back. That left only the exterior painting for now, which was partially done and should be finished by next week. Half of the parking lot had been roped off to prepare for the new pavement. She'd decided to only fix the worst cracks, since the pavement guys had told her that curing an entirely new lot might take two weeks. With the outside nearly finished, she ordered all the slipcovers for every suite, and put in an order including rush delivery with a local company for seventy-five new comforters for the single and double bedrooms.

Stephanie and Mitchell's wedding flowers had been ordered, the officiant paid and completely reserved, and a string quartet booked that luckily had a single cancellation that day—everything was coming together beautifully.

Dave and his crew were busy outside, filming the wedding party as they all arrived and checked in to the inn. Lauren sat back in the new desk chair and fiddled with her bracelet. Was it good luck after all? She never imagined she could plan a wedding and shoot a pilot in the amount of time she'd been given, yet somehow it had all happened. And she felt that she'd definitely found her place there in the Outer Banks and at the inn. She couldn't remember the last time she'd felt so productive, as if she were really making a difference.

"Knock, knock," Stephanie said at the door.

Lauren stood up and went around to the other side of the office desk.

"Mary said I'd find you in here."

"Morning," Lauren said.

Stephanie came in and dropped down into the chair across from the desk. "Brody and Melinda have both agreed to let me invite Chuck."

"They have?"

"Yep." Stephanie folded her arms and slumped back happily. "I was so worried, but they said that it's really up to me. I doubt he'll come anyway, but I got his address from Melinda. Can we get an invitation out to him?" She reached into her pocket and pulled out a slip of paper with his address, sliding it across the table.

"Of course." Lauren opened her email and requested one final invitation, typing in Chuck's address in Boston.

"I also stopped by because I was wondering if you'd go with me to my final dress fitting today. It's in twenty minutes." She sat up, scooting to the edge of the chair. "It would be nice to have you there to give the final approval."

Stephanie had been the biggest surprise of all. They'd fallen into a friendship easier than Lauren had with anyone else in her life—even Andy. She hadn't felt this close to any of her former clients, but

Stephanie just had that way about her. "Of course," she said. "Let me make sure that it's all right if I leave Mary."

"I beat you to it," Stephanie said with a grin. "I asked if she'd mind if I stole you away and she said she's fine. And the film crew is coming."

Lauren clicked off the light in the office. "I'll just get my purse."

"Are you ready?" Stephanie called from behind the pink velvet curtain of the dressing area in the small bridal shop in town.

Lauren sat on the tufted bench, facing the platform in front of a large, three-way mirror, the portable stage lights for filming set up just out of view. A crew member, dressed in a T-shirt and black jeans squatted down next to her, the camera on his shoulder as he zoomed in on Lauren's face and then focused toward the closed curtain.

"Ready," Lauren called.

"Okay, here I come. Honest opinion."

Stephanie pulled back the thick curtain and stepped out in a stunning, form-fitting, lace-over-satin ensemble. The neck was a delicate V with tiny beading along the edge. The lace slid down her body effortlessly, giving her a perfect silhouette. As she turned, her long, dark, wavy hair fell down her bare back, the dress scooping all the way down to below her waist. The two camera guys pulled in for opposing angles.

It was perfect.

Lauren should've jumped for joy at the sight. Even with all her experience, she couldn't have chosen a better dress. It was tailored perfectly for Stephanie, and it was going to be the most elegant addition to the wedding. But, just as she'd feared, that familiar plume of dread smacked her in the face, waking her up to the fact that, if she squinted her eyes, the woman in front of her could've been *her* in the same style of dress, preparing for her forever, taking the next step to have a family of her own.

Lauren caught the flash of interest in Dave's eyes and he motioned for the cameras to focus in on her, only serving to cause her more anxiety. The dress, the show, the wedding—she was stuck once more in the jaws of her old life and she couldn't escape it. Her pulse pounded in her ears and her heart raced. She needed to get out of there.

Taking in slow breaths, with Stephanie still waiting for an answer, Lauren tried to force a smile, but it got caught on a sob. She thought she'd come so far since arriving, but this moment had opened her old wounds. As the cameras turned entirely on her, she attempted to shove it all down into the depths of her soul, that place where she'd pushed all her emotions over the last year, but it was proving difficult to do. Her vision blurred with the tears that were beginning to brim.

"What do you think?" Stephanie asked, her voice quivering with unease.

She'd left weddings behind, sold everything she'd worked for, and gotten out of TV for a reason: because she could no longer manage any of it. What had she been thinking, taking this on? She should've known that she wouldn't be able to do it. She'd only *just* left Sugar and Lace; it was too soon.

"It's… everything it should be. But—I'm sorry—I can't do this." The cameras moved back to Stephanie just as tears spilled over Lauren's eyes.

All of it caused Lauren to feel as if the room were swallowing her up, pulling her away from all the progress she'd made. She wanted to be strong for Stephanie and not make a scene on camera, but it was too late for that. Her skin prickled with apprehension as she got up, her body on autopilot. Lauren ran across the room, pushed open the door and gasped for air, the thick heat doing nothing to help her. She leaned against the brick wall of the shop, her hands on her knees, feeling lightheaded as her tears dropped onto the pavement by her feet, making little gray circles of wetness on the sidewalk.

What if she never recovered? What if, no matter how far she'd come, she'd never be able to manage this? And now, she had just run out on Stephanie, very likely ruining her day when the poor woman had done nothing to deserve it. The guilt and shame penetrated every crevice of Lauren's being. She'd ruined this, and she couldn't fix it.

"I can't do it," Lauren said to Mary later that evening, after telling her the whole story. "I haven't even faced Stephanie yet. Dave's been texting me all afternoon and I've been avoiding him. And Stephanie's called twice. I don't know what to say. Dave will get over it, but I have no idea what Stephanie's probably thinking."

Mary had been a sounding board for Lauren the whole time while the film crew had finally taken a meal break, all of them pulling out of the parking lot in their rental van. Now the two of them were preparing the table in the main room and entryway for the dinner crowd, adorning the tables with fruit-infused water and lemon meringue pie cookies. The sugary citrus aroma filled the newly decorated space, but it did nothing to lift Lauren's utter worry over the situation.

Mary scooted the silver tray of cookies to the right and then scrutinized the placement. "I think the first order of business is to talk to Stephanie."

"After how I reacted to seeing her in her dress today, I don't know how I'd be able to manage it."

Mary turned to face her. "Lauren, you *are* capable of doing this."

Tears filled her eyes and her chest tightened with emotion. "I don't think I am." Mason's voice floated into her mind: *Come on, kid, the sunshine's stronger than the storm. Know how I know that? Because if it wasn't we'd all have drowned by now.* She was officially drowning. Lauren looked down at her bracelet. "I was hoping the luck was real. You know, my fiancé, Mason, mentioned that he'd like to move to the beach and he even said he wanted to collect sea glass. *He* didn't have very good luck…"

"I wouldn't read too much into it," Mary said, still fiddling with the water glasses.

"Why?"

"He never got a chance to explore his luck. Maybe that's why you're here. To explore it for him."

Lauren stood, unmoving, and took in what Mary was saying. It had just been a quick observation, but the meaning of it impacted her. Mason hadn't had a chance to live out his life. He'd missed out on their marriage and their time together too. And for some reason unknown to her, she'd been spared that day when she didn't go with him. But now, she was broken beyond repair. She wasn't strong enough to live for the both of them. And she had very possibly ruined the wonderful friendship she'd started with Stephanie. How would she explain to her new friend that it was impossible for her to go through with organizing the wedding? Maybe she could explain and then offer up the Sugar and Lace staff.

Her phone buzzed in her pocket and she pulled it out to check the call. "It's Brody," she said. "Mind if I take it?"

"Of course not, dear. I'm off to handle the dinner crowd anyway."

Lauren let herself out onto the porch and answered the call.

"Hey," Brody said. "Is Stephanie with you?"

"No, why?"

"Thank goodness. Would there be any way that you could come over? I have a little problem."

"What is it?" she asked.

"Come over and you'll see."

Lauren squeezed her eyes shut to alleviate the burning from crying earlier. "All right. I'll be there in just a few minutes."

She cleared it with Mary and then jumped into her car and headed to Brody's. When she arrived, she parked next to the Winnebago and ran up to the front porch, ringing the bell.

Brody answered the door wearing a tattered T-shirt with a fishing logo on top and his tuxedo trousers and shiny shoes on the bottom. "The tuxes for Stephanie and Mitchell's wedding came today." He opened the door wider to let her in as Milton greeted her. The tuxedo shirt and jacket were draped on the leather sofa.

"What's wrong?" she asked, giving the dog a pat on the head.

"Well, take a look at this."

He stripped off his T-shirt, causing her to stop breathing at the sight of his bare, toned chest and arms. When he turned toward the sofa, she forced herself to take in a gulp of oxygen. He slipped on the shirt, and it was about two sizes too small.

"The jacket is the same way."

Lauren had learned to stay calm in these kinds of situations. But with the wedding in a mere two days, her jumping ship at the last minute, and no idea where they'd find a tuxedo with Brody's broad build, her pulse quickened. "Did they send the wrong size?" she asked, walking over to the jacket and checking the tag.

"Yep," he replied, taking the shirt back off.

Lauren tried to keep her gaze off his biceps. No matter how hard she tried, though, all she could think about was his touch, and given her day today, and the fact that he was leaving at the end of the summer, she needed to look away and focus on the task at hand.

"*And* I called them, and the other two tuxedo rental companies on the island. None of them have my size in stock at the moment. The guy said he'd refund the money, but that's not going to do me any good at the wedding." He slipped his T-shirt back on, to her relief. "So, what are we gonna do?"

"Okay, let's think," she said, more to herself. But as she did, the tears that she'd worked so hard to stuff down surfaced, and to her complete mortification, she found her bottom lip wobbling.

"We could all go shirtless," he said as he went around the bar that separated the living area from the kitchen and pulled two glasses from the cabinet, filling them with lemonade. Milton followed and loafed on the floor beside him.

Lauren scrambled to get herself together.

"Stephanie's a pretty relaxed person, but if we tell her this, I can almost guarantee that she's going to freak out." He handed Lauren a glass of lemonade, clearly not noticing her inner thoughts.

"Brides usually do," she heard herself say, but she was distracted by the warning alarm in her mind that was screaming for her to get out of there before she fell apart.

"Yeah, I guess for most of them it's the one day in their lives that they've planned for since they were little girls, right?" He gestured for

Lauren to take a seat on the sofa, but then his face came into focus. "You okay?"

She sat down before her knees buckled. "I told her I can't do this," she said, her voice quivering. Brody's empathetic stare only made her feel worse.

"Do what, the wedding?"

She nodded, the tears that she'd somehow managed to keep at bay springing to her eyes.

"Hey, it's okay," he said.

She shook her head, unable to speak for fear she'd blubber all over him.

Tentatively, he put his arm around her, her head resting on his chest, under his chin. She felt even worse now. And it wasn't the wedding. It was the fact that she held on to the guilt over moving on with her life, as if it were some kind of gift that she'd been given, but she was messing it up, and the whole ordeal was now making her feel like an utter failure. She looked up at him, but not for an answer. She just needed to know that someone could see her.

He took her hand, his thumb stroking her fingers. "You're doing great," he said.

She looked into his eyes, shaking her head. More tears flowed.

"You've singlehandedly helped Mary with the inn and planned a wonderful wedding for a good friend. You're changing lives." He wiped her tears away. "You've definitely changed mine."

She wasn't sure what came over her, but without a thought, she wrapped her arms over his shoulders, giving him a hug. He pulled her into his embrace, his strong arms around her, the scent of him filling her lungs.

"How can I get someone to do the wedding at this late date?" she asked through her sobs.

"You can do it," he whispered into her ear.

"I don't know if I can."

He lifted her chin, those blue eyes swallowing her. "I'll be right there with you every step of the way." His gaze locked with hers, and, his face serious, he whispered, "I won't let you fall." Then he leaned down cautiously, hovering as if asking her permission to kiss her.

Lauren swallowed, oddly calmer than she probably should've been. She closed her eyes, and his soft, gentle lips met hers in an explosion of electricity through her body, making her feel alive for the first time in a year. His hands found their way to her face, caressing it lightly as his lips moved on hers. It felt new and right at the same time. It was such a wonderful feeling that there was no room in her mind for anything but the present. What was happening? She pulled back and stared at him in wonder. He was like magic for her soul.

He offered her a soft smile.

Milton jumped up between them, lightening the mood considerably, and it got both of them laughing. Lauren sniffled as she rubbed the dog's head.

"We both really like you," Brody said, giving Milton a pat.

Milton barked and they laughed again. Lauren soaked in the feeling of it, never wanting to let go of that relief.

"I don't know how to be with someone," Lauren admitted to her mother on the phone. She'd originally called to elicit some advice about the wedding, but she'd been stalling, telling her mom about her new feelings for Brody.

"You don't have to do anything. Just enjoy yourself."

"I don't know how," she repeated. The dress she'd ordered online to wear for the wedding had been delivered and was now draped across her bed. It was a deep shade of beachy turquoise with a fitted waist and flowing hem that would fall perfectly just above her ankles. She turned away from it.

"It'll come back to you." Her mother seemed surer than Lauren.

"I have something else to tell you. I've just been so busy that I haven't had a chance to call," Lauren said, rushing the discussion to an end to avoid that subject as well. What Joe had said was much more baffling. She filled her mom in on how Joe had called her Grace. "How did he know your name?"

"Maybe it's just a really odd coincidence."

"Maybe. It just seems like an awfully big coincidence. He could've said any name. But he said yours." Lauren stuck to the notion that she didn't believe in fate or good luck or any of those things, but the longer she stayed at the Tide and Swallow Inn, the less secure she was in those beliefs.

Chapter Eighteen

The unique cocktail of fear and shame had waited to rear its ugly head until Lauren had managed a full night's sleep. It had surfaced in the wee hours of the morning, probably because she'd admitted her feelings about Brody to her mother on the phone, coupled with the fact that the wedding had no official planner. She'd texted Stephanie late last night and told her to come over today. Stephanie was on the way, and she still didn't know exactly what she would say to her. She'd busied herself with office tasks all morning, and now the sun had fully risen and was streaming through the window, but it didn't do much to lighten her mood.

"Hey," Stephanie said, coming in.

Lauren quickly got up and locked the door behind her to keep the film crew out, returning to Mary's desk. She braced herself for whatever Stephanie had to say to her, but instead, Stephanie sat down silently, looking both exhausted and overwhelmed.

"I owe you an incredible apology," Lauren said.

The rims of Stephanie's eyes were red, which made Lauren feel like the lowest person on the planet. How could she have allowed her grief to get the better of her like this?

"You haven't explained or anything. I have no idea what's going on."

"I'm so sorry. When I saw you in that beautiful dress, I lost it."

Dave drummed on the locked door, interrupting them. "Let me in, Lauren. You're in breach of contract."

Stephanie went to get up, but Lauren stopped her. "We're doing a confidential fitting and you can't film her while she's unclothed," Lauren lied.

Stephanie's face crumpled in confusion.

"If he doesn't get this conversation," she whispered, "he most likely can't use the footage of me running out of the bridal shop because he won't have a way to tie up the storyline, and neither of us want that in the episode."

Stephanie sat back down.

Quietly, she explained to Stephanie why she left Sugar and Lace and her reason for running out of the shop. When she finished, both of them sat across from each other, tears in their eyes for different reasons.

"I can try to get my old partner, Andy, to send someone to fill in for me," she said, feeling awful about putting Stephanie in this position.

"I don't want someone else," Stephanie said.

"Stephanie, if I try to go through with it, I might ruin your wedding day and I couldn't live with myself if I did."

Stephanie leaned forward, locking eyes with her. "You can do this."

"That's what everyone is telling me, but I'm almost certain that I can't. You saw me at the bridal shop. If I can't handle that, how will I manage when you're actually standing at the altar?"

Stephanie softened. "I know how."

Lauren frowned, confused. "How?"

"You'll handle it just fine because I'll help you through it. And Brody will be by your side. I know he'll support you. He's crazy about you. And Joe. And Mary. We'll all be there."

"But this shouldn't be about me. It's your day."

"I *want* you there. It wouldn't be the same without you."

Dave pounded on the door again. "You almost done?"

They both ignored him.

Stephanie stood up. "Please. Do this for me. And cry if you want to! Blubber like crazy! I'll tell everyone you're emotional at weddings—they'll all believe it," she teased, making Lauren smile.

"I've already seen you in the dress. There's nothing more to fear, right?" Lauren said, feeling a little stronger with Stephanie's support. And she needed to be resilient for her new friend. No matter what Stephanie said, this was her new friend's day and Lauren needed to make it great.

"You've got this."

Lauren broke into a smile. "I'll give it everything I've got."

After Stephanie left, Lauren tried to continue working. But despite the fact that she kept telling herself that she was okay, she still carried the weight of her thoughts while considering the final details for tomorrow's big event. Grief wasn't that easy; it couldn't be fixed with a single pep talk. There was still the fear that, while today she felt strong, tomorrow she might make a spectacle of herself. Could Brody save her from that? Should he have to? She propped her elbows on the desk and leaned her forehead on her fingers.

Brody floated through her mind more than once. The wave of unease used to come because she missed Mason too much to move forward. Then it arrived in the form of remorse whenever she considered moving on, but now it was the shame and fear that she was making a decision that Mason wouldn't agree with. Would she ever get loose from the web of sorrow, or would she overcome one obstacle of thought, only to be faced with a new one?

Brody was so different from Mason. He worked with his hands, whereas Mason was analytical, more introspective. Brody was tender in his affection while Mason was more playful. Would Mason approve of Brody? Even more important: would Mason feel slighted by her moving on?

"Lauren?" a deep voice called to her.

She looked up to find Brody, her face flaming at the fact that she'd just been thinking about him. "Hi."

"I'm going to pick up Joe from the hospital. Wanna take a break and come with me?"

"I have so much to figure out," she said, not feeling herself today.

Brody took a step into the office. "Joe lit up when he saw you. I'm sure he'd love to have a diversion right now."

"You still have no shirt for tomorrow. I have to at least figure that out for Stephanie and Mitchell," she reminded him.

"I promise, we'll come up with an answer."

She deliberated. While she'd love to see if she could find out more about the person Joe had thought she was when he'd first met her, she worried about spending too much time with Brody. She didn't trust herself with him, and she wanted to be sure that she was making the right decision. It might be better to allow things to cool off with him, let him take his cross-country trip, and then see where she was in a year or so.

"Plus, Mary was going to drive, but she's caught up in the lunch crowd. The truck might be tough for Joe to climb up in, so I was hoping I could use your car."

She looked at her computer to avoid his blue eyes.

"And I know you'd jump at the chance to escape the TV crew."

He got her.

His woodsy, spicy scent tickled her nose as he took another step and kneeled next to her at the desk. "I can see you're struggling with an answer to my question, but I'm willing to bet that it has nothing to do with Joe or your responsibilities with the wedding or the inn." He commanded her attention. When she made eye contact, she saw nothing but sincerity. "We don't have to be anything, you know. All we have to worry about is *today*." He stood up and offered her his hand.

That was the problem: she wanted more than today, but she didn't think she could offer it yet. Still not entirely sure, she took his hand, the sea glass bracelet gleaming in the bright summer light. At the very least, she'd found someone who didn't want a thing from her, and he was gentle with her shattered heart.

"I've got your medications," Brody said, gathering up Joe's things and closing his suitcase. "The doctor cleared you for lunch. Wanna go out somewhere?"

Joe didn't answer from the wheelchair the hospital staff made him use. He was clearly too busy looking Lauren over. After seeing him with Mary, Lauren struggled to understand his curiosity. He seemed so interested in her, even now. She stepped behind the wheelchair and began to push Joe out of the room and toward the hallway.

Lauren leaned over the chair to address him. "Brody asked if you wanted to go to lunch," she said.

"Absolutely," he replied, snapping out of whatever it was.

Brody slung a couple of bags onto his shoulder and pulled Joe's suitcase behind him. "Where do you wanna go?"

"Anywhere that doesn't serve hospital food. I need some fresh local seafood."

"Done." Brody patted his shoulder.

Joe tilted his head back in an attempt to view Lauren once more. "I'm only just now noticing how you resemble Stephanie."

"Yes, I've been told that." Lauren wheeled Joe around, heading down the hallway to the double doors that led to the parking lot. She leaned over to catch his attention once more. "I heard that you've known Stephanie since she was a baby, is that right?"

Joe nodded.

"He knew her mom, too, didn't you, Joe?" Brody held the door open and Lauren pushed the wheelchair into the sunshine.

"Yes, very well. I was… a friend of the family." He cleared his throat. "And yours, right, Brody?"

"Yep," he said with a grin.

"Your dad coming to the wedding tomorrow?"

"I don't know. Stephanie invited him."

"I might have to call him and ask," Joe said.

That look of irritation that formed whenever Brody spoke of his father surfaced. "Be my guest. I doubt you'll get anywhere."

Joe glanced up at him. "It was a good thing I was invited into Stephanie and Brody's families, since I didn't have one of my own." He seemed affected somehow, and, given Lauren's situation, she immediately wondered if he was still dealing with the death of Stephanie's mother. Or perhaps his wife's. She remembered Mary telling her he'd experienced loss at a young age.

"No family?" she asked gently, curious as to whether he and his wife had planned to have children. She came to a stop by her car and Brody opened the trunk, lumping the suitcases inside.

"Penelope passed away very young."

The news that he'd lost his wife before their family had ever had a chance to start hit Lauren like a punch in the gut; their situations were so similar. But before she could react, Brody was at her side, his attention on her. Even with his quick reaction, her thoughts had already gone to the fact that after losing his wife as a young man, Joe *still* had no family, after all these years. Would her fate be the same?

Joe tried to get up himself, and Brody redirected his energy from Lauren to the old man, reaching out for his arm to help him.

"How did you keep going?" she heard herself ask.

Brody's gaze moved over to her as he assisted the man into the back seat.

Joe leaned forward and put himself into her line of vision. "I had to relearn who I was. It took me a while to figure out that I wasn't the grieving man I had become. I was still the man *she'd* seen in me."

"That's a big job," Lauren said, having no idea how to change herself back into the person she'd been.

"The transformation began with something small—something I could manage. I used to go by Joseph, but I began to go by Joe."

"Oh?" She went around and climbed into the driver's side, peering at Joe in her rearview mirror.

"There was only one person in my life who called me Joe, and that was my wife. It took me a long time, but eventually, I realized that I was more me with her than with anyone, so the next time I introduced myself to someone, I said my name was Joe. I've been Joe ever since."

She twisted around while Brody got into the car. "Do you still miss her?"

"Like crazy. But she's right here with me. She sends me signs."

"What do you mean?"

"I was having a low moment one night and in my anguish, I cried out, 'Penelope, I miss you so much. Are you here?' I fell back onto the bed and, out of nowhere, a penny rolled down the pillow toward my cheek, hitting it like a little kiss. It wouldn't be a big deal except that 'Penny' was my nickname for her."

Lauren immediately thought of Mary's story about Frank and the quarter. Certainly, the two of them finding coins couldn't be their loved ones from heaven. "And you don't think it was a coincidence?" she asked.

"At first I did. Until I told her to show me more. That day, I was walking along the street when I noticed a fountain that we'd never gone over to. A gut feeling told me, 'Go over there and look inside.' I did, and it was full of pennies. No other coin—only pennies. Every time I need her, she sends me pennies. They show up whenever I think about her—on sidewalks, tables, everywhere. I even saw one shining at the end of our favorite pier once."

"I've never heard that story," Brody said.

Joe shrugged. "It's sort of personal. I don't just offer it up to people."

"It's lovely," Lauren said, everything in her body wanting to believe it could be true.

Chapter Nineteen

"Here's your cell phone," Brody said. "It's fully charged in case you need me. I'll be back to check on you later tonight." Lauren made her way to Joe's front door, the two of them leaving the old man in his favorite chair, armed with a few healthy snack options and a large bottle of water.

"You don't need to do that," Joe called.

"I will anyway." Brody winked at Lauren and opened the door.

"Think he'll be okay?" she asked, looking back at the small fishing cottage that Joe called home as they headed to her car.

"Yeah, he'll be fine. We're only a few streets over from my house if he needs anything at all, and I'll swing by a couple of times to make sure." He opened the passenger door to her car and got in.

Lauren drove toward Brody's house, taking the two turns to drop him off.

"I have an idea for the tuxedo. Why don't you come in so I can show you what I'm thinking?" he offered.

"All right, but I should text Mary to be sure she doesn't need me." Lauren pulled up next to the Winnebago and fired off a message. Mary came back, telling her business was slow and to take as much time as she needed, so she thanked her and dropped the phone into her handbag.

"All good?" he asked.

"Yeah." She opened the car door. "I did check with the other groomsmen. They all have white button-down shirts. You all could go casual and ditch the jackets. It's a beach wedding so you could pull it off. Do you have a white shirt of any kind?"

"I don't think so, but I might have something that works."

"Okay, well, it can be different, since you're the best man. The bridesmaids are wearing pale blue. Do you have a blue or light gray formal shirt, by chance?"

"That's what I wanted to show you. I do have a blue one at the back of my closet that my dad bought for me. I wore it once to a museum exhibit he asked me to attend."

She walked around the car, and met him on the porch. "Speaking of your dad, how do you feel about him coming tomorrow?"

Brody shrugged. "It's fine, if he even shows. Stephanie always liked him. I think they bonded because she's the academic type like he is. She spent time with him, going over all the colleges she wanted to apply to while I threw out a few applications just to appease him and went on about my business."

"Did you ever try to see his point of view?"

"No." He unlocked the door and Milton greeted him with a bark and a wagging tail. "Why would I, when he never tried to see mine?"

"Fair enough." She followed him inside.

Milton jumped onto the sofa and rolled onto his back when Lauren sat down. While she rubbed the dog's belly, Brody went into his bedroom and returned with a dry-cleaning bag. He pulled the plastic off and set it aside, revealing a powder-blue, pressed shirt.

"That's perfect," Lauren said, utterly relieved.

"Glad to hear it." He hung the shirt on a nearby doorknob. "While I've got you here, I've decided that I'm ready to show you something."

He opened the back door to the deck and beckoned for her to follow. "It has to do with the question you'd asked about what I'd do if I weren't a fisherman. And it also has to do with my dad."

Lauren got up and Milton tagged along behind her.

A soft breeze rustled the trees as she walked the stepping stones leading to the detached garage. Brody unhitched the two barn-like doors and swung them open. Lauren had been expecting something resembling the interior of a large woodshed by the look of the building, but when he opened the doors, it was more like an artist's studio. She stood, in shock, as she took in the shelves of lacquered wood artwork, and the neatness of the desk with a row of shiny tools all organized by size. A large wine barrel flanked each side of a long workbench that held a wooden saw and a few other contraptions she didn't recognize.

"Come on in," he said, flicking on a studio-style light that illuminated the space.

When she stepped onto the polished cement floors, she zeroed in on the wall opposite her and then walked over to a line of wooden trunks with iron hinges and latches, each one revealing the grain of the wood. "Brody, this is incredible." They looked like the old trunks her grandmother had kept blankets in at the foot of the bed, except these were sleeker, more modern, and stylish. She ran her hand along their shiny surfaces. "I've never seen anything like this."

"It's just a little something I do in my time off."

Excitement bubbled up. He'd surprised her.

He leaned over her shoulder and lifted the large latch of the trunk in front of them. "Open it."

She pushed the heavy lid upward, the hinges moving with ease. The interior was painted in vibrant colors, like a mural. She looked over at Brody, stunned. "Did you paint this?"

He nodded.

"You have such a gift." The intricate way in which he blended every color was like visual music. Everything was perfect—every line, the curve of the swirls, the vibrance of the artwork. It was as if he'd harnessed the sun, the moon, and the stars in one bright piece. There was so much depth there that if she owned it, she'd never want to fill it. Instead, she would want to leave it open so that she could take in the magnificence of it every time she walked past it.

Then she remembered what he told her before taking her out there. "What does this have to do with your father?"

Brody stared at the artwork, his thoughts clearly elsewhere. "Guess how many classes I took in college to be able to do this."

She pursed her lips, thinking. "I don't know, ten?"

"Zero."

He closed the lid and she turned to face him. "I don't understand."

"I showed one of these to my dad when I was eighteen and he said, 'What, are you going to be a trunk-maker?' That was his response. So I went to college just like he wanted. I got a degree in a finance career I'll never work in. And I did it all on *his* dime. And then I became a trunk-maker because, forget him. He wouldn't know happiness if it bit him in the—"

She put a finger to his lips. "It's okay."

"Not to me, it isn't." He looked down at her. "I never want to find myself with someone who thinks there's no merit in being a trunk-maker."

"Well, I see merit," she said, walking over to the next one and lifting the lid to reveal another stunning painting set under high gloss. This one had birch trees, and it might have been her favorite of the two. "But I don't think you're a trunk-maker at all."

He stared at her, clearly waiting for some sort of explanation.

"I think you're an *artist*."

The corners of his lips turned upward and he looked as if he were drinking her in.

"Maybe your dad just isn't an artist, and you need to teach him what you see."

"Maybe," he said, but the hurt in his eyes made her wonder if he ever would. "I made you something."

"Me?"

He walked over to one of the shelves and pulled a small box from it, handing it to her. It was a mini version of the larger trunks, so compact that it fit in her hand. She unfastened the small iron latch and lifted the lid, revealing a swirling, lacquered pattern of seafoam green, cream, and blue.

"It's for your sea glass."

For an instant, she didn't know what to say, her feelings for Brody welling up and nearly overwhelming her. She'd never had anyone take this kind of time for her. There was so much more to Brody than she'd ever imagined. "It's so beautiful, Brody, thank you."

"You're welcome."

Lauren and Brody arrived at the Tide and Swallow later that evening and met Mary finishing things up at the front desk. The film crew was noticeably absent. "Where's Dave?" Lauren asked.

"He told me that he went to film Mitchell at work for a few clips to use when he introduces them."

Happy to have a little time to herself, Lauren and Brody walked Mary to her suite and filled her in on how Joe was doing.

"I'll have to make him a casserole, so he'll have something to eat," Mary said, her warmth for the man evident.

"Well, he's eaten lunch," Lauren told her, "and Brody's stopping by his house later, so you can rest easily."

"Thank you, you two." Mary reached up and gave each of them a hug.

After they said their goodbyes, Brody walked back down the hall with Lauren. "Mind if I come in for a minute so I can see the sea glass in its new home?" he asked, as she slipped her key in the lock and opened the door.

"Sure," she replied. She was tired and wanted to sink into a bathtub full of bubbles, wrap herself in her fluffy robe, and curl up in bed. Also, the intimacy of having him in her personal space made her nervous. But she'd focus on the work she still had to do before Stephanie and Mitchell's big day. She offered Brody a spot on the sofa and went into the bedroom, scooping up the sea glass, along with the ring she'd bought with Stephanie.

When she returned, Brody opened the box and she gently placed the sea glass inside. "Look at how perfectly the colors match," she said. "They're almost camouflaged against the painting."

With a satisfied look, he closed the lid and handed it to her, their fingers brushing as the box changed hands. Lauren set the small chest on the coffee table, trying not to look into those sapphire eyes of his. There was an air of electricity between them that they were both trying to navigate. Lauren was the first to break the spell, turning away to put the box back on her dresser.

"Think Joe will still be able to walk Stephanie down the aisle tomorrow?" Brody asked, plopping down on the sofa.

"I'll have a chair for him at the front, so the minute he's finished walking her, he doesn't have to stand," Lauren replied, lowering herself down beside him. Even sitting next to Brody was difficult. She wasn't sure how to act, or what she was feeling exactly. It would feel so normal to drape her legs over his and lean her head against his shoulder as if the two of them had been together for years. But there was nothing telling her that it was okay to take that step and she wasn't even sure if she should.

Brody rubbed the scruff on his chin and changed the subject. "Speaking of Stephanie, think she's gonna freak about the shirt and no jacket?"

"You know better than I do." After what she'd put Stephanie through, something like this should be a piece of cake.

"Yeah, it's hard to say…" He turned toward her, his eyes full of interest. "So with my clothes taken care of, what do you have left to do for the wedding?"

"I still have to map out seating arrangements for the dinner. And I need to get the final place cards organized. Then, early tomorrow morning, I'll set them out and make sure everyone who's decorating and preparing the space shows up." She rubbed her shoulder, a pinch forming. She prayed she could do this.

"You're putting together the seating thing tonight?" He looked at his watch. "It's getting kind of late."

"I know. But I've had worse schedules, believe me." She rubbed her shoulder again.

"Turn around," he said gently.

"Why?"

"Because you've rubbed your shoulder twice." He put his strong hand on the base of her neck and guided her to face away from him. Moving her hair, he placed his thumbs right on the two spots that had been giving her trouble and began to knead the pain away.

Lauren closed her eyes, unable to remember the last time someone had done something like that for her. She let out an exhale of relief.

"Feeling any better?" he asked, his voice soft.

"Getting there," she said.

A little huff of a chuckle escaped his lips.

"What?"

"I won't talk," he replied.

"Why?"

"Because when I speak, your shoulders raise back up." He applied a bit of light pressure, and her shoulders slid down into the relaxed position once more.

"Sorry," she said. "I've just got a lot on my plate with the wedding." It was the first thing she could come up with to explain why his easygoing, masculine voice made her anxious. If she was being completely honest with herself, it wasn't even that. It was the way his voice and his touch made her feel. She pulled away. "Thank you. I should probably get to work."

"I can help."

"It's all right." She struggled to look at him for fear that her feelings for him would show.

"I *am* organized, you know," he pressed. "I planned an entire cross-country trip entirely by myself. I've bought all the tickets to the museums in each state already. And I reserved all the campgrounds. Everything. Signed, sealed, delivered, and paid in full."

She tensed again slightly at the mention of the trip, and, to her mortification, the look in his eyes told her that he'd noticed. To avoid his gaze, she got up and grabbed her laptop, setting it in front of him on the small table in the sitting area. Then she went into her bedroom to get the seating cards.

She didn't know how to do this anymore. She should play it cool. He could certainly take a trip if he wanted to without her weighing in. And she should be able to let him go without feeling all sappy about it. She went over to the small table in the bedroom. The cards weren't there. She remembered moving them, but with the muddle of thoughts going through her mind, couldn't remember where she'd put them. She stared out at the dark-purple sky and chewed her lip.

"Need any help?" Brody called from the living area.

"No, I'm just..." She peered around the room, her mind still on Brody instead of the task at hand. She should've forced the issue that she was fine to work alone.

She pulled out the drawer of the nightstand where she'd been stashing a few things since she'd gotten there. She rifled through the items, but the pack of cards wasn't there. Had she taken them to Mary's office?

"Sure you're okay?" Brody asked from the doorway.

Flustered more because he was so darn handsome standing there, she shuffled through another drawer. "I can't find the place cards."

"These?"

She turned around and found him holding the pack. "Where were they?"

He pointed to the dresser. "Right there." Next to where she'd had the little pile of sea glass. She remembered that she'd set them down on her way into the room when she'd gone in there earlier today.

"Thank you." She plucked them from his hand. "You saved me." She grabbed the calligraphy pen that was in the same spot and went past him into the living area. Forcing herself to focus on the task at hand, she sat down on the sofa, across from her laptop. "If you could call out these names," she said, tapping the screen, "I'll find the corresponding cards and write the table numbers in calligraphy, and then we can order them by table, using Stephanie's descriptions."

"Easy," he said. "We just need some music or something while we work." He clicked on the radio that sat next to the TV. A beachy southern song that she didn't recognize played softly. He came back over to the sofa, picking up the laptop and pulling it into his lap. "Ready?"

"Mm-hm," she said, keeping her concentration on the cards.

"Janice Phillips," he began, "table one."

Sitting on the floor in front of the coffee table, Lauren located the card for Janice Phillips. She steadied the marker in her hand and then began her signature calligraphy script, spelling out the table number.

"Wow." Brody leaned over her shoulder. "You're so talented." His breath was at her cheek, his woodsy scent making it difficult to breathe. The way he said the word "talented" reminded her of Mason's assessment of her: *We'll scour the beaches for shells and sea glass. You're so talented with everything you do that you can make beautiful things with it.* Brody was only the second person to point out her artistic ability. Even though Brody and Mason were different people, they were similar when it came to her.

"Thank you." She could barely get the words out. She cleared her throat. "Next name and table number please?"

Brody scooted down onto the floor beside her, making her pulse race. "Michael Fisher, table one."

She took in a long breath and began hunting for Michael Fisher's name. She found it and drew the swooping number on the card. When she finished, she could feel Brody looking at her, so she turned toward him. The way the corners of his mouth twitched upward in amusement only made her more uneasy.

"What?"

He broke into a full smile. "Am I making you nervous?"

"No," she replied, her cheeks blazing with heat.

Brody reached over and took the pen from her, capping it, and set it on the table.

"What are you doing?"

He stood up and took her hands. "Making you less nervous." He guided her to a spot in the middle of the suite and wrapped his arms around her. Then he began swaying to the music.

Stunned by the move and unsure of what to do, she had no other option but to put her arms around his neck. "Would you like to tell me why we're dancing in the middle of my suite?" This was *not* helping her to achieve a calmer state.

He leaned down and put his mouth next to her ear, making all the hairs on her arms stand up. "Because if we just get this tension out of the way, we'll be able to finish all those names and tables."

"What tension?" she asked.

"The tension that you have sitting next to me tonight." He pulled back and looked her in the eyes. "And the tension that I'm feeling from wanting to kiss you again."

"I don't know if that's a good idea," she said, but her words withered as he leaned toward her.

His lips hovered over hers, a gesture she was already used to. She loved how he silently asked for permission, allowing her to make the first real move. "What do you think? Good idea?" he asked, his breath intoxicating.

She closed her eyes and pressed her lips to his, the act instantly calming every buzzing nerve in her body. It was as if she'd been born to kiss him, which made no sense at all, given who the two of them were. She'd been building an entirely different life until last year, and he was leaving for months. But she kissed him anyway. His hands moved affectionately along her back, the feel of his lips on hers like fireworks.

She knew that, in time, the remorse would swarm her, but there was no way she could deny how he made her feel in this moment.

Chapter Twenty

Today was the day. The inn looked incredible. Cass and her team had outdone themselves. She'd cleared the furniture in the main room. Rows of white chairs filled the space, leading to the large wall of windows where the French doors were open. The florist had dressed the doorway where Stephanie and Mitchell would say their vows below cascading white roses and magnolias with trailing ribbons to the floor. The wedding party had all gathered, dressed immaculately in their attire, and Dave was busy getting the final release forms signed with his team all in place.

Stephanie had taken the news of Brody's tuxedo in stride, to Lauren's relief, and everything else had gone off without a hitch.

Lauren wore the new turquoise dress she'd bought online, hoping when she'd ordered it that wearing something different would help her forget the fears she'd had during all the weddings she'd planned over the last year. She'd curled her hair, put on her best makeup, and continued to focus on the events that would occur *after* the wedding, to get her through. She would grab a glass of champagne and maybe even get a dance or two in with Brody. But even with her positive mantra going through her head, she could feel the cracks forming in her well-orchestrated façade. Her heart racing, she squeezed her eyes shut to keep from getting lightheaded, the familiar feelings of loss and doubt surfacing.

Lauren leaned against the wall, trying to pull herself together. She had a job to do. She just had to get through this one day and then it would all be over. She knew Brody would calm her, but he was at the front of the main room and the crowd had begun to file into their chairs.

Given what Joe had told her about his "Penny," she decided today was a good day to try to *believe*. It went against everything she'd done before, but she silently called out to Mason. The act of it felt odd, and she forced herself to trust that he could hear her. *Mason, if you're with me, I need you to let me off the hook. I'm about to go into this wedding and I want to be strong. Please send me some sign to show me that I'm doing the right thing.*

"Lauren?" Stephanie called from the doorway of the suite they'd set up for the bridal party, down the hall.

She blinked and focused on her breathing—her coping strategy—still trying to manage her emotions. She stepped into the hallway. "Yes?"

The musicians began the processional music.

"Could you come here for a minute?"

"Yep." She paced toward the bridal suite, her head feeling as if she were submerged in the Atlantic. When she got there, the bridesmaids were primping in their powder-blue satin gowns behind Stephanie, who was holding a small gift bag.

"It isn't much, but I wanted to give this to you to say thank you for everything. I know how hard this is for you, and I'm more thankful than this little gift expresses, but something told me you'd like it anyway." She held it out to Lauren with her manicured fingers.

"You're so sweet," Lauren said, her skin prickling at the sight of Stephanie in her dress. Her mouth dried out and her vision blurred—all the signs that she wasn't going to make it. She worried she was having a full-blown panic attack. *Keep it together.* She needed Stephanie to get down the aisle so she could stand at the back of the room and work on keeping herself from making a scene. Then, hopefully, Brody could swoop in and take her mind off it. "The music's started. I'll open it as soon as the wedding's over. I promise I won't peek."

"It's okay," Stephanie said, shaking her head. "You can open it now. We can steal a few seconds."

The music continued to play, and Lauren knew that they needed to get out there. If they didn't, she might fall apart. *Mason, I'm going to falter.* She pushed back tears, her silent words floating up to the sky with no answer. She looked around frantically for something, some sign from Mason, but all she got was silence.

"Go on. Open it."

Deciding it would be faster to accept the gift now than to try to convince Stephanie to wait, she fought through her growing anxiety, opened the small bag, and pulled out a box. Was Mason even around to see what she was going through? She wondered as she held the box. Angry that he couldn't answer her, she sent up the thought, *Do you even think of me?*

Her heart still drumming in her chest, her eyes aching with grief, she lifted the lid and her breath caught. The music in the main room suddenly faded to a distant murmur and everything stopped.

She pulled out the gift. Hanging from her finger was a keychain made of varying shades of sea glass in the colors of the ocean. In gold script over the shiny surface read the words, "Wish You Were Here."

Every nerve in her body fired as Mason's words came back to her: *You'll love the beach so much… We'll send everyone postcards that say, "Wish You Were Here," drink piña coladas, and lie in the sun until we're as red as lobsters.*

It was as if Mason had answered her.

"I know it's just a little touristy thing, but Mary mentioned that you decided to stay here, and I know how much you like sea glass. When I saw this, I was compelled to buy it for you. I thought you could put your inn key on it."

"Thank you," she said, tears surfacing for a different reason. "This is… unbelievably perfect," she said, breathless. She tried to process the fact that Stephanie might have just delivered a message from beyond. Could it be?

"And," Stephanie continued, picking up her flowers, "I should tell you that I've added a little something to the bouquet."

"Oh?" she said, the word barely coming out on her breath, tears spilling her lashes at a rapid pace now as she blinked them away, gripping the keychain as if it had just saved her life. She barely heard Stephanie.

"I feel like our loved ones are with us—even when they aren't actually here," Stephanie said, and gestured to her flowers, but her words meant more than the surface of whatever she was saying.

Lauren tried to pull herself out of the feeling that Mason was there, wrapping her up in his arms and telling her, *Go—your future is waiting.* Could he really be there with her? Were all their loved ones around? She peered down at Stephanie's bouquet, and nestled between two roses was a photo of a couple.

"It's a picture of my parents, William and Anne."

Stephanie moved a sprig of baby's breath and the blood ran out of Lauren's face. She stood there, motionless, the sounds of wedding chatter muffled, her vision tunneling toward that photo.

"Now I know why we look alike," Lauren whispered.

"Why?" Stephanie asked.

"Your mom looks *exactly* like mine."

Stephanie's mouth hung open. "How…?"

Only then did Lauren realize that the musicians were improvising. With a rush of adrenaline, she snapped into gear. "We've got to go. We've got a wedding to get to."

Late Fall, 1960
Kill Devil Hills, North Carolina

"I've been over and over this, and I truly don't know what's best for them," Joseph said to Phillip, his voice breaking. Tears brimmed as he looked down at the twin baby girls, Grace and Anne, in the bassinette that Penelope had left behind when she'd passed away that fateful day in the hospital. They had dark eyes and a patch of black hair just like their mother. "Penny would never have wanted me to put them up for adoption, but with the cutbacks at work, we'd be living in poverty. I want to give them the best life I can offer them."

They cooed when he ran a finger over their milky cheeks.

"I can try to get you some money," Phillip said, "but I've got to go back home to do that." As soon as he uttered the words, he wondered if his parents would even give him the money. But he wouldn't worry about that now. He felt he had to do something. He'd give him all his inheritance if he had to.

Joseph shook his head. "That's very kind of you, but you can't fund them until they're adults. Even with all the money you say your family has, a handout wouldn't be enough." He stepped away from the infants, staring blankly, looking absolutely empty. He put his head in his hands and sobbed. "I have to let them go."

He slumped forward, appearing completely overwhelmed by grief. Phillip wasn't sure of the best way to handle it. He wanted to make it better, but he knew there was no way to do that.

"So you're putting them up for adoption?" Phillip asked.

Joseph cleared his throat and let out an anguished groan. "Yes. I spoke with a woman at an agency who can place them with good families. She travels to different states, finding suitable homes." His breathing became shallow, his chest barely moving in his obvious anxiety. "I'd have to just hand them over to her. My sweet angels, gifts from my darling Penny." He collapsed into a fit of tears.

Phillip reached into his pocket and grabbed hold of the bracelet. He'd carried it with him everywhere—the last remnant of their love. He felt as if he'd been left behind as well, and it was his burden to pick up all the pieces that remained. He was angry about it at first, thinking how she wouldn't have even been in the situation had his parents allowed them to marry. Who even knew what they'd be up to. They could be traveling the world. Now, he felt hollow, void of all emotion because if he actually allowed himself to feel something, he'd probably be right there on the floor next to Joseph.

Rodanthe, North Carolina

Clutching the keychain, Lauren ushered the bridal party and Stephanie to the double doors of the main room, where Dave and the film crew were ready and waiting. The bridesmaids began to file down the white runner that cut the room in half, the place full to the brim with Stephanie and Mitchell's family and friends. Joe was waiting and offered Stephanie his arm, already choking up at the sight of her.

"You're like a grandfather to me," she said into his ear. "I've always thought that."

Joe cleared his throat, his bottom lip wobbling, and kissed her cheek. Then the crowd stood.

On Joe's arm, Stephanie walked slowly toward the officiant, where the wedding party had gathered.

At the front, Mitchell's eyes glistened with fondness for his bride.

Lauren watched it through a different lens, her mind consumed with whether or not she'd gotten a message from Mason and why her mother and Stephanie's looked just alike. Her time in the Outer Banks ran through her mind, step by step. Whenever she'd thought about Mason, the messages *had* shown up.

When she moved to the beach like he'd wanted to do, she'd gotten the sea glass bracelet. At Brody's, when she let loose a little for the first time in a year, she received sea glass. When she wondered if Mason could hear her thoughts about Brody, Brody had given her the yellow piece—yellow for happiness. And then another piece of sea glass had washed up after that, just to drive it home. As tears filled Lauren's eyes, she remembered when the sea glass that she'd thrown out had shown up right in front of her "where it belonged," Mary had said.

They all belonged together.

Mason had been with her the whole time, watching over her and helping her to rebuild her life. She just hadn't asked him to show her that he was there. As she stood at the back of the wedding while Stephanie and Mitchell said their vows, it suddenly hit her that she was home. She was still planning weddings. She was still doing TV shows. Those were the things she was great at. And now, she could do them during the next chapter of her life because she knew that Mason would want her to, because she loved her work. Right then it was as if the burden of it all had been lifted, and she could take in the wedding with no fear.

Her tears surging for a new reason, she quickly wiped them away. When she finally swam out of her thoughts, she zeroed in on Brody, and was surprised to find his protective gaze upon her. Their eyes met, and he smiled, calming her. She turned inward one last time, knowing now that Mason was showing her exactly what to do without him. Finally, she felt like she had his blessing to move forward and to live the life he would have wanted for her.

The beading on Stephanie's gown shimmered in the setting sun, the sky painted in vibrant pinks and oranges behind them, as Mitchell twirled her around on the new decking for their first dance as husband and wife. Mary was dressed in a lovely pink dress with a new, pearl-colored cane in her hand, her other on her heart as she admired the couple. Melinda was beside her, telling her something sweet in her ear, making her smile. Joe sat in a chair, chatting to some of Mitchell's family members, and Milton, sporting a black bowtie, was loafing in the setting sun next to his bowl of water.

Lauren had made it through the rest of the wedding easily, and now, it was party time, just like she'd always done with Sugar and Lace. She watched the couple with a different perspective now. She didn't have a clue how her own life would turn out, but she knew that everything would be okay if Mason had anything to do with it. He would always be a part of her, and she swore she could feel him there today.

When the first dance ended, the DJ launched into another slow song and Brody walked up to her. "It's wonderful to see you smiling."

"I'm happy," she said, raising her eyebrows in excitement. "At a wedding!" She laughed, a big burst of release escaping. She ran her hands down the blue shirt he'd found, her affection for him overflowing.

He wrapped his arms around her in a strong embrace. "I'm so glad," he said before kissing the top of her head. He held out his hand. "Dance with me?"

She allowed him to lead her onto the porch's makeshift dance floor.

He gave her a spin and then pulled her toward him. "I'm proud of you."

She looked into his eyes.

"When I met you, you seemed completely broken. And now, look at you, making it through the wedding with barely a flinch."

"Well, I wasn't perfect, but I'm definitely getting there."

"None of us are." He pulled her close and she reveled in his hold on her. He was the best thing to happen to her since she left New York, and she couldn't imagine what her time here would've been like without him. They danced together in the salty summer air, the coastal breeze at her neck, and she suddenly didn't want to let him go. But she knew that in a few weeks, she would have to.

A man at the end of the deck, sitting alone and looking back at them, distracted her from her thoughts. "Who's that?" she asked.

Brody's jaw clenched before he answered. "It's my dad."

"He came? I can't believe it."

"You and me both."

"You should go talk to him." Lauren wrapped her arms around Brody's neck.

"And ruin this moment? No way." He gave her another spin and dipped her dramatically in the center of the floor, making her laugh.

"You should at least acknowledge him. He's staring right at you." She gave the man a friendly wave, and he offered a tentative nod in return.

"If it makes you feel better, I'll do it for you, but it's wasted time."

When the song ended, he took Lauren by the hand. "I'll need a drink for this. Want anything? Cocktail? Champagne?"

"I'll take a glass of champagne," she said. "And I'll be your out. If you need to escape him, just squeeze my hand and I'll make up an excuse for us to leave the conversation."

He smirked before turning to the bartender and asking for three flutes of champagne.

"Three?" she asked, hopeful that he'd thought of his father.

"Yep." He downed one, set the glass on the bar and then picked up the second, taking a small sip. "Ready?" He offered Lauren the third.

"He doesn't look like that awful of a person," she said, second-guessing her request and beginning to worry if she'd made the right decision by coaxing him into talking to the man.

"He's not. We just don't see eye to eye."

Lauren stopped Brody in the center of the wedding crowd. He faced her, his brows pulling together.

"If I can offer you one piece of advice, it would be that none of us know how long we have on this earth, and I'm learning that no matter what, we should make the very most of the time we're given. Even if that man never understands you, he's your dad. *Try*."

He shook his head as he looked adoringly into her eyes. "The things I'll do for you."

Happiness fizzed inside her like the glass of champagne she was holding. "You'd do things for me?"

"It seems I build whole decks and make little boxes for sea glass these days," he replied lightheartedly as he laced his fingers through hers and moved through a group of wedding guests. "And now you've got me spending time with the one person I really don't care to see, instead of taking you back out on that dance floor. So, yeah, I'd say I do." He winked at her.

When they got to Brody's father, the man stood up. He held out his hand to Lauren. "Chuck Harrison."

"Lauren Sutton. It's nice to meet you." She let go of Brody and clasped her hand around Chuck's.

He regarded Brody hesitantly. "It's good to see you, son."

Brody nodded a hello as if the mere act of it pained him.

"Please, have a seat," Chuck offered, gesturing to the chairs around his table.

Brody complied, taking a large drink from his champagne flute. Lauren sat down next to him and reached for his hand under the table, ready for the squeeze.

"I'm surprised you came," Brody said before taking another long drink.

"Joe convinced me."

Brody looked out at the ocean, his solemn expression not matching the merriment around him. Joe was a table down, chuckling with a group of bridesmaids.

His father coughed, clearly to fill the awkward silence. "He told me that family is everything."

Brody's gaze slid back over to Chuck, but he wasn't showing a single emotion.

"Yeah, I didn't really buy it either," Chuck said, reading his son's reaction. "Until he told me a story I've never heard before. It made me realize how lucky I was to have had you and your mom in my life."

A slight break of interest showed on Brody's face, his expression softening.

Chuck stood up and waved Joe over. Joe carefully walked the few paces to their chairs while Chuck pulled another chair to their table for him so that the old man could sit down. "Do they know what you told me?"

Joe shook his head.

"Would you tell them?"

Joe leaned in and started at the beginning. "Well, as you know, I lost my wife, but what you don't know is that she left me these two gorgeous little girls…"

Chapter Twenty-One

Late Fall, 1960
Kill Devil Hills, North Carolina

"I've found Anne a home here in the area," the head of the adoption agency said. She'd introduced herself as Rhoda Perkins, and had a folder full of forms for Joseph to sign. "They'd prefer if you weren't involved in the parenting, but you would be able to see her at least. They said you could visit any time you like. And they've agreed to keep the name Anne, as you've asked."

"Thank you," Joseph said, his face white as a ghost, as he consulted Phillip.

Unsure of how to handle such a situation, Phillip nodded his approval, but he really had no idea if Joseph was making the right decision in giving up the children. Was this what Penelope would have wanted? No one knew. But with every paper that Joseph signed, Phillip decided that the Penelope he'd known would have wanted the very best for her children, and this was the most logical option that they had for giving the girls a better life.

"And what about Grace?" Joseph asked.

"I've found a lovely family in Tennessee. They, too, will keep her name."

Fear swam around in his face, his cheeks turning pink. "They're going to be split apart?"

Phillip couldn't imagine what it would be like to find out one day that he had a brother he'd never met. He couldn't fathom it. The little babies were so young; they'd never know the difference, but it seemed awful to split the sisters up. They would become girls, then teenagers, then women, have families of their own, and never know that they had each other out there. Would they ever find out the truth?

"Both families are amazing, loving people, Joseph," Rhoda said. "These girls will be treated like princesses in their new homes."

Joseph ran his hand along their names on the forms as a tear streaked his cheek. "I can't even afford to feed them," he whispered, his lips quivering and his face empty from the pain that seemed to have drained him of every expression he had. He'd lost his wife and now he was losing their children.

Phillip wanted to tear up the papers, figure out how to save Joe from this. He had all the money Joe needed and yet he couldn't give it to him. It belonged to his family and Joe had been right: they weren't about to give it up as charity for the rest of their lives. He should have known; they'd made that abundantly clear with Penelope. Phillip stood by, helpless, as the grieving father's pen hovered over the paperwork, the last shred of Penelope's love slipping away from them both as Joseph signed his name.

Rodanthe, North Carolina

When Joe had finished telling the story, Lauren was frozen in her chair, all of the events now coming together. It was slowly dawning on her—the real reason that Stephanie's mother in the photo had looked exactly like her own mom. She peered over at the bride—her cousin—who was dancing with her new husband, as Dave and his crew caught every move. A wave of wonder washed over her at the fact that Stephanie had actually had their own grandfather walk her down the aisle. It was incredible, something that could only have happened with a little help from above.

"I got to see Anne grow up, get married, and have Stephanie. I had to grieve on my own when she passed away. I never knew Grace or met her children. And it has always been a hole in my life."

"I think I can help you with that," Lauren said, finding her words as she looked her grandfather in the eyes. She pulled out her phone and scrolled through her photos until she located an old snapshot of her mother a couple of Christmases ago. She turned it around for Joe to view. "Does this person look familiar?"

Joe peered at the phone, his eyes filling with tears. "Grace?"

Every hair on her neck stood up. "I'm Grace's daughter."

His mouth hung open, a look of utter astonishment in his eyes.

"I knew I wasn't crazy when I saw you that day and thought you were Stephanie," Brody said with amazement.

Lauren smiled at him, still in a fog of delight and disbelief.

Joe looked over at the bride and then back at Lauren.

"When are you going to tell her?" Lauren asked.

The man smiled wistfully at his granddaughter. "I was afraid to tell her for so long, afraid to change her world even more after her parents' death. I thought about it so many times… But now, the day is here. It's right. I'll tell her after the wedding."

"Okay. I'd love to be there with my cousin, when you do." She liked the sound of the word "cousin" when referring to her new friend.

Clearly incapable of hiding his emotions, Joe stood up and opened his arms. Lauren followed and embraced him. "I have my family again," he said with a sob.

Lauren gave him a loving squeeze, her heart overflowing. "Yes, you do. I can't wait to call my mother."

Brody shook his head. "I can't believe this, Joe. You've had this secret and you haven't shared it with anyone at all?" Then his face crumpled. "If my grandfather witnessed all this, why wasn't he…" He seemed to struggle to say the words, Lauren hanging on every one of them to figure out what he might be thinking.

Chuck spoke up. "I asked Joe, too, if my father had witnessed all of this, why wasn't he a better father himself?" Remorse fell over his face. "You can say it: and I followed right in his footsteps."

Joe sat back down. "Your father was a very complex individual. He confided in me that when he married Alicia, he held on to a lifetime of guilt for being able to have a family when Penelope couldn't. He told me once that he couldn't love you all in the way you deserved, so you were better off if he just stayed away."

"I never understood that about him," Chuck said. "I always thought he put work above us because taking care of people meant working to provide for them." He addressed Brody. "And I was scared that your interests wouldn't give you what you needed to be a provider, and I was hard on you because of it. I'm sorry."

Brody nodded, still obviously hurt.

"What I didn't understand then, which I do now, is that I should've trusted you to follow your passions and make them a success."

"Thank you," Brody said.

"Sitting in Boston alone, I realized what I'd lost, and I, too, felt as if I didn't deserve to have it back."

"You deserve it," Melinda said, coming up behind them.

Chuck stood and turned to face Melinda, uncertainty in his stare.

"And I did want you to pick us over work," she said.

"I'm sorry I didn't," he said. "But I will, if you'll let me show you."

Melinda's eyes glassed over, a smile forming on her lips. "I'd love for you to show me."

"Sorry to butt in," Dave said, slicing through the moment. "The sun is setting perfectly for the cameras right now. Think we can push the cake-cutting forward a few minutes?"

Lauren stood up. "Sure." As she left them, a new feeling washed over her: hope. With the glowing sun on the horizon and laughter lifting into the air, there was nothing but hope around her. And she had a very real feeling once more that Mason had something to do with it all.

Lauren sat in a chair that Brody had brought down to the beach and dipped her sore feet into the cool sand. The wedding had been an amazing success, and afterward the crowd all headed for their homes and their rooms at the inn. The bridal party was inside, and Dave and his crew had rushed off to catch the last flight out of town, planning to return in a couple weeks after editing their rough cut to shoot narration footage with Lauren. And Chuck had decided to go back home with Melinda. The only ones left on the beach were Stephanie and Mitchell, Mary, Joe, and Brody.

Stephanie hiked up her wedding gown and plopped down into one of the beach chairs, holding a glass of wine. "I'm exhausted," she said, her cheeks rosy with happiness. "Who knew that getting married was so tiring."

"It's on purpose," Joe said from across the bonfire in the center of the circle of chairs. "That way, married life will seem like a walk in the park."

They all laughed.

But then Joe sobered. "It's actually better than a walk in the park. It's… heaven."

Brody offered Lauren a thoughtful grin, the little group falling into a quiet, happy silence.

"What was your wife, Penelope, like?" Stephanie finally asked from behind her wineglass while Mary puttered over with a glass of water and took a seat between her and Lauren. "You've never really spoken about her."

They all looked around at each other, excited for this moment. A hush hung in the air and all eyes were on Joe, ready for what he was about to tell Stephanie.

The corners of his eyes creased as his weathered face broke into an enormous smile. "She was radiant. Penny was a spitfire of a woman. She was small but feisty and playful." He leaned forward in his chair. "And there's something that I think you should know."

As Joe told her the story, Stephanie's face became brighter with every word. She put her manicured fingers to her lips in awe, her gaze moving from Joe to her husband to Lauren, in utter disbelief.

"I have a family again?" she asked, her eyes wide.

Lauren pulled out her phone and showed her a picture of her mother. "This is my mom."

Stephanie sucked in an excited breath, staring down at the photograph. "Oh my gosh," she said in a whisper, her body still with the shock of it. Then suddenly knocking her wineglass into the sand, she stood up and draped her arms around Lauren. Mary threw her head back in delighted laughter.

"You said Brody's grandfather drove all the way from Alabama that day he showed up. How did he end up living in the Outer Banks?" Lauren asked, her curiosity getting the better of her. Ever since she'd shown Joe the bracelet, he hadn't taken his eyes off her.

"I'm not sure," he said. "He stayed with me for a couple of weeks and then promised he'd come back, before he went home and got married. A little less than a year later, he brought Alicia and they moved into a big ol' beach house down the road. He never really told me what it was that made them come. Did your grandmother ever tell you, Brody?"

Brody shook his head.

Spring, 1961
Fairhope, Alabama

"What?" Alicia stood in the kitchen of the home that Phillip's parents helped them buy, her hands by her sides, her face slack in surprise.

"I bought us a house in the Outer Banks."

"It's a summer home, right?" she asked.

Phillip took a step toward his new wife. "No, it's going to be our home. I'm meeting with the agent today to put this one on the market."

"Phillip, I've never even set foot in the Outer Banks of North Carolina. Why in the world would you buy something so far away and not at least consult me?"

Phillip ran his hands through his hair in frustration. "I'm miserable in this town, Alicia." He threw his hands up. "There's nothing at all keeping me here."

She stared at him, silent, unblinking, long enough for him to turn his attention to her in an attempt to decipher her reaction. "What about *me*?" She jabbed her chest. "*I'm* not keeping you here? I grew up here. I love it here. Our *home* is here."

"You can be happy anywhere," he said, irritated that she wasn't elated. But his crossness was more with himself than with her, if he was being honest. After promising Joseph that he'd come back to North Carolina, he returned home and married Alicia out of duty. He didn't want to let her or her parents down, but now, he was struggling to know his own place in all of this and be the husband he wanted to be.

"I can't be happy plonked in the sand in the middle of some *fishing* village!" She put her hands on her hips adorably, her cheeks red, only making him feel guiltier. But the truth was that when he lost Penelope, he'd lost a piece of himself—that little slip of freedom that he felt with someone who understood him inside and out. And now, he was torturing himself and Alicia, completely adrift as to his purpose.

She deserved a better man. One who could love her like she should be loved. It wasn't her fault that he'd been irreparably broken. Fairhope only reminded him of the love that had been ripped away from him and the innocence that he'd lost, and he needed to get back to the Outer Banks to take care of Joseph, a place he could do some good in Penelope's honor. The poor man was completely on his own.

He left the room, unable to look at Alicia's disappointment in him anymore. He had no idea when or if he'd ever figure out a way; but somehow, he planned to make it right for everyone, even if it took until his last breath.

Rodanthe, North Carolina

"Gosh, you two look like you could be Grace and Anne, all grown up," Joe said as Stephanie and Lauren sat by the flickering flames of the bonfire. Both barefoot, still in their formal gowns from the day, the two of them were giggling together like schoolgirls, the thrill of connection and the wine making them giddy. "If only your grandmother were here to see this."

Just then something distracted him, his attention moving to the sand. He bent over, running his fingers through the grains. "Ha!" He righted himself. "I saw it flashing at me in the light of the fire." He held up a shiny penny. Then he tipped his head up to the star-filled sky. "I've never told a single soul about her sending me pennies until you all. I suppose she's happy that you know." He smiled, gripping the penny in his fist and pressing it to his heart, emotion brimming in his eyes. "And I'm happy to think that maybe Phillip is up there keeping her company until I arrive."

Stephanie's lips wobbled. "We *all* have family now," she said, standing up. She pulled her gown into her fists and paced across the sand to Joe, putting her arms around him. "I can't believe it. This is the best wedding gift I could've ever gotten." She squeezed his neck, the two of them crying happy tears.

Lauren, still trying to wrap her head around it all, stared at the man who was most definitely her grandfather with a lump in her throat. Brody came over and stood behind her, draping his arms around her shoulders. He bent down. "You okay?"

She nodded. "I need to call my mom."

"It can't be. There's no way. I mean, what would be the odds?" Lauren's mother said, her words coming out breathy and unsteady over the phone, obviously wanting to believe it but not sure if she could.

"Probably one million to one," Lauren replied. She ran her finger over the glass pieces of her bracelet and then scooted closer to Brody. He put his arm around her.

"Are you hearing this, John?" she asked Lauren's father.

"I'm speechless," her father said in the background.

Lauren cradled the phone as she sat next to Brody in the sand, the wind tickling her cheeks. "I think Mason planned it all along. He wanted to give us the big family we've always wanted the only way he could."

"Mmm," her mother said, with fondness behind it. She'd always adored Mason. "I think you're probably right. Sounds like something he'd do."

"You'll love Joe. He's the sweetest man."

"I'd like to meet him." Her mother let out an excited huff on the other end of the line. "I had such a wonderful family. I don't know what I did to deserve more than that."

"And I want you and Dad to meet Brody. He's someone very special." She leaned against him, putting her head on his shoulder and he gave her a squeeze.

"I can't wait," her mother replied.

The surf slid up the sand, reaching her toes with its cool foam. "When can you come?"

There was a rustle on the line and then her mother came back with an answer. "Your dad and I can leave tomorrow. He's already looking up flights."

"I'll buy your tickets," she offered.

"Don't worry your pretty little head." Her dad's voice sailed through the phone. "It's worth every penny to see you. I'll text you with our flight information once I've got it all squared away."

Lauren cradled the phone against her ear, happiness bubbling up. "I can't wait to see you two."

"I know, my sweet baby girl. I can't wait to see you either."

Lauren said her goodbyes and hung up the phone.

"I'm meeting the folks?" Brody asked with a playful smirk. "And you said I was 'special'? You're building me up. I'm going to have a lot to live up to."

She slipped her phone into her pocket and cuddled up next to him. "All you have to be is yourself. You're pretty special all on your own."

He leaned down and pressed his lips to hers. "So are you," he whispered.

Chapter Twenty-Two

When the sun rose, Lauren was awake and ready for the day, but this time, her usual guilt and anxiety had floated away on the breeze. She made herself a cup of coffee, opened her French doors, and took in the golden morning light until the sun rose high into the bright blue sky.

With a new sense of purpose, she settled on the sofa and called Andy to fill her in on everything.

"So are you going to do the show?" Andy asked.

"I might," Lauren replied, tucking her feet underneath her and reaching over to the coffee table for her mug. "I'd like to suggest to Dave that, if he wants to do more episodes with me, we retitle the show from *Wedding Scramble* to something else. I'm only planning weddings at the inn and I will be much more prepared from here on out."

Andy laughed. "If you're willing to do it, Dave would probably jump at the chance to have you, so I'm pretty sure he'll change it as long as he can sell the pilot. If you and I split into two entities, each with our own series, he's just doubled his production."

"I know. We probably have a lot of power if we want it." She took a sip of the warm, rich coffee and then snuggled in on the sofa.

"Did you have anything in mind for a new show concept?"

"Yeah, I was wondering if I could restore the inn and have the show revolve around the weddings but include the revitalization of the area and the community. It would be an easy pivot, given that his footage began with the wedding and early renovations."

"That would work nicely with what the network is already doing, but it would also include the weddings you're known for with Sugar and Lace."

"Bingo."

"I can't wait to hear what Dave says. But I can already guess. I know he'll be over the moon."

"And given that I'm considering agreeing to it, I want to be very clear with him about when he can and cannot film. If I agree, it's not going to be a circus."

"You're a different person, Lauren. I wish I could say I had something to do with it, but I think leaving home might have been what you needed."

What Andy didn't realize was that Lauren hadn't left home, she'd *come* home. "Being here has taught me so much about myself and it's also what Mason wanted for me from the beginning. Maybe he could see something about me that I couldn't."

"He always knew you best," Andy said.

"Yes, he did." Happiness washed over her as she thought of him. She still missed him, but now, she knew he was there with her and all she could feel when she thought of him was love—a love so strong that it had stretched all the way from the great beyond to get her where she needed to be. That love would stay with her forever, which was just what she'd promised him when she'd said she'd marry him.

After the call to Andy, the excitement of her parents' arrival fueled her. She fastened her earrings and slipped on her sea glass bracelet and the matching ring she'd gotten with Stephanie. Then she took a moment to admire the little box Brody had made her. She would miss him terribly while he was gone, and she didn't want him to leave just when they were starting to build something together. What if the time away changed things? Could it? Would she be able to talk to him on his travels, or would he be busy taking in all the sights on his journey? No matter how it went, she'd have to be strong.

After supervising the staff, Lauren went down the hall to the main room to help Mary with the guests while she waited for her parents to arrive.

"I'm blown away by everything that happened last night," Mary said in Lauren's ear as she nodded hello to a couple guests. "I've known Joe my whole adult life, and I've never heard any of that. I had no idea he had children."

Lauren leaned on the window ledge, the bright summer sunlight shining through the panes, warming her. "I can't imagine what he went through, giving them up."

"I can't either." She turned to Lauren. "You know, I wasn't able to have children, and I've always wondered what it would be like; I've always wanted to be a mother. That's one of the reasons I enjoyed being around Brody and Stephanie when they were growing up."

Lauren nodded, following Mary outside onto the front porch.

"If only I'd been around back then," Mary said. "I'd have adopted both those baby girls." She shook her head, evidently contemplating Joe's hardship once more. "He never showed once that he was carrying any of the weight of it."

"I didn't think I would ever understand it, but I know now how you both came through your losses and made it safely to the other side. It's because you carry the love with you. You know they're here."

"Yes," Mary said. "Exactly. Frank is always with me."

"I've learned more than you know from you and Joe. And now, I carry that love too. I truly believe that Mason is around me. All the time. I can feel him now." She looked around them, wishing she could see him just as the breeze from the open door blew over her skin, as if he were letting her know where he was.

Mary smiled.

Just then Lauren caught sight of her parents in a rental car, pulling into the parking lot. She grabbed the luggage cart, and then she and Mary made their way down to greet them.

They wrapped Lauren up in a tight embrace as they met her in front of the inn. "It's so good to see you," her mother said into her ear.

"You too." She gave her a big smile and then planted a kiss on her father's cheek.

"You look incredible," her mother said. "I haven't seen you this vibrant in a long time."

"It's because I've found where I belong." She gestured toward Mary. "This is Mary Everett, the owner of the Tide and Swallow."

Mary shook their hands as she stared in awe at Lauren's mother, Grace, while Lauren helped them with their bags. "I'll make sure we've got enough glasses for cocktails," she said as she headed inside.

"How was the trip?" Lauren asked, piling the luggage onto the cart.

Her father grabbed the heaviest suitcase, placed it next to the ones Lauren had organized, and shut the trunk. "It wasn't bad; we enjoyed it," he said, wheeling the cart up to the main porch of the inn.

Mary poked her head out. "I just called Brody to pick up Joe. He said he's already on his way, and he's bringing Stephanie."

Lauren's mother lit up.

Eagerness prickled Lauren's skin. Her mother was about to meet her biological father and niece for the first time. "I'm so excited for you to get to know them. They're great people." She opened the door and helped them guide the cart inside.

Her mother put her shaking hands over her mouth, already overcome with emotion.

Mary wobbled through on her cane. "It's incredible," she said. "You standing here—it's like seeing Anne again. It takes my breath away." She placed her hand on her heart.

Mary's comment only seemed to increase Lauren's mother's anticipation. Her mom was nearly bouncing with observable energy.

Lauren picked up one of their suitcases. "Let's get your bags to your suite and then we can settle in. Mary, are the cocktails ready?"

"You know they are," Mary replied with a wiggle of her shoulders. "I'll get us a round."

"Thank you," Lauren called back to her.

"This place is wonderful," Lauren's father said as they made it down the hallway to the office, where Lauren ducked in to grab their key.

"I'm glad you like it! It's a wonderful place. You're staying in unit eighty-six, next to mine."

They went down to the suite, let themselves in, and dropped their bags.

"We haven't had a vacation in years, John," Grace said, putting her arm around Lauren's father before she drew open the new sheers and opened the French doors. "I'm already so relaxed." The shushing sound of the ocean filled the room.

Lauren understood exactly what her mother was feeling. "It has that effect on people."

Lauren's phone buzzed in her pocket with a text. She pulled it out and peered down at the message. "They're here," she told her parents. A zinging sensation shot through her, and as her parents met her at the door, she took their hands for support and walked back down to the main room.

Stephanie was the first to see them when they entered. She immediately gasped, tears filling her eyes as she looked at Lauren's mother. She gawked at Grace, her whole body trembling. Brody put a protective hand on her shoulder to let her know that they were all there for her.

"Oh my God," Stephanie said and then ran over to her. "You look exactly like my mother—you two are identical." She fell into her aunt's arms, bawling.

Joe's knees buckled and Mary quickly helped him to sit down.

Grace held Stephanie the same way she'd held Lauren whenever she faced something difficult, with her hand on the back of Stephanie's head, comforting her as the tears flowed from her eyes as well. "I wish I could've met her," Grace said when they parted.

Stephanie stared at her. "You even carry yourself the same way. You walk like her, stand like her, talk like her. It's amazing."

"I'm in just as much shock to see someone who resembles my daughter. You two could be sisters." Grace reached out for Lauren's hand and squeezed it.

Then, as if the three of them shared the same thought, Lauren, Stephanie, and her mother turned to see Joe, who worked his way to standing and slowly moved over to them. His eyes brimmed with tears as he took in the sight of his daughter. "Grace." He blinked to clear the emotion, but the tears slid down his weathered cheeks anyway. With his arms stretched wide, he held them out to her. "My little girl."

She embraced him, and he wept like a baby into her shoulder. "My sweet Grace... I never thought I'd see you again. It's a miracle." He pulled back and gazed at her, completely mesmerized. "Have you had a good life?"

"Yes," Grace said. "I've had a wonderful life."

He put his face in his hands and cried, his relief palpable. "That's all I could ask for." He wiped his face and turned to Mary. "I need some fresh air."

"I'll get the cocktails, and we can all go out to the back porch," Mary said. "Brody, will you help me get them?"

"Of course," he replied.

Lauren assisted Joe through the doors, stepping out into the bright light of summer. As they all settled on the back porch, Lauren, Stephanie, Joe, and Grace—now a family—walked to the railing and looked out at the glistening water while Mary, Brody, and Lauren's father took a seat in the shade. Under the warm orange sun, the waves shined like diamonds.

Like little pieces of sea glass.

Thank you, Lauren said silently to Mason. *Wish You Were Here*. But she knew he was. He was right there beside them, along with Penelope and Phillip. And she could be sure that Mason was cheering for her. All she had to do was look around. He'd been showing her, one sparkling piece of sea glass at a time.

Chapter Twenty-Three

A Week Later

The last seven days with her parents had gone by in a flash. Lauren had shared so many good moments with her new family and her old one, and they'd all promised to get together every holiday. After seeing her mom and dad off, hugging them both fiercely, she settled into the newly decorated main room of the inn with Mary and Joe.

"I don't think my heart could get any fuller," Joe said. "All those years, I had to keep quiet. I wasn't allowed to tell the girls who I really was."

"What finally prompted you to do it?" Mary asked.

"It just felt right. As if Penny was urging me to do it." He flashed a big smile at Lauren. "Penny and Anne got you here just so that I could tell you—I believe that."

"I believe it too," Lauren said. "I'll bet they're with Mason. They're going to love him." She was able to speak of him without sadness today, and she could feel the love and hope radiating from inside. He used to say she was stubborn, and she definitely had been when it came to moving past his loss, but, just as he had in life, he'd managed to get her to change her mind.

Brody's voice cut in from the front of the inn. "Hey, could I steal Lauren for a second?"

Mary twisted around. "Of course."

He walked over and held out his hand to Lauren, an undecipherable look in his eyes. Curious, she took his hand and followed him out the front doors, where the Winnebago was parked, idling. Her heart dropped into her stomach. She'd just finished one of the best weeks of her life and now she was facing Brody leaving them. It was time to say goodbye. She didn't want him to go, but she couldn't stand in his way either.

He led her down the stairs to the parking lot. "I got it all clean, gassed up, and ready for the trip, and I wanted to bring it by to show you." He opened the door and gestured for her to step inside.

Lauren entered the large vehicle and took in the renovated space. Brody had installed hardwood-style floors in a stunning gray throughout, he'd upholstered the small sofas and chairs along the side in a complementing gray color, and across from them he'd built a miniature kitchen, complete with white cabinetry and stainless-steel appliances.

"This is beautiful." All his choices were perfect.

"Watch this." He hit a button and the top cabinet door rotated, revealing a flat-screen TV, perfectly positioned for watching from the sofas.

"That's great," she said, admiring his handiwork.

"And this footstool opens up." He unclipped the latch and pulled out the leaves of a full-size breakfast table, lacquered like his boxes.

She ran her fingers over it. "You did all this?"

His toned chest puffed out proudly. "Yep."

"I shouldn't be surprised," she told him. "But even still, I am. You never cease to amaze me."

"I'm glad you like it." He took her hands. "But I think it needs one more thing."

"What's that?"

He looked into her eyes with a mischievous sparkle, a bolt of excitement swimming through her. "You."

"Me?"

"I'd like you to go with me across the country. We could see it all, from the mountains to the deserts and everything in between. I want you with me."

A pulse of hope shot through her, but then she considered what it would mean to go with him. "I can't leave Mary and the inn."

"Yeah, I thought about that. What if I told you that I've figured out how to get her some help just while we're gone?"

Lauren waited for the explanation, wondering how he'd managed that.

"Stephanie's job is only part-time and she told me once, a long time ago, that she'd love to work at the inn. I explained what I was going to suggest to you and I asked her if she'd want to fill in for you. She said she would."

Suddenly, Lauren's future stretched out in front of her in a way it never had before. Mason's voice floated into her mind: *...sell it all and travel the world.* He was giving her a little push to do even more of the things he'd planned for them, and to do them with someone wonderful.

"I'd love to," she said.

Brody scooped her up into his arms and spun around in the little space, making her laugh. Real joy that she hadn't known was possible filled her. He set her down, put his hands on her face, and kissed her lips. "What have you done to me?" he asked softly, his eyes opening.

Instead of an answer, she kissed him again, knowing she hadn't done a thing. Finding him had changed them both.

She pulled back. "When do we leave?"

"Well, I only have a few date-specific reservations, so it's really up to you. Do you have any renovations that you want to get done before we set off?"

"The sand's being brought in next week and Dave's going to want to film that when he does my final interview. And they're redoing the parking lot in a couple days."

"How about we leave right after that? Would that give you enough time to get the ball rolling so that Stephanie can oversee the construction?"

"Yes. All I have to do is finalize everything. Stephanie can keep me posted on progress. We could probably leave next week."

He picked her up again in excitement, nuzzling her neck and making her squeal. "Let's call Stephanie right now and tell her."

She wriggled free, giggling. "Let's go inside and talk to Mary so she knows about our plan. Then we can call Stephanie."

They stepped out of the Winnebago and he stopped her. "Oh, I forgot." Brody dug into his pocket and pulled out a shiny green object. "I found it this morning while I was fishing. I was nervous about asking you to come on the trip with me, but when I saw it, I took the boat straight home, got in the Winnebago, and drove over." He took her hand and placed a piece of sea glass in her palm. "Green for go." He winked at her.

With a plume of delight, Lauren held the glass up to the sun, admiring the sparkle of it. "Green for go," she repeated with a nod to Mason. Then she took Brody's hand, and, together, they stepped into their future.

Epilogue

Lauren's heart felt as if it might explode at the sight of the small crowd of family and friends that had gathered by the Winnebago. Melinda and Chuck were there, along with Mary, Joe, Mitchell, and Stephanie.

"Everything's packed." Lauren dropped her bags at Brody's feet as everyone inched closer to see them off. Milton barked from inside the vehicle, his head hanging over the open back window, his tail wagging furiously. "I've brought a few outfits for each season, just to be safe. You've got a washer and dryer in there, right?"

"Yep." Brody slid the bags in the compartment under the camper.

Chuck was the first to step up. He'd really taken the time to talk to his son since the wedding. Brody told Lauren that his father had even come by the house to see his projects and they'd talked for over an hour about Brody's artwork. Chuck had confessed to Brody that he hadn't been the best father, and while he couldn't get those years back, he wanted to do everything he could to make the time they had ahead happy.

"I'm proud of you, son," Chuck said before reaching out and giving Brody a hug.

Brody returned the gesture. "Thanks, Dad."

Melinda looked on with tears in her eyes.

Chuck moved back next to Melinda and took her hand.

"Y'all be good, okay?" Melinda said, wiping her eyes.

Brody kissed her cheek. "Love you, Mom."

"I've made you all lunch," Mary said, emotion showing in her face, handing Lauren a handled bag full of containers. "There's chicken salad, crab cakes, biscuits, a cheese tray, and a bottle of wine." She leaned over to view the contents while attempting to list the final items.

"You didn't have to do all that," Lauren said.

"Of course I didn't. But you all need to be fed, don't you?"

Brody put his arm around Mary. "Thanks."

"You're welcome," Mary said with a wink.

"You gonna be okay?" Brody asked Joe.

He gave Brody a good-natured slug on the arm. "I've managed for this long."

Brody chuckled, giving him a warm hug.

"You and Stephanie have my number," Lauren said to Mary. "If you need me for anything at all, just give me a ring."

Stephanie stepped forward as the palm trees rustled when the warm coastal breeze blew. "Don't worry about us! We'll be just fine. You'll be too busy on your adventures to have time to think about what's going on here."

"We *will* be very busy," Lauren agreed, while Brody gave Mitchell a handshake to tell him goodbye. "We're visiting my old Sugar and Lace partner and friend, Andy Jacobs, in New York just in time to see a little of the shooting for her next show."

Stephanie bounced up and down. "Oh, that's exciting! Think you could video call so I can say hello?"

"Definitely." Lauren laughed. "And by the time we get across the country, we'll be in California just in time to see the premiere of the new series, *Bait and Switch*." She gave Stephanie a conspiratorial grin.

Stephanie and Mary had been with Lauren while she'd chatted with Dave, and the two had kept the secret until today.

"*Bait and Switch*?" Joe asked.

"The name of my new TV show. Dave had an idea to do a show about how my life as a wedding planner took a turn in the total opposite direction and how I fell for a fisherman. The network loved it. The series is going to follow us along on our journey across country to document how I rebuild my life. They even have more episodes planned for the next season to cover restoring the inn. Which is good because I'm competing with Andy's show and I hear the Maxwell wedding will be an absolute smash of an episode."

Mary turned to the group. "Isn't that wonderful?"

They all agreed enthusiastically.

"I had a long conversation with Dave and decided that maybe telling my story could help others who have lost someone wonderful not to give up."

Mary reached out and took Lauren's arm, jingling the sea glass bracelet. "Still don't believe in good luck?"

"I believe in luck now," Lauren admitted. "And so much more." She put her arm around Brody and he kissed the top of her head.

Milton whined from the back window, making them all laugh.

"Well, I guess this is it," Brody said just as the sun came from behind a white billowy cloud, casting a golden light across them all.

Lauren stopped for a second to take in the moment. When she'd imagined packing back up, she never would've believed that she'd be where she was right then. While the last year had been trying, what she'd learned was that if she just held on through the hard parts, she'd make it to the other side. Mason's voice floated into her mind: *The sunshine's stronger than the storm.*

Brody opened the passenger door for her. As he pulled out his keys, Lauren stopped him, reaching out for them. "Wait. May I see those? I brought something."

He handed them over, watching her. She pulled the *Wish You Were Here* sea glass keychain from her pocket and slipped the keys onto it, leaning in through the passenger door and pushing the key into the ignition, the sea glass sparkling in the sunlight.

After one last goodbye to everyone, the two of them climbed in with Milton and pulled off, driving away.

"Where are we headed first?" Lauren asked Brody.

He looked over at her as if he were drinking her in. "Somewhere further south, down the coast."

Lauren leaned back, her elbow out the open window, the wind against her face. She wasn't sure when they'd arrive at their first destination, but it didn't matter. She was already right where she was meant to be.

A Letter from Jenny

Hi there!

Thank you so much for reading *The Magic of Sea Glass*. For all of those who have lost someone dear, my aim was to provide hope that our loved ones are around us all the time.

If you'd like to know when my next book is out, you can **sign up for my monthly newsletter and new release alerts here:**

www.itsjennyhale.com/email-signup

I won't share your information with anyone else, and I'll only email you a quick message once a month with my newsletter and then whenever new books come out. It's the best way to keep tabs on what's going on with my books, and you'll get tons of surprises along the way like giveaways, signed copies, recipes, and more.

If you did enjoy *The Magic of Sea Glass*, I'd be very grateful if you'd write a review online. Getting feedback from readers helps to persuade others to pick up one of my books for the first time. It's one of the biggest gifts you could give me.

If you enjoyed this story, and would like a few more happy endings, check out my other novels at www.itsjennyhale.com.

Until next time,
Jenny xo

9 7201437.Jenny_Hale

f jennyhaleauthor

@jhaleauthor

jhaleauthor

www.itsjennyhale.com

Acknowledgments

I am forever indebted to Oliver Rhodes for shaping me into the author I am today and setting the bar for my own publishing journey. His example has inspired every choice I've made along the way and continues to inspire me even now.

I owe a huge thank you to my amazing editors: the fabulous Lauren Finger, who shaped this book right up, Mira Park, my copyeditor, and the most wonderful proofreaders, Becca Allen and Liz Hurst. I couldn't have had a better team to help me get this story ready than these women.

The amazingly talented cover designer Kristen Ingebretson is the best of the best. I'm so very thankful to have her for cover direction.

And to my husband, Justin, who is always by my side in this wildly unpredictable career I've chosen. He handles my crazy with ease and is always rooting me on.

30642176R00165